**He r**

before Mrs. Flanagan shuffled to the door tying her robe at her waist as she came. At first glance, he thought her eyes were red-rimmed from sleep, then realized the woman was crying.

"Is something wrong?" He put the professional tone in his voice, hoping to make the question sound less invasive.

"Oh, yes, David. Everyone in town's just sick about the news this morning. That precious Memory Smith is dead."

"What?" He choked on the word and blinked to focus.

"Killed right out there on the highway, she was. Run over. They found her body not two miles down the way." She indicated the highway in front of the motel. "The poor, sweet thing. She was so tore up, they figured it must have been one of those eighteen-wheelers that got her." She mopped her nose with a tissue. "Tore all to pieces, they tell me, layin' right there by the side of the road. That precious, precious child."

**Praise for Sharon Ervin**

Contest judges said of *MEMORY*:

"Well written…"

"Intriguing premise…"

"Strong writing style…"

"…the dialogue has an ease about it…"

"Delightful…"

For Nancy and Doug, writer friends and colleagues!
Sharon Ervin

# Memory

by

Sharon Ervin

**Memory**


Contact Information: info@thewildrosepress.com

Cover Art by *Kristian Norris*

The Wild Rose Press, Inc.
PO Box 708
Adams Basin, NY 14410-0708
Visit us at www.thewildrosepress.com

Publishing History
First Crimson Rose Edition, 2017
Print ISBN 978-1-5092-1290-3
Digital ISBN 978-1-5092-1291-0

Published in the United States of America

**Dedication**

To Bill,
for all the usual reasons,
and Brandi, Joe, Cassie, and Jim,
my best backers

**Acknowledgements**

I would like to thank Ronda Talley and Jane Bryant,
able, eagle-eyed friends, for improving this book;
McAlester's McSherry Writers
for astute critiquing;
And Laura Kelly,
one of the world's most patient, persistent editors.

## Chapter One

The windshield wipers slapped faster, clearing glimpses of shiny blacktop highway. They had waited two months for a good rain. Now, here it was, all at once, midnight the first day of August.

"Careful, David." Laurel's voice sounded hollow. "Someone's walking. Over there. On the shoulder."

David McCann saw a shimmer as his headlights reflected off the wet pedestrian not twenty yards ahead. He tapped the brake again, slowing to a crawl on the four-lane.

The walker's pace looked purposeful and vaguely familiar. David strained to identify the woman as his Lexus rolled by her striding form. He pulled onto the shoulder and stopped. By remote, he lowered the passenger window—Laurel's window—and leaned toward it.

Passing briskly on the passenger side, the walker ignored them.

"Memory?" David shouted.

Laurel covered her ears. He had put some volume behind it, but he doubted his raised voice did more than annoy Laurel. Ten years after their senior class play, the woman was still the consummate drama queen.

The pedestrian stopped and turned to face them, pushing strands of her dark, bedraggled hair away from her face as she squinted against the headlights. She took several steps back to put herself even with the car, bent, and peered inside.

"Hello, Laurel. David."

A car roared by, spewing water as its taillights danced crazily in the spray. David frowned at Memory's face, visually trying to sort out the features which had once haunted his dreams.

She never dated, of course. Not the wondrous creature known in Astrick as "The Miracle Child." Regarding her more closely, it looked to him as if the angelic Memory Smith's full bottom lip was cut and swollen.

"Get in." He tapped the automatic door lock, releasing the latches.

She fumbled with the handle to open the back door, then hesitated, shivering. "I'm filthy. And soaking wet."

Laurel cleared her throat to draw his attention before she spoke in a stage whisper. "We can send someone back for her."

"Get in," he repeated, more forcefully, ignoring Laurel. "The seats are leather. You won't hurt them. Hurry up, before we get rear ended."

As the sodden hiker stepped into the car, Laurel folded her arms across her chest and slouched. There was nothing subtle about Ms. Dubois. He didn't know what she was being so haughty about. She was bumming a ride herself.

David had pretended to be pleased when Laurel asked for a ride home, but he knew from experience that the lofty Laurel was a rigid, unresponsive lay, always desperate to protect her flat little breasts and her tight little butt. Too, he had heard the rumors. She had told people they were getting serious. With him she'd made broad suggestions about marriage.

McCann hadn't been Laurel's social equal in high school, but at twenty-eight, it appeared she had lowered her standards. He, on the other hand, ranged a long way from that kind of commitment, and with someone like Laurel…well, that wasn't happening. Not now. Not ever.

With Memory secured in the back seat, David guided the car back onto the highway before he readjusted his mirror. He wanted a better look at the woman, but her features were distorted and only partially visible in the strobe lighting provided by oncoming traffic.

"Are you staying at your dad's place?"

When she hesitated, he glanced over his shoulder, straining to see her face which was shrouded in the shadowy corner of the back seat. He gave up and turned his attention again to the roadway. She seemed to give his ordinary question an inordinate amount of thought.

"Yes." Her voice wavered as she added, "but not tonight."

"Okay, where to tonight?" He waited, listening closely for any telltale inflection, but her voice sounded stronger when she responded.

"Take me to Flanagan's. It's only a mile or so up the highway, isn't it?"

"Why a motel?" He squinted into the mirror, again trying to read her facial expressions as they passed under white ways that lighted the bypass closer to town.

Her eyes met his in the mirror and she attempted a smile, a lopsided one, as if she'd been to the dentist, or taken a punch. It was too late in the day for a dentist, but who in Bacone County would have had the gall to pop Memory Smith? Her clothes were splattered, certainly soggy, but they didn't appear to be torn or damaged, didn't look as if she'd been forced to defend herself. Her voice came again, muted by the car noise.

"I lost my purse."

His attorney's instincts sounded their alarm, ever attuned to a witness avoiding the easy question. Probably she was only thinking out loud. He continued driving in silence, allowing her time to reflect. At the moment this usually winsome woman looked and sounded oddly defeated.

The prolonged silence ended abruptly when Laurel snapped her head around to stare at Memory in a delayed reaction. "Lost your purse? How in the world did you do that?"

Memory didn't seem to hear the new question as she stared out the window. Several moments ticked by as the rain continued peppering the car, but the deluge had lost its ferocity. David adjusted the wipers again, slowing their rhythm and reducing the noise level inside the car. The steady slap of the wipers punctuated by occasional fading claps of thunder were the only sounds in the enveloping silence as David pulled under the overhang in front of Flanagan's office behind the red neon "Vacancy" sign. He opened his car door and thrust his flattened hand toward Memory, signaling. "Stay put. I'll get it."

He went inside and returned almost immediately, trotting from the office door with a key in one hand and a bed sheet draped over his other arm. Both women regarded him quizzically. He got back in the car and offered Memory the sheet before he answered the unasked question. "I thought you could wrap up in it while your clothes dry."

She nodded, took the offered sheet, and reached for the key dangling from a metal ring circling David's index finger. Pulling it back out of her reach, he shook his head and studied her.

Memory had always been a beauty. Long and lithe, she moved with the supple grace of a cat. And here she was, in the back seat of his car, close enough to touch. But this particular feline was wet and didn't look like she'd take well to stroking at the moment.

"Answer me a couple of questions first," he said, using the colloquialism intentionally, hoping to ease her tension.

She lowered her hand and regarded him coolly as her puffy bottom lip joined the upper in a grim line. She winced and lifted a hand toward her mouth, then stopped, apparently at some mental scolding. In her expression, he recognized the stubborn cast of a hostile witness. She seemed to be overcoming the defeat, clawing her way toward defiant.

He had never before seen this woman combative. She had been serene through elementary, junior high, and high school. Their paths hadn't crossed in the ten years since, and idly he wondered why not.

"You weren't at the reunion." Maybe the innocuous observation would breach the barrier she'd thrown up.

Memory shook her head. "No. I work in Metcalf. I couldn't get back that weekend."

Metcalf was the nearest metropolitan area, less than two hours' drive from Astrick. "But you're here now."

"Since Dad died I've come down once or twice a month to check on his place and sign papers. Quint Ressler is doing the probate." One eye twitched when she spoke Ressler's name and her burgeoning confidence seemed to nose dive. David might not have noticed if he hadn't been watching the rearview mirror so intently. She wasn't the first attractive female to develop harsh feelings toward Quint.

Laurel glanced from David to Memory and interrupted the rhythmic give and take David was trying to establish. "What do you do?"

He saw the flicker as Memory's expression again became guarded. Damn Laurel anyway.

"I'm a paralegal." She eyed Laurel skeptically. "An attorney's assistant."

Laurel returned a pained look. "I know what a paralegal is, thanks."

Memory attempted a smile, but flinched with the effort and fisted her hand, again overcoming what looked like a reflex effort to touch her swollen lip. She covered the awkward moment with rhetoric.

"I came Wednesday to update the computers in Ressler's office. He suggested it as 'sweat equity,' a way to reduce the fee on the probate." Her voice had taken on a brittle quality, as if she were annoyed.

"Oh, I see." Laurel sounded relieved. "You're a computer nerd."

"I wish." Although the words were pleasant enough, Memory's face assumed a look of solemn concentration. "I know something about legal pleadings and forms. Not as much about computers, but I can put two and two together, if it's simple."

"Was it?" Laurel asked.

"Yes."

David had a hunch and went with it. "Then you were out with Quint tonight?"

Memory snorted and he got the impression her thinly veiled derision was directed at herself even though he caught the brunt of her wrathful glare in the rearview.

Suddenly she was all business. "David, please give me the room key. I need to go inside. I'm cold."

"Okay. Do you want me to drive out to the house and bring you a change of clothes?"

"No. I want you to give me that key and go away."

Maybe she was afraid Quint would be at her dad's house looking for her. Actually, David's running into Quint out there might not be a bad thing. He would like a shot at Quint in a remote setting, alone. If Ressler were responsible for Memory's busted lip, or her intimidation, David would like to be the one to square things. Oh, yes, the Smith's isolated farm would be perfect.

But right now, Memory was his main concern and her shivering was getting worse. Was her discomfort only from the cold or was fear adding to her distress? He held out the key and she took it. Before she could grasp the door handle, he jammed the accelerator, made a quick U-turn, drove down and pulled in directly in front of Room 107.

"Thanks." There was no smile, but some of the tension seemed to leach from her face as she glanced from David to Laurel, both craning their necks to face her.

Clutching the sheet, Memory flung the car door open, ducked into the rain, unlocked the door to room

107, and disappeared inside.

Even dirty and disheveled, Memory was gorgeous in the exotic way David remembered: the full mouth, the prominent cheekbones, the Polynesian cast to her dark eyes which gave her that ethereal, foreign look. Of course, she still had the firm, ample breasts that had beguiled every male in school—teaching staff included.

Bright and friendly, Memory Smith was untouchable then. Everyone in Astrick called her “the miracle child.” She was neither designed nor intended by the gods to mate with any sweaty, swaggering adolescent, certainly not a perpetually horny goof-off from the wrong side of the tracks like David McCann.

Small town lore had it that her parents, devout Catholics, had no children until they were forty-five years old. In a town the size of Astrick, stories of Memory Smith’s birth were local legend. If their name had been anything but Smith, her parents would have named their daughter for the blessed mother, but “Mary Smith” was too plain a name for a miracle, so they named her Memory, an unusual name for a unique being.

Both parents waited outside piano and dance lessons, cheered her at ball games, traveled as sponsors on every PTA, band, and debate trip. The perfect child blossomed into an enchantress, allegedly without ever exchanging a cross word with her parents or objecting to their suffocating attention. Recalling her storied perfection, it was hard to imagine that tonight Memory Smith had gone out with a married man, particularly a man of Quint Ressler’s ilk. Of course, she might not have known Quint was married, even though the man’s very public, very volatile union was broadcast in every beauty, barber, and coffee shop in Astrick, accounts issued practically as part of a daily bulletin.

Staring at the closed motel room door, David felt a disquieting urge to stay; to maneuver his way into Room 107 using any means necessary; to look at her, listen to the soft cadence of her voice, comfort her, maybe even hold her—chastely, of course.

Suddenly aware of Laurel's eyes burning into him, he remembered he was not alone. He sat straighter, shot a sidelong look at Laurel, and jammed the car into reverse.

"My daddy is such a tightwad," Laurel said.

"Hmm."

"He raised my allowance to thirty-five hundred a month, but he won't give me an advance when I'm in a pinch."

"Oh." David listened to her complaint, but it didn't get his attention. When she remained quiet, he thought she might be waiting for him to comment. "Is your rent too high?"

"No, Lame-o. He owns the apartments. I don't pay rent. He won't give me my money until the twentieth of the month. He's trying to make me budget."

"Hmmm." If she needed a loan, she'd have to tap someone else. He'd fallen for her sad story once and forked over two hundred bucks. He'd waited for repayment without mentioning it. Apparently she considered the money a gift, not a loan. Rich kids had no regard.

Laurel didn't speak the rest of the way until after she handed him the keycard and he pulled through the security gate at her apartment complex. He wound around to her building and parked but didn't turn off the engine. The rain had become a drizzle.

"Come on in. I'll fix you a cup of coffee…or a nightcap." Laurel flashed him a plastic smile, obviously struggling to control the sulk that had become her trademark. Her brooding expression threatened again as he shook his head. She leaned close and her second invitation came as she brushed her lips against his cheek and caressed the back of his head, both gestures to suggest she was offering more than beverages.

He felt embarrassed for her, but had other things on his mind. "No thanks, Laurel. Not tonight." He might have relented if he'd been able to jettison the mental image of Memory Smith wrapped in a bed sheet, injured and alone in that room at Flanagan's.

Laurel got out in a huff, then slammed the car door, hard. David watched her all the way to her apartment, saw her insert the key, open and go inside, without so much as a wave or a glance back. That door cracked like a minor explosion when she hurled it shut behind her. That door slam vindicated him. There was nothing subtle about Laurel Dubois. Revving the car engine, David figured he'd just trashed any future opportunity in Laurel's bed. He gave up a grim smile and shrugged. Maybe that was not altogether a bad thing. She could tell everyone she had broken it off with him. Being the gentleman he had become, he would not dispute the claim.

He drove through a shabby residential neighborhood, then to a nicer area to cruise by his grandmother's house and assure himself the crusty little woman was buttoned down for the night. He liked to do that, swing by the dilapidated old house, then on to the small brick home he was buying her, pleased at the difference between structures and neighborhoods, a little smug that he was providing better than she'd ever had before.

He heard sirens in the distance—ambulance and police—rare in the usual small-town quiet. Probably a car accident. Rain-slicked blacktop could cause hydroplaning if a driver failed to control his speed on the abrupt curves in and out of town, intentionally put there by city fathers to slow approaching traffic.

The drizzle became intermittent sprinkles as David drove to the only all-night convenience store in town. He bought a hairbrush, a toothbrush, and toothpaste. He glanced at packaged ladies' briefs, but decided that might be taking chivalry to a tasteless extreme. Donnie Rutherford talked on a cell phone the whole time David was in the store, even kept the device at his ear as he rang up the purchases. With a sense of mission, David drove back to Flanagan's.

Caught up planning his campaign for the siege of Room 107, David heard more sirens. Another accident? Maybe. Or the earlier commotion might have involved more than one vehicle. And injuries. It could even be a fatality. But he had other plans. He'd get details at the office Monday, which would be plenty soon enough.

He rapped on the motel room door several times before Memory, her muffled voice just at the other side, asked who it was.

"David McCann."

"What do you want?"

"I brought you some things."

The security chain rattled. There was a brief pause, then the chain rattled again as she reattached it before she released the dead bolt, turned the knob, and cracked the door, which opened only as far as the chain allowed.

David tried not to stare as he passed her the sack from the convenience store. All he could see of her was one firm, smooth, bare arm and shoulder, and part of her facc, twisted into a frown.

"Give me your wet clothes." He intended to capitalize on this opportunity, take it as far as he could.

"What? Why?"

"I'll take them to the motel office. Get Mrs. Flanagan to run them through her clothes dryer. It probably won't take an hour."

Memory stared into his face, the almond eyes narrowing. She closed the door and shuffled away, then returned, and opened, again only as much as the chain allowed, and squeezed her denim dress through. It was wrapped tightly as if it contained other clothing.

David smiled. "Be right back."

"Why?"

"You can't go get them later wearing a bed sheet and I didn't think you'd want me to sit in the car for an hour, in this." He glanced skyward, ignoring the fact the fickle sky was clearing. "Mrs. Flanagan can ring the room when the clothes are dry and I'll run pick them up for you."

Without giving her time to think of an alternative plan, he took off for the office.

Mrs. Flanagan sat slouched on the rumpled sofa in the front office staring blankly at the TV screen on which there flickered an ancient episode of "Happy Days."

"I have a load of towels to run anyway," she said, responding to his request. Immediately she began struggling to pull herself up from the pillowed confines of the sofa. David stepped closer to offer her a hand. When she took it, he tugged her to her feet.

She seemed surprised to find the clothing belonged to a female but recovered quickly enough to cast him a jaundiced eye. “I can throw her things in right now, but if I dry them with the towels, it may take a while. ‘You in a hurry?” She raised her eyebrows.

He intentionally hadn’t mentioned when he’d taken the room that it wasn’t for him. No use starting unnecessary speculation or loose talk. Also, if Quint were looking for Memory, David didn’t want to make it easy for the jerk to find her.

He flashed a secretive smile and handed Mrs. Flanagan a ten-dollar bill. “No rush.” As an afterthought, he picked up an unopened deck of playing cards from a display on the glass counter. “How much?”

She waved the ten at him and grinned. “This’ll cover it. I’ll ring you when her clothes are dry. Like I said, it could be a while. But you don’t look to be in any particular hurry.”

His smile broadened to indicate she’d guessed correctly. “Thanks.” He pocketed the cards and trotted back to Room 107. Thunder rumbled. He hoped it signaled more rain coming.

## Chapter Two

Memory opened the door slowly, mincing backward in the sarong she had improvised by wrapping the sheet around her body once, then draping the ends over her shoulders, concealing entirely the satiny flesh he had admired earlier.

David closed the door, flipped the dead bolt, and turned to find Memory settling demurely into one of the two arm chairs at the small table near the draped picture window.

He felt damp, was chilling a little. Heat blew from the unit under the window on the far side of the room, promising an increase in temperature, eventually.

Memory had been soaked, probably all the way to the bone. He wondered if she had recovered. Did her arms have goose bumps? If so, was it the cold or his presence stimulating her beneath the sheeting? Disregarding those inappropriate thoughts, he kept his eyes on her face as he produced the new deck of cards from his coat pocket, exaggerating his movements to lighten her mood.

Memory's eyes widened and a tentative smile eased the corners of her mouth, which definitely showed signs of recent injury. His questions could wait. He'd bought himself a little time. There was no need to press.

David chose the other chair, broke open the

cellophane packaging on the cards, removed the jokers from the deck, and began to shuffle. "Gin rummy?"

Allowing a full lopsided smile, and drawing a breath, obviously relieved, she nodded.

"Dealer gets ten cards," he said. "I give you eleven and you discard first."

She nodded again.

"First one to get to a hundred points wins."

"Right." Her funny smile appeared to be genuine, if not exactly symmetrical.

He grinned in return. "Do you want to play for something?"

She glanced down at her scant attire, flushed, and smiled sheepishly. "I don't have any money. My purse…you know. Nothing else I can afford to lose. Besides, aren't you still an assistant D.A.?"

"I am."

"It probably wouldn't do your reputation any good to get busted in a motel room gambling with a scantily clad woman."

She was kidding him and, in spite of unpleasant events or company earlier in the evening, her being playful indicated a lift in her spirits. The lighter atmosphere was definitely a good sign. He liked this aspect of her, which he did not remember from their formative years.

"Probably wouldn't do your reputation any good either," he said, fanning and studying the cards in his hand, his concentration a ploy to keep himself from looking at her.

Her lilting laugh tickled his ears. "My reputation can probably take a hit better than yours can. In case you don't remember, I'm the miracle child."

Faking a grimace at her inference, he said, “Meaning my reputation can’t afford to drop any rungs on the wobbly ladder of community esteem?” He pretended a scowl, stimulating her laugh that chimed again. Her expression indicated she was suddenly aware of the conversational corner she’d painted herself into.

He wanted to pursue their chitchat, keep her from lapsing back into self-consciousness. “My reputation has improved since high school, you know.”

“Thank goodness.” She giggled at her own little taunt and bit her lips. The gesture sobered her and she tenderly fingered the swelling around the split in her lip.

Determined to keep her spirits buoyed, he flashed a quick smile. “Okay, go ahead and say whatever wicked thing it is you’re thinking. Spit it out. You think my reputation couldn’t be any worse than it was after I stuck Glover with the shiv I made in metal shop, right?”

Her shoulders moved up and down, but his comment appeared to draw her back from the gloomy place where the reminder of her busted lip had taken her. “I didn’t say that.” She arched her eyebrows. “You did.”

“It was an accident. Rick and I were friends. We were goofing around.” He didn’t know if it was his confession, the peculiarly intimate circumstances, or the constant reminder of her injured lip, but something was easing the tension between them.

“Do people still call you ‘Mac?’”

“Yeah, ‘Mac the knife.’” His spirits soared as her demeanor lightened again.

Mac McCann prided himself on his rich imagination, but even he would never have foreseen that an evening with such dismal prospects could wind up with him in a motel room playing gin rummy with Memory Smith, and her wrapped in a bed sheet.

The rain came again and Mac smiled to himself. What a great way to spend a rainy night.

As they played out the first hand, Memory called, “Gin,” and laughed, a peal that increased when he glowered and slapped his cards down, face up to allow her to count the points. To heighten his reaction, which seemed to delight her, he grumbled.

“Beginner’s luck,” he complained, enjoying each of the gurgling giggles she tried valiantly to muffle. “I only needed three or four more cards and I could have ginned.”

“Not good enough, McCann.” She was really getting into this. He was liking this situation better and better.

He tallied her score out loud, making himself sound disgruntled without stifling her sputtering laughter, all the while studying her. Her pleasure filled him with a peculiar joy that increased as she shifted the sheet enough to allow her to gather the scattered cards.

“Winner shuffles and deals.” She glanced up at him and hesitated, apparently waiting for confirmation.

Watching the sheet tighten, emphasizing the swell of her hips and upper legs as she moved in the chair, he took a quick breath. “Right.”

Trying to redirect his explosion of imaginings, he got up to retrieve a promotional pad of paper and ball point pen from the bedside table. It took heroic effort for him not to react when he noticed the pillows stacked and the indention that must have been made by Memory’s sweet, nearly nude body lounging against them during the time he was taking Laurel home and shopping for sundries.

He battled to banish thoughts of Memory peeling out of her wet clothing, enjoying a warm shower, drying herself, then wrapping her voluptuous body in that bed sheet.

She gave him a sidelong look and her eyes followed his to the impression in the pillows. “The lawyer in you is showing, McCann.”

He slipped back into his chair, angry with himself and his evocative visions of this gentle woman. “I’m not like Quint, Memory. I’m an entirely scrupulous lawyer.”

She nodded, sobering, and dealt the cards in silence.

“Tell me,” he ventured, pursuing a new thought, “is there a boyfriend in Metcalf who could come busting in here and misunderstand our…ah…our circumstances?”

“No.”

Her quick response sounded definite enough. Hard to believe, but definite. As he fanned his cards, he shivered involuntarily. He wasn’t sure if the movement was prompted by the chill of his damp clothing or a reaction to the excitement of being here—like this—with her. Regardless, his shudder drew Memory’s attention. She leaned forward to touch the sleeve of his blazer and scowled. “You’re all wet.”

Resisting the word play the comment invited, he folded his gin rummy hand and stood. “I might take off my jacket, hang it here on the back of the chair, if you’re okay with that.”

“Are your trousers wet too?”

Patting his thighs, he pretended he’d been unaware

of how damp the legs of his slacks were until she mentioned it. "Yes, but it's no big deal."

She didn't say anything for several heartbeats. He waited. He wanted her to come up with a suggestion on her own. After a long moment, she did. "You could probably use a sheet off the bed, if you wanted to take them off."

He couldn't help smiling at her sincerity. She didn't have a clue about how her badly concealed curves teased him with her every move; that he was painfully aware of the rise and fall of her breasts when she breathed, of every swell and hollow of her anatomy so lovingly encased and strikingly defined by the sheet. Could she honestly not know how she looked, her delectable body swishing, whispering invitations with every motion. And the scent of her, the fragrance of fresh air and damp woods and warm female, subtle aromas that stimulated every nerve feeding his male appetite.

He cocked an eyebrow as a villainous chuckle burbled from him involuntarily. "Are you making up a party game where the guests trade their clothes for bed sheets?"

She laughed lightly, a whispery sound that seemed directed at herself, before she blushed.

"I think your game will catch on." He tilted his head sideways, studying her as she avoided returning his look. If this innocence were an act, it was damn believable.

Mac had succeeded in life by recognizing an opportunity and taking advantage of an opponent's momentary lapse. He wasn't going to let one this good pass without at least taking a stab at it.

He walked to the bed, tossed back the spread and blanket, removed the top sheet, and carried it into the bathroom, flashing her a playful smile before quietly closing the door.

He removed his shirt and tie, which were dry; his shoes and socks, which were not, then his trousers, which were only slightly damp. Smiling at his reflection, he delayed a moment before slipping off his shorts, which were dry as dust.

This might work out, he thought, wrapping the sheet around his waist and grinning approval at his image in the mirror, flexing, pumping his muscles like a teenager, and silently mouthing the words: "To-ga. To-ga."

His facial features, the prominent jaw, made him look rugged, but not pretty, certainly not handsome by most standards. His look was enhanced by the muscled arms and chest and the flat abs, all honed and maintained by jogging most mornings and three sessions a week at the gym. Tonight might make those tedious workouts more worthwhile than ever. His physique was definitely the best part of his looks. His sexiest anyway. He tugged the wrap below his belly button. The bulk of sheeting bunched around his lower body would help hide his arousal which kept responding to her, in spite of his mental efforts to control it.

He placed his shoes and socks on the vanity, hung his trousers over the shower rod, his dry shirt, tie and shorts on the hook on the back of the door, and snapped on the overhead heater.

With one more quick glance in the mirror, he straightened and took a deep breath, then pulled the sheet up to his waist. Better. Less likely to offend. He patted his stomach, and opened the door.

Mac watched her face as he emerged from the bathroom, curious to read her response to his bare chest. He didn't want to make her uncomfortable. Well, maybe a little.

When she looked up, her expression remained guarded but she inhaled and sat straighter, pulling her shoulders back and thrusting her breasts high. Her movements signaled primal interest. A good sign. Very good.

Apparently realizing her body might be conveying more information than she intended, Memory suddenly looked abashed and slumped, rounding her shoulders and staring fixedly at the cards in her hand.

Mac pretended not to notice her reactions but was inordinately pleased to see he stimulated her, her curiosity, if nothing else.

He sat down, cleared his throat, and opened up the new gin rummy hand before he realized how difficult it was going to be to concentrate in their "reduced circumstances."

In turn, they drew from the deck and slapped down discards without speaking.

As a precaution, he sent his eyes to her bare toes, thinking those a benign enough target. In a moment, however, he was thinking his way up her trim, exposed ankles and mentally climbing those long, shrouded legs. His fingers twitched at the thought of her legs, which he imagined soft and smooth and naked beneath the sheet.

While their card play continued, he turned his attention to his own toes, the safer target, but was quickly, uncomfortably aware that they, too, were bare all the way up to the appendage throbbing between his legs.

"Gin," she said, a little breathlessly. His gaze cruised to her face. Already flushed, she shivered when their eyes met.

"You're cold," he said, pretending genuine concern, but reflexively seizing another maybe fleeting opportunity. "Stand up." He grabbed the castoff bedspread and positioned himself squarely in front of her.

When she rose, he moved deliberately, as if he were in complete command of his faculties. He draped the spread around her shoulders and knotted either end in his fists at her throat. There he froze, staring at his own hands, making a Herculean effort to steady them.

Memory, her head bowed, stood as if she were paralyzed, her timidity even more convincing evidence that there was no boyfriend.

Without his willing it, his index finger brushed her chin. She tilted her head slightly, enabling the lone finger to caress her cheek all the way to her ear. Her eyes glazed as if she were under some hypnotic spell. Her breathing became slow and shallow.

Encouraged, Mac caught both ends of the spread in one hand, freeing the other to make a sweeping survey of her face, brushing curlicues of her dark, damp hair back behind her ears.

Her flush heightened and her skin warmed beneath his touch, but she didn't attempt to pull away.

The bedspread hung about her shoulders on its own as Mac laced the fingers of both hands into her hair. His breath burned in his chest, coming and going in sporadic gulps. Leaning, he pressed his lips to her forehead in what he hoped was a non-threatening gesture, one she could interpret as a display of genuine affection.

She shuddered but didn't retreat.

He nibbled feathery kisses down the side of her face to a spot beside her mouth and lingered. He didn't know how far to go with this. He didn't want to frighten her. His lips touched the edge of her mouth to tap another series of innocent, staccato little kisses, then held. He didn't want to take things too far too fast. He wanted more, at the same time he needed to make conscious concessions to allow for her obvious lack of experience and, of course, the cut and swelling on her lip.

When she tipped her mouth to his, he congratulated himself. Her increasing enthusiasm for the game seemed enhanced by her own bold move. He had been wise to wait, let her take the lead. She didn't seem to notice as the bedspread slid to the floor.

He kissed her slowly, carefully, allowing her to set the pace, reminding himself again and again of the cut and the swelling.

Her compliant body nestled into his. Taking that as encouragement, his fingers plucked at her wrap until he coaxed a corner of the sheet off of her shoulder. She shivered and retreated a step, giving him a puzzled look.

He set the expression on his face, the serene one he'd practiced, formatting it in front of the mirror, a look designed to inspire confidence in clients and jurors.

Memory surprised him by lowering her eyes, at the same time raising her hands and lacing her fingers into his chest hair. When she flashed a quick, startled glance at his face, he remained stoic, intentionally limiting his response to a practiced, benevolent little smile.

Emboldened, he supposed, by his apparent lack of excitement, she flattened her hand against his chest and drew it down. He tightened his stomach muscles in anticipation of her gliding touch. Focusing on his stomach, she used both hands to brush the dark hair from his ribs toward the center, redefining the natural trough that ran vertically from the well-honed plates of his chest down…and down.

When she risked another breathless glance at his face, her eyes rounded with a look he thought was surprise and veiled innocence, totally out of place in a woman her age. Could he be her first? Nah, this had to be an act. But, if it were, it was a convincing one.

She stepped over the bedspread at her feet as he arrested her roaming hands, covering them with his. She tilted her head to one side, watching their hands as he slowly escorted hers to the edge of the sheet at his waist. He paused for one pregnant moment, then guided her right hand lower over the sheet.

Fighting his own eagerness, Mac's breath quickened as she acquiesced. He kept a tight rein on his mounting desire, amazed at the unique pleasure of her wonder. It looked as if this were a brand new experience. If that were true, he sure as hell wanted her to enjoy it.

"Stop." She pulled her hand from under his.

He groaned. The lower part of his torso twitched. "It's not that easy to turn my interest off, you know."

Their gazes locked. She looked bewildered. "You mean you can't make it stop? That?" She glanced toward the area of the sheet bulging over the swollen appendage. “Even if you want to?”

With a half laugh, half cough, he shook his head and removed his hands from her warm, smooth skin. “I think ‘if you want to’ is the operative phrase. I’m a healthy, warm-blooded adult male aroused by a beautiful woman, and I am fully prepared to behave as healthy, warm-blooded adult males are designed to behave in these circumstances.”

As if oblivious to his need, she again touched his waist, her hands caressing his over-stimulated flesh. “Does that mean no, you can’t make it stop?” She asked the question as if hers were academic interest.

He caught her wrists and guided her hands away from him. “I have exemplary self control. I can wait.”

“What does that mean, you can wait?”

“Until you’re ready.”

“But what will you do about that?” She glanced at the area where the bed sheet continued to spike prominently.

“If you think it’s going to be a while before you’re ready, the first thing I’d better do is put my clothes back on.”

Memory looked disappointed at the suggestion.

Mac studied her. “You don’t want me to put my clothes on?”

She didn’t meet his gaze. “I’d really like to see…what you look like.”

“We’re a little old to be playing doctor. Did you skip the part of fourth grade where girls and boys check each other out?”

“I guess.” Her grin was still lopsided and she blushed. “Can I help you, ah, well, you know, set it off?"

He laughed as he considered her question and what it revealed. "Apparently you think what I've got under here is a mousetrap." They both laughed a little self-consciously. He needed to think—for both of them—without scandalizing her or tormenting himself. Tall order.

He looked at his watch, then at the bed. "Tell you what. It's ten after two. How about if we grab forty winks."

"Take a nap? Here? In this bed? Together?"

He avoided looking at the bed. "I didn't mean it quite the way you think. You lie down and cover up. I'll take a quick shower, then I'll join you." He swept the fallen bedspread off the floor and threw it back over the bed, smoothing it before he beckoned her.

As directed, she sat on the side of the bed. Mac propped the pillows against the headboard for her, then went into the bathroom. He paused, then opted not to lock the door.

In the steady stream of tepid water, David Mac McCann closed his eyes. Allowing his imagination to run, he visualized her slipping into the bathroom, the sheet falling away and her naked form, distorted by the plastic curtain, coming toward him. Telepathically, he commanded her to walk through that door and do everything he imagined, relieving him of any responsibility for what might occur.

He needed to quit thinking like that. There was something pathetically naive about the woman's questions and her curiosity. Sexual tutoring with her needed to be approached with sensitivity by someone in complete control of his libido. At the moment, he was not that someone.

A dozen pounding heartbeats later, he relieved himself, then leaned against the ceramic wall, allowing the cascading water to soothe both his mind and his body.

Memory was stunning, and very bright. If she were curious about sex, there were men in Metcalf who would leap at the opportunity to school her. Here in Astrick, Quint certainly was willing. Hell, *he* was willing. He just wasn't sure exactly how things were with her. She was twenty-eight years old, for heaven's sake. She couldn't possibly be as virginal as she acted.

Mac turned off the water, dried himself, put on his boxer shorts and his trousers, which were still damp at the seams.

Memory lay close to the edge of the bed leaving three-quarters of the far side for him. She stretched under the covers, which she held clutched at her chin. Her eyelids were closed but twitched, indicating she was only pretending to sleep.

Clothed and temporarily sated, Mac realized the bearable condition wouldn't last long. If he were staying, he needed to get comatose in a hurry. He walked around the bed without taking his eyes off her and was still watching as he doused the one lamp she'd left burning. He eased down, and stretched on top of the spread. Flat on his back, he cradled his head in his hands.

****

The jangling phone jarred Mac awake in the predawn darkness. Not sleeping deeply, he knew exactly where he was and who was there with him. The rain had let up. The call had to be Mrs. Flanagan about the clothes but the phone was on Memory's side of the bed. She struggled up to an elbow, fumbled and snapped on the bedside lamp as she picked up the phone and groaned, "Hello."

Her eyes popped wide and darted to Mac's face as she listened to what sounded like a man's voice rumbling over the phone—a familiar voice.

"How did you know I was here?" she asked.

Mac glanced at the digital clock at the bedside. Five-fourteen a.m.

"No. I didn't call the police, but so help me, if you show up here, I will." She listened again as the rosy color of sleep drained from her face. "Don't use that language with me. You've had too much to drink." She trembled and fumbled the receiver. Mac took it out of her hand, put it to his ear and listened.

The man's words were vile suggestions of sexual stimulation he would use to excite her to performing certain lurid acts with him. His words were lewd and very specific.

"Hey, Ressler," Mac said, cutting into the vivid description, "I don't care where you beat your meat, buddy, but you're disturbing my sleep. If you're that bad off, run over to Barbarella's and buy yourself a couple of rounds with one of the girls."

The voice on the other end of the line bellowed like an injured animal. A large one. "McCann? What're you doing there?"

"I was sleeping. And I'd like to get back to it. I'm really surprised you're this kind of desperate, Quint. Aren't you the guy who's always bragging about how much action he gets? I thought you had to beat the women off with sticks. Maybe I can help spread the word. Find you a willing woman." Mac lowered his voice to a threatening tone. "But this one's not." He glanced at the pad marks on Memory's face and her tousled hair. She looked like a little girl. "This one is taken. Do I make myself clear?"

The caller hung up.

Mac leaned across Memory to cradle the phone. "Quint's been defending criminals and riffraff so long, he's picked up some colorful street lingo. It's just bad boy talk, Memory. The guy's still a wuss. Don't put up with it. Not that you did, but…" He couldn't help smiling. "I still scare the hell out of him, like when we were kids. If he bothers you, threaten him with me. I broke his nose once and blacked his eyes several times. I might need to remind him how tentative our relationship is—his and mine."

Memory lay back stiffly, clutching the covers to her throat. "Thank you, I think."

"He's not in any position to blab about our being here or my threat." He paused a moment, then threw back the end of the bedspread which he had wrapped over him sometime in the night. "I'll go get your clothes from Mrs. Flanagan."

Waking up in a bed beside Memory Smith was something David McCann might have dreamed but would never have imagined. He needed to hurry, not get caught up in a lot of nonproductive fantasizing.

He went into the bathroom and returned fully clothed and shod. He grabbed his blazer off the back of the chair then darted out and jogged through the early morning stillness to Flanagan's office. The thunderheads were gone, replaced by feathery clouds drifting over a pink-streaked sky, heralding the dawn.

He rang the night bell several times before Mrs. Flanagan shuffled to the door tying her robe at her waist as she came. At first glance, he thought her eyes were red-rimmed from sleep, then realized the woman was crying.

"Is something wrong?" He put the professional tone in his voice, hoping to make the question sound less invasive.

"Oh, yes, David. Everyone in town's just sick about the news this morning. That precious Memory Smith is dead."

"What?" He choked on the word and blinked to focus.

"Killed right out there on the highway, she was. Run over. They found her body not two miles down the way." She indicated the highway in front of the motel. "The poor, sweet thing. She was so tore up, they figured it must have been one of those eighteen-wheelers that got her." She mopped her nose with a tissue. "Tore all to pieces, they tell me, layin' right there by the side of the road. That precious, precious child."

## Chapter Three

"Who told you that? Who said it was Memory?" Mac couldn't seem to form questions bombarding his brain fast enough, and didn't allow time for Mrs. Flanagan's faltering answers.

"Everyone at the country club. She had an argument with Quint Ressler. He took her there for dinner. They said it was all perfectly proper and above board. Of course, they all know…knew…Memory. Knew she wouldn't be involved in anything bad, especially not with someone like Quint Ressler." Mrs. Flanagan spat the name as if it had a bad taste. "Martha Pearl said he had too much to drink."

"Wait, Mrs. Flanagan. Who found the body and why did they think it was Memory Smith?"

"Oh, it is. It was that rascal Ressler himself that said it was."

"When did all this happen?"

"After midnight. People calling back and forth…well, the whole town's been up all night."

Mac shifted, struggling to be patient. He needed to get this story from the beginning, get the full account, non pertinent details along with the rest. He took Mrs. Flanagan's arm, escorted her to the cushy sofa and indicated they should sit.

"Now, tell me, did anyone mention anything about Memory leaving the country club without Quint?"

"Oh, yes." Mrs. Flanagan stared intently into his face. "Even as sweet as Memory was, she couldn't put up with that kind of behavior."

"What kind of behavior?"

"Why the drinking, of coursc, and what always comes next with that awful man." She arched her brows above the rims of her eyeglasses. "They say he gets real lovey-dovey, totally obnoxious and doesn't care who's there or who knows. The problems start if the lady he's with objects. If she raises a fuss, they say he gets mad and even abusive, depending on how many other people are around and who they are and…" she blinked at him.

"And what?"

She stared at the floor. "Well, he gets pushy, if you know what I mean."

"Sexually?"

Her voice dropped almost to a whisper. "That's what they say. And poor Memory, with no more experience than a babe in the woods." Mrs. Flanagan sniffed twice, then broke into a new cycle of sobbing and nose blowing.

Watching in disbelief, Mac almost laughed, but the humor was too dark to be funny. "You're telling me that Quint had too much to drink and got fresh with Memory Smith?"

Mrs. Flanagan glowered. "It's too early in the morning, David McCann, and I'm too upset for you to be obtuse on purpose. And you putting the question that way doesn't show proper respect for Memory or for me either."

Uncertain exactly how he had offended her, or Memory, David tried to look contrite and said, "I see what you mean," though he didn't. "I apologize for any disrespect. Now, please tell me exactly what you heard happened. I promise I'll try not to interrupt."

"Well, Ressler got soused, like he usually does out at the club every weekend he's in town, and wouldn't eat his supper. Memory wanted to leave, but she didn't want him to drive her. Everyone knows she was too smart to get into a car with someone who'd had too much to drink." Suddenly the woman's eyes met his and her brows arched again. "Memory was too smart to do anything as stupid as that, even when she was a little child, you know. No one in her right mind would get into a car with a drunk behind the wheel. I wouldn't. You wouldn't."

He held onto his patience and the effort was rewarded because Mrs. Flanagan blew her nose and returned to her story.

"She stumbled in the doorway and banged right into a doorjamb, at least that's what he told everyone. Someone said it was him and he'd done it intentional because he'd done that to ladies before. The same doorjamb, too. Of course, no one saw it happen, not this time nor any of those times before this. It busted her lip. They say her…her beautiful lip, bled like a stuck pig."

Mrs. Flanagan mopped her nose again and gave David an accusing look. "When he saw the blood, he upchucked right there, all over that new parquet. The directors are going to have something to say about that. It'll serve him right if they toss him out of the country club once and for all, I say. But they won't do it, his granddaddy being a charter member and all. Pushing Memory Smith around…well, he deserves a whole lot worse than any slap on the wrist he'll get from the country club."

Mac took a deep breath and didn't know whether to laugh or shout at her. Before he could decide, she was back on track.

"Well, before anyone knew it, Memory was gone. Took off walking, they said. It's probably three miles down this highway to the shopping center, and raining cats and dogs like it was. You remember how bad it was a while before you checked in?"

He nodded, glad he knew exactly where Memory was and in what condition, which was most decidedly not dead. Then another thought: Quint Ressler damn well knew that.

"Then what happened?"

"It took her a long time, nearly an hour to get to where she got run over. It appears like someone hit her on the shoulder of the highway. Either they didn't know they'd hit her, or they didn't want to own up to it, because they left her, tore up there on the side of the road.

"Some others on their way home from the country club saw the body, I guess after the rain let up enough for a person to see, and they stopped to help, but it was too late."

David studied the woman. "And who said it was Memory?"

"He did. That Ressler. He drove up while they were all gathered around the body and he said it definitely was her."

"I thought he was drunk."

"He was, but they say he was still positive. Memory's sweet, pretty face was tore up so that no one else could recognize her. But when Mr. Ressler said it was her, they all remembered her being at the country club and leaving in a huff right there in the middle of that awful rainstorm. And they remembered that beautiful white cardigan she was wearing because by then it was muddy and shredded near to pieces, they said. They said there was no sign of her purse anywhere."

Mac thought back. Memory hadn't had a purse when he and Laurel picked her up, or a sweater either. She had even mentioned the purse.

Mrs. Flanagan was again mopping tears and had developed a case of hiccups. "She always seemed like such a—hic—a lonely girl."

The woman glanced at him as if wary of Mac's opinion of her comments. She didn't appear threatened by his expression, and continued. "Awfully independent—hic—particularly since her mama and daddy passed, bless 'em. Now she's gone to heaven to be with them, long before her time."

Mrs. Flanagan's narrative ended abruptly as she dissolved into tears, smushing her nose into her tissue.

Ressler had called the motel room to talk to Memory just after five a.m. Peculiar if he had identified a dead body as hers only hours earlier. What was the story on that? How did Ressler know Memory was there? Did he ask Mrs. Flanagan to ring Memory's room?

Mac thought maybe he himself was not fully awake. He couldn't get that part of the night's events straight in his mind.

"Of course," Mrs. Flanagan rambled, as if she were speaking to herself, "everybody who had seen her before wondered about her changed clothes."

"What?"

"Ones who remembered, said she was dressed different on the highway than she was at the country club."

"Did anyone say what she was wearing at the country club?"

Mrs. Flanagan peered into his face. "Why, yes. Someone said she had on a denim dress with smocking."

There was a long silence before Mrs. Flanagan suddenly flashed Mac a hard look, narrowing her eyes. "That dress in my dryer—the one you gave me to dry—it's denim and it's got smocking." The woman suddenly began flapping and scrambling to work her way out of the confines of the too-soft sofa. "Fred!" she shrieked.

Mac tapped an index finger against his lips, shushing her. "Listen to me." He hesitated, giving her a moment to stop flailing. "Come down to my room with me for a minute."

"Not on your life, mister."

"Come on, Mrs. Flanagan, you're not afraid of me. You've known me all my life."

"Yes, and you were a very naughty little boy. And you got naughtier."

"People change."

"Usually not for the better."

"I did. I promise. Now come on down to my room. I've got something I want to show you."

"I want Fred to go with us."

"There's no need to wake him. There's someone there you need to see." He glanced toward the laundry area and stood up. "Oh, yeah, and bring the clothes you dried, if you will."

She regarded him suspiciously for several beats.

"David McCann, your grandmother and I are in the same church circle."

"Yes, ma'am, I know that." He stood.

Arching her eyebrows, she slanted him a familiar, maternal warning look. "If you're up to something you shouldn't be, I am going to tell her every bit of it."

"I would expect you to do that, Mrs. Flanagan. It'd be your duty."

Huffing, she hoisted herself to the edge of the sofa before she finally, reluctantly took Mac's offered hand and let him pull her to her feet.

"I'll get those clothes. You stay here."

"Yes, ma'am, I'll wait right here."

Seeming better satisfied that he didn't insist on going with her to retrieve the clothing, Mrs. Flanagan didn't wake her husband before she accompanied Mac to Room 107.

He knocked and identified himself. They heard someone remove the security chain before the door opened.

Mrs. Flanagan gasped and stumbled back a step. Standing directly behind her, Mac caught her shoulders to steady her.

"Memory?" Mrs. Flanagan said. "Is that you?"

Memory regarded the older woman strangely before she shot an accusing glare at Mac, then she looked back at the woman. "Yes, Mrs. Flanagan, it's me. How did you know I was here?" Pursing her mouth, she narrowed her eyes for another harsh look at Mac.

"I didn't tell her, Memory, but I had to bring her to verify that you were alive and well."

"What? Why?" Memory's annoyed look deepened.

Obviously she didn't want people to know she'd spent the night in a motel room with him. On this particular morning, however, there were other, more serious rumors which needed to be squelched, even at the risk of the town knowing about their overnight together.

"Let's go inside and sit a minute," he said, escorting Mrs. Flanagan by Memory and offering her a chair. The motel owner clamped both hands on the chair's arms and lowered herself into it, still staring at Memory.

Mac waited until Memory was seated in the other chair, then he continued to hold his silence. He wanted Mrs. Flanagan to relay her startling news to Memory. The older woman didn't speak immediately, studying Memory oddly before she began explaining in a whispery tone. "The radio is saying you're dead, Memory. It's all the news. Of course, I can see perfectly well with my own two eyes that you're not."

"Dead?" Memory cast an alarmed look at Mac. "What's she talking about?"

"They found a woman's body beside the highway this morning. She'd been run over and apparently was mangled so badly, they couldn't recognize her. Quint identified the body as you."

"Quint? But he…"

"I know. He identified the body sometime after midnight and called you here at five." Mac looked at Mrs. Flanagan. "How did you happen to ring this room when he called?"

"I didn't know that was Quint Ressler on the phone." Mrs. Flanagan looked flustered, then annoyed. "He asked if a woman had checked in here sometime around midnight. I was half asleep. I thought about the clothes in my dryer and said, yes, one had. He told me to ring her room. If I had recognized his voice, I wouldn't have, but I didn't, so I did. Then I went right back to sleep. A person learns to do that when they're in the motel business."

Memory looked genuinely perplexed as she turned to Mac. "If he knew the woman killed by the side of the road wasn't me, why did he say it was? Does that make sense to you?"

Having had more time to consider the events that prompted her question, Mac had reached that bottom line, several times. No matter how he approached it, he couldn't come up with a reasonable explanation. "No, it doesn't."

## Chapter Four

Not everyone in Astrick had heard she was dead, therefore, the counter rumor on Saturday morning that Memory Smith was still alive caused considerable confusion.

After daybreak, David drove her out to the farm. He insisted she let him go inside first. He swept the place, checking closets and under beds. When he gave her the all-clear, she went upstairs alone to shower and change clothes, fix her hair and put on fresh makeup. Personally, he liked the freshly scrubbed look: her hair down, no makeup, exactly the way she'd looked in high school.

"And your car is where?" he asked, when she came down the stairs. He did a double take. She had always been beautiful but that morning, he decided, she had never looked better.

Her mouth stretched to a thin line, still a little crooked. "My car is in the parking lot at Quint's office. We went to dinner from there." She gave him a sheepish look. "It wasn't a date. I mean, I didn't think of it as a date. A couple of coworkers working late is what I thought."

He must have looked annoyed because she frowned and her voice became urgent with appeal. "Mac, he's married, for heaven's sake. There's no way…" She looked surprised. "I don't know why I suddenly began calling you Mac again."

"That's what you called me in high school."

"But not everyone did. Who used to call you that? Not the teachers." She looked enlightened. "Oh, yes, it was the coaches. And some of the guys. Your buddies. The ones you played football with. Probably the people who knew you best?"

His voice dropped. "And you."

She bit her lower lip and winced. Apparently it was still tender. "And me. Coach called you that in algebra class. I didn't know the name was reserved for your intimate friends."

Harkening back to the difference in their status and reputations, David Mac McCann nodded. "I liked your calling me that. It made people think we were close, which was okay with me." Guiding them back to the more pressing subject, he said, "I knew you didn't think of going to dinner with Quint as a date."

She smiled and nodded.

Oh, yeah, he knew what she'd been thinking when she agreed to go to dinner with Quint. He also knew what was on Ressler's mind.

"Are the keys in your car?" he asked.

"No, they're in my purse."

"Which is?"

"Which was in Quint's car." She looked at Mac as a slow smile of realization stole over her face. "No, it isn't. I took it into the country club dining room. I left it on the table when Quint asked me to dance." She looked away from him as if again caught in the throes of guilt. "I know I shouldn't have, but there were lots of people around and I hadn't danced in a long time. I should have known better. Even in junior high, Quint was famous for his moves on the dance floor. But there were dozens of people…I just never…I didn't realize…"

Mac snorted, then allowed a reluctant smile, marveling again at how rare it was to find a grown woman with Memory's naiveté.

"Okay, we'll swing by the country club first to see if your purse is still there and pick it up. Then we'll go downtown to get your car." He thought a moment, then recanted. "No, we'll pick up your car later. I think it'd be a good idea for you to keep a high profile, let people continue to see you around town, doing regular stuff."

"Like?"

"Do you need groceries?"

"I could use a few things."

"After that, you can be my guest at a special Lions Club luncheon." He liked this, coming up with legitimate reasons to prolong their time together. And although she seemed to be onto his game, she didn't appear to mind the prospect of a day in his company.

"I've got some estate checks to put in the bank. The drive-in's open until two on Saturdays." She rolled her eyes grimacing. "Of course, the checks are in my purse."

"That's fine. We'll pick it up before we go to the bank."

"And I need to run by Blevins' Hardware and find nine porcelain drawer pulls and a globe for a broken light fixture."

"Good. We'll trot you around and show everyone you're alive and kicking. When you're ready to go home, we'll pick up your car and you can be on your way."

Her expression darkened.

"Now what?"

When she didn't answer immediately, he took a shot at easing her concern.

"Naturally, I'll follow you home, check out the premises, make sure the bogeyman didn't sneak back during your absence."

A slow smile eased her scowl. "Would you be going to all this trouble with just anybody or is it me bringing out the chivalry in you?"

He could guess what she was fishing for, though he couldn't tell for sure, but he seemed to be pretty good at reading her. He was reluctant to tell her that her facial expressions were like a picture book, providing direct access to her every thought. No woman liked to hear she had no mystique, even if, like Memory, she had everything else.

She dismissed his non verbal response—a crooked, knowing grin—with a huff of disdain.

Obviously, he'd guessed right, again.

She turned and began walking toward his car. "You don't have to follow me home. You've already gone far beyond the line of duty."

He fell into step behind her. "I know, I know. I'm gallantry on the hoof, and don't you let anyone tell you different, but maybe I have an ulterior motive, did you think of that? Maybe I'm interested in doing more than my duty where you're concerned."

She tried to stifle a smile, but the laughter bubbling inside her had too strong a start to be squelched. "Maybe I have ulterior motives, too." She tossed a playful glance back at him. "Did you think of that?"

He arched his brows, doubting their reasons were

even in the same ballpark.

"I sure hope so." He grinned and his pleasure was amplified as she blushed. Was it possible they were on the same page? Nah. He might have elevated himself socially to Laurel Dubois' level, but it would take heavenly intervention to reach Memory's. Following her to the car, he thought again of how she looked wrapped in the bed sheet, inviolate, a pure, innocent female. She had looked like a gift, without the bow, but looks could be deceiving.

Come on now, he chided himself. Get real. No woman can be as perfect as you're imagining her. Still…

"Earth to Mac." Facing him, she peered into his face as if trying to make contact.

He laughed. "Another stop on our schedule: Quint Ressler."

Memory retreated a step and bowed her head but, to his delight, she didn't argue.

****

For practical reasons, they decided to do errands and lunch first, then pick up groceries when they were ready to go out to her house.

Her purse had been turned over to the country club manager who had locked it in his desk for safekeeping.

"Delighted to see you, Ms. Smith," George Cleaver said as he strode several brisk steps closer, his arms open wide. A quick glance at Mac's glower and the fifty-year-old club manager retreated a couple of steps, reducing his enthusiastic welcome to an affectionate pat on her shoulder. "We were pretty torn up around here this morning when we heard you'd been run over out on the highway."

He seemed to be using the editorial we.

"We were super pleased to learn that the early report was a mistake. Now, of course, it's like waiting for the other shoe to drop, wondering who the dead woman might be."

Memory turned a sudden querying look on Mac. Apparently, she hadn't thought of that. Unable to suggest a name, he shrugged.

Her purse was intact, drivers license, credit cards, and cash present and accounted for.

"We don't even open purses," Cleaver said. "We've got too big a turnover in employees to trust them to rifle through someone's personal information. Besides, we always figure whoever left one will call in a day or two or be by to pick it up. If we have one several days, I check out the I.D. and call the owner, but that doesn't happen much."

Cleaver returned Memory's sweet smile before her expression darkened. "Did you see anything of my white cardigan sweater?"

"No, but it may turn up."

"I think I left it on the back of my chair."

Mac didn't mention the fact that the Jane Doe reportedly was wearing a white cardigan, similar to the one Memory described to Mr. Cleaver. He did make a mental note to double check that information.

Memory was quiet as they drove to the hardware store. He could tell as she got out of the car that her attitude had taken a turn for the gloomy. Her shoulders slumped and her eyebrows veed over the bridge of her pert nose.

"Now what?" he asked as he caught up in time to open the glass door for her.

She whirled just inside, almost making him bump into her. “Who do you think she is?”

“I don’t know,” he said. “She’s not you. That’s enough for me.” He caught her shoulders to move her out of the way of other customers entering and exiting.

“What woman in her right mind would be walking on the highway late at night in the middle of a thunderstorm?” she asked.

Marveling at her sincerity, he stared into her face.

She did a double take and swallowed hard. “I had a good reason for being there.”

“Maybe she did too.”

“Meaning you think Ressler keeps the highways crowded with disgruntled ladies trudging along through sleet and snow and dark of night to make good their escapes?”

He laughed out loud at the mental picture of the imaginary lines of women making their way along the sides of roads.

Watching him, Memory’s scowl lightened and she began to laugh too. “Well, I suppose anything’s possible.”

He draped an arm around her and gently pushed her down the aisle they had blocked during their exchange, but he allowed the laughter to continue rumbling from his throat. “You, Memory Smith, are unique. You really are one-of-a-kind.”

Lions Club members, predominantly male, were unusually well behaved from the moment Memory walked into the meeting room.

“It’s nice to see this bunch still has the manners your mamas taught you,” Mac said when he introduced his guest. Their laughter at that comment was the most boisterous of lunch.

"Things seem to be breaking well so far," Memory said as they drove to Quint's law office finally to retrieve her car.

Mac flashed her a smile. "Has it occurred to you that we might just be good together?"

"I guess." Her voice fell. "But facing Quint will be the test. Is there any reason why we have to go inside?"

"Don't be chicken. It's the polite thing to do, to tell him you're picking up your car. You have to face him sometime and having me along might stiffen your backbone."

Memory bristled at the insinuation, just as Mac had intended. "I have all the backbone I need to confront Quint Ressler without any backing from you, McCann."

Mac laughed lightly, pleased that it was so easy to bait her. "I know that. I just wasn't sure you did."

Quint rarely appeared at his office on Saturdays, the receptionist said, eyeing Memory suspiciously. "You look fine. Weren't you in an accident or something last night?"

Memory gave Mac a quizzical look, then glanced back at the office girl. "No." She sounded genuinely mystified by the question.

The girl's face twisted. "Sorry. I must have misunderstood. That's what I get for eavesdropping."

They said good-bye, but before the outside door had swung closed the receptionist called loudly to someone further back in the building. "Hey, I thought you told me Memory Smith got killed in a car accident last night."

Mac's gaze locked with Memory's and they exchanged a smile as both hummed an acknowledging,

"Hmmm." Mac expanded his with: "That's sure what I heard."

"Yeah, me, too." Memory laughed. "People in small towns are so prone to gossip. You remember the old Mark Twain quote when he heard he was supposed to have died."

"About the reports of his death having been 'greatly exaggerated'?"

"I know how he felt."

"Yeah."

Memory caught his teasing look and laughed, as if she were happy just to be with him.

He kept the stop at her house brief, just gave it a quick run-through, in spite of Memory's objection. He didn't want to be a pest, but he did want to assure himself she was safe in her own home.

## Chapter Five

No one missed Laurel Dubois at first.

Supported handsomely on an allowance from her father, Laurel lived alone in a posh apartment building on the boulevard. Since she didn't have to earn a living, she didn't bother with the inconvenience of holding down a job. Instead, she devoted her sporadic energies to charity work. She volunteered in the church thrift shop, sometimes several days in one week, when the fancy struck. Occasionally she took a trip, but was never gone overnight without notifying her parents.

When her mother wasn't able to contact her in twenty-four hours at home or by cell phone, the older woman called the police.

What might seem obvious to an outside observer, did not dawn on local law enforcement until Mrs. Dubois, who obviously had some dark premonition, asked if there could be a connection between the Jane Doe found beside the highway and Laurel.

Even then, the suggestion was not taken seriously. Women like Laurel Dubois, a former debutante from a wealthy family, did not wind up unidentified and mangled on the side of a highway. It was the kind of thing that happened to transients, homeless people, or those heavily into booze or drugs.

After the idea became a possibility, it took only half-an-hour for Laurel's father to drive down to the hospital morgue Sunday to identify his only child by a tiny birthmark and a tasteful tattoo on the victim's left ankle.

Witnesses remembered having seen Laurel leave the country club on Friday night with David McCann.

As first assistant district attorney, right arm of the chief law enforcement officer in a three-county district, McCann was above suspicion. Cops who worked with him balked at the suggestion he might be involved.

His boss, Cliff Horsely, summoned Mac to his office on Monday morning before his number one assistant heard that the Jane Doe had been identified and that the body was Laurel.

"Sit," Mac's boss said brusquely. "We need to talk."

Mac sank into the chair, glad of a respite from the mountain of paperwork perpetually shifting across his desk. "Shoot."

"I have it on pretty good authority that you and Laurel Dubois have been thinking seriously of tying the knot."

Mac groaned. "Not true."

Cliff looked surprised. "I actually got that tidbit from her dad on the golf course a couple of weeks ago."

"Well, it isn't so. I don't even like Laurel much. Anyway, what's that got to do with anything?"

Cliff's somber expression grew more dreary and his shoulders drooped. He stuck out his bottom lip as he often did when he was fretting. "The woman…the unidentified body beside the highway?"

Mac felt his earlier relief sour. "Spit it out, Boss. Are you suggesting Jane Doe could be Laurel?"

Cliff raised his squint to Mac's face, studying his

assistant's expression, his body language, all of his reactions, as Mac himself would have done if the situation had been reversed; as most able prosecutors with well-honed instincts might do.

Horsely's voice was almost a whisper. "It is Laurel, Mac. Her dad identified her. Laurel is our Jane Doe."

Mac stood quickly, hovered a moment, then paced to the window, wrapping one hand around the other fist behind his back as he moved.

Cliff kept his voice low. "People saw her with you. As far as we can tell, no one saw her after that."

Mac turned to face his boss. "She asked for a ride home from the country club. I was leaving. She was ready to go." He didn't want to drag Memory into this but saw no reason to keep secrets from Cliff, who would honor the confidence if he could. Besides, Mrs. Flanagan knew and probably had spilled the beans already anyway.

"We saw someone walking on the side of the road. It was pouring down rain. Laurel actually saw her first. Pointed her out. I would have been sympathetic toward anyone out in that weather—besides that, the temperature was dropping. Of course, she was moving at a pretty good clip, straight ahead, obviously not under the influence." He hesitated, wondering again if there were any reason to try to protect Memory, and decided there wasn't anything incriminating about those circumstances…exactly.

"And?" Cliff prodded. "Did you stop?"

"Yes. It was Memory Smith."

"And you know Memory Smith well enough to recognize her from the back, walking beside the highway in a downpour?"

"We were classmates from kindergarten through high school."

"Are you suggesting you dated the miracle child?"

"Are you kidding? I was the scourge of the school. I came from the wrong, wrong side of the tracks. Memory was considered some kind of heavenly being. No, I didn't date her, but that didn't keep me or any other guy from worshiping the ground she walked on."

"And Laurel?"

Mac shrugged. "Date her then? No, I wasn't good enough to get a date with her either…then. I didn't get good enough to go out with Laurel until she got desperate and I had taken on some respectability."

Cliff smiled and nodded as if he understood. "Yeah," he whispered, almost under his breath. "Laurel didn't have much use for strays."

"What makes you say that?"

Horsely gave Mac a startled look. "I know she had a cat she was crazy about. It disappeared. Nearly broke her heart. A friend gave her a replacement, a Persian. Laurel insisted the new cat come with registration papers. She liked her animals and friends with pedigrees. Anyway, that's neither here nor there. Go on."

His thoughts going off in all directions like popcorn, Mac had a hard time concentrating. He paid little attention to Cliff's comments, which seemed to reflect a wide-held opinion of Laurel Dubois. "Memory asked us to take her to Flanagan's."

Horsely seemed to dismiss whatever tangent that had drawn his thoughts away and returned to the subject. "Did you ask why?"

"Yes. She didn't want to discuss it. She had a busted lip."

"Did you ask about that?"

"No." He regarded his boss seriously. "If you knew Memory, even knew her by reputation, you would know she's a very private person."

Cliff puckered, looking as if he were pondering nuclear fission. In an effort to keep his mind from wandering again, Mac continued. "I thought maybe she'd fallen while she was walking, but I knew that wasn't so. Whatever the problem was, she wasn't talking about it, or much of anything else at first."

"Where was she coming from?"

"The country club."

"Had you seen her up there?"

"No, but I was in the bar, not the dining room."

"Had she been with a group?"

"No." He hesitated again, not wanting Cliff to get any wrong impressions. "Quint is doing her dad's probate. In order to reduce his legal fee, she…"

Cliff was on his feet and waving a hand to stop Mac's recitation. "I don't even want to hear this. According to legend, Memory Smith is the only saint Astrick ever produced. Her dad was…"

"No, Cliff, don't go jumping to conclusions. That's why I was reluctant to tell you this, but she's my alibi, so I pretty well have to." He eyed his boss until Horsely looked reconciled to the last statement. "What I'm going to tell you next… Well, I don't want it to leave this room. Now take a seat and try to listen with an open mind, damn it."

Cliff propped himself against the corner of his desk, folded his arms over his chest, and assumed an expression that fairly dared Mac to say anything derogatory about Memory Smith.

"In order to reduce the bill on the probate, Memory upgraded the computers in Quint's office for them. She's a paralegal in Metcalf, works for Hydro and Fitch." Mac lowered himself onto the front edge of the client's chair he had vacated moments before. "She did the upgrade to get a break on the cost of the probate."

Cliff's arms appeared to relax and he was at least willing to look at Mac, which encouraged the assistant to continue.

"Laurel and I drove Memory to Flanagan's, which is where she insisted she wanted to go. I got her the room. She didn't have her purse, or a wrap, or anything else for that matter. I left her there and took Laurel home.

"When we got to Laurel's, I stayed in the car. Laurel was mad. She had invited me in. I had other plans. I watched her all the way to her door. I saw her go inside. My recollection, the mental picture, is vivid. She was storming and I wondered if she'd cool off between the time she slammed the car door and the time she got to the condo. She also slammed the door to her condo. I know because I was watching and wondering."

"What was she mad about? Did you know?"

"Yeah. She was fuming because I turned down a nightcap."

"Why didn't you take her up on it?"

Mac scowled at his boss as he decided to come completely clean. "I couldn't get Memory off my mind. I had to go back to that motel. I wanted to see her. Talk to her. Find out what had happened. Hell, I didn't even walk Laurel to her door."

"Could someone have been waiting inside Laurel's apartment? Someone you didn't see?"

"I don't know. As I said, I didn't go inside, but I watched her unlock the dead bolt to open the door. The lights were on and things looked like they always do, as far as I could tell. I didn't see any signs of anyone else. There are always a few cars in visitor parking, but nothing that grabbed my attention. Of course, I was focused on something else right then. I guess Laurel got her car and went out again."

"No. She'd never have taken her new car out on a night like that. She wouldn't have wanted to get it dirty. It's still there in her covered parking place."

"Oh, yeah, I forgot the Camry. That pale yellow color wasn't real practical for a fussy female like Laurel."

"No, but it was a perfect color for her." Cliff smiled as if recalling a pleasant memory. "She loved that lemony color. Said it matched her hair. And it did." Horsely flashed Mac a guilty look, as if rudely awakened, then reclaimed the scowl. "So where did you go from Laurel's? Did you go straight back to the motel or did you have the good sense to go on home?"

Mac frowned at the toes of his shoes. "No, I didn't."

"You went back to Flanagan's." Cliff's shoulders slumped with his own guess, which was more of a statement than a question. The district attorney seemed disappointed that Mac might have an alibi, and Mac wondered at that random impression.

"I stopped at Kitchell's first to get some things for Memory: a comb, a toothbrush and toothpaste, you know, stuff she'd need."

"Can someone verify that?"

"Yes."

Cliff nodded, studying his protégé. "Okay. Then what happened?"

"I went back to Memory's room. She kept the chain on the door at first, even after she knew it was me. I handed her the sack of stuff from Kitchell's and told her if she'd give me her wet clothes, I'd ask Mrs. Flanagan to dry them for her in the clothes dryer."

"While Memory wore what?"

"A bed sheet. She was all wrapped up in a bed sheet, covered up like a bug in a rug."

"And did she go for that?"

"Yes. I took her wet clothes down to Mrs. Flanagan and asked her to call me at Room 107 when they were dry."

"Memory was going to let you wait in her room?"

"Well…" He flashed Cliff a silly grin. "She's not real sophisticated." He tried to change the grin to a sincere look, but apparently wasn't all that convincing, judging by Cliff's caustic snort. "She's known me all her life, Boss."

"Sounds a little cozy to me. So how long were you there?"

"A while."

"How long a while?"

"Well, it was already after midnight."

"What time did you leave?"

"Sunup."

Cliff stood, inhaled a harsh breath, and straightened to his full five-foot-ten. Mac noticed that the district attorney had clenched his beefy hands into fists. "You and Memory Smith shared a motel room at Flanagan's from midnight until sunup? Do you expect me to believe that kind of slander about the finest young woman this town has ever produced?" Cliff took several steps to draw within arm's length of Mac.

The first assistant kept his seat. He didn't want to stand up or give any appearance of challenging his boss, or present too tempting a target. The D.A. prided himself on having a mind for justice and could get pretty pumped with righteous indignation when he was riled. And he definitely was riled.

Mac was taller, younger and in much better shape than Horsely. He wasn't afraid for himself physically, but he didn't want his revelations about his and Memory's night together to precipitate something he and the older man would both regret.

"I bought a deck of cards from Mrs. Flanagan, Cliff." Mac offered that salvo in his most placating voice. "We played gin rummy, for heaven's sake."

"All night?" Cliff was obviously open to any plausible explanation, but was having a hard time swallowing that one completely.

"Well, no, just until we got sleepy."

"Were there two beds in the room?"

"No, sir."

"Did you sleep there? In the bed?"

"Yes, sir, I did, but my grandmother could have stayed in that room with us. You, too. It was perfectly innocent."

"Mac, why in hell didn't you go home?"

Mac grimaced and took a deep breath. "I didn't want to. I just flat didn't want to leave her. I've waited all my life for some uninterrupted minutes with Memory. I just couldn't let the opportunity of a lifetime slip by me."

"Or let Memory slip by either, it sounds like."

Mac shrugged.

Cliff puckered and squinted, staring at his first assistant. "Are there people who can verify any of this? Help us establish the time frame?"

"Yes. Mrs. Flanagan was watching a 'Happy Days' rerun when I got the room. That might help establish what time I dropped Memory off. I took Laurel home and went directly to Kitchell's to buy the toothbrush and stuff shortly after midnight. Donnie Rutherford was working. Donnie knows me, but I don't know if he'll remember specifically what time I was there. He had a phone in his ear, even when he was checking me out at the register."

"Do you have a receipt? It could show the time."

"I might be able to find it, depending on whether Memory kept it or the sack. Anyhow, I took Memory's clothes to Mrs. Flanagan right about one o'clock. I figured she'd call the room to say they were dry in an hour or so and I glanced at my watch to check the time. I think there was a different episode of 'Happy Days' by then.

"I was in the room with Memory from then until daylight. Do you have an idea about what time the Jane Doe…I mean…what time Laurel was killed?"

"Shortly before her body was discovered, about two. I wonder if Mrs. Flanagan will be able to verify that you didn't leave the motel during that time."

"Anyone going in or out has to drive under that porte cochere in front of the office. It depends on how long she was up front watching TV, I guess."

Then he remembered the phone call. "There's one

other thing I need to mention."

Horsely sat straighter, obviously bracing himself.

"Quint called the room a little after five a.m., to talk to Memory."

The district attorney's face fell to a scowl of disbelief. "Did she tell you that's who was on the phone?"

"No, I was right there, close enough to hear him shouting. He was cussing and saying some pretty raw stuff, being damned abusive. I took the phone out of her hand and listened a minute before I had a word with him myself."

"And how did he take that, your being there at the motel with her?"

"Not well."

Cliff set a hard stare on Mac who guessed the older man was thinking of something else. "What is it?"

"Quint identified the body originally. He's the one that said it was Memory. He was definite. I wonder why he did that right after two a.m., if he knew it wasn't her? And he must have known it, if he called her motel room at five. Are you sure it was five?"

Mac nodded. "Five-fourteen. There was a digital clock on the bedside table."

"What the hell kind of game was he playing?" Cliff stood and began pacing, pinching his bottom lip between his thumb and index finger. He continued talking, muttering to himself. "Someone should have checked dental records. Laurel had just had all four wisdom teeth extracted. Hadn't healed completely."

Damn, a body couldn't buy a new car or get dental work done in this town without everybody and their brother knowing about it. But Mac had a theory of his own about Quint's peculiar behavior. "I figured maybe it was because he was the one who busted Memory's lip and goaded her to the point she preferred hiking in the rain to riding in a car with him, rattled so badly she didn't think to pick up her sweater or her purse."

Mac suddenly again had his employer's full attention, as Cliff froze mid stride and said, "What do you mean?"

"Memory left her purse on a table at the country club and her sweater on the back of her chair. We picked the purse up Saturday morning while we were running errands."

"That's good." Cliff walked around behind his desk looking determined, sat in his chair, then immediately stood again. "That may help. Odd thing, though. One of the things that fouled up identifying Laurel's body was that she was wearing a white wool cardigan with a 'Smith' dry cleaning mark, which several people had seen Memory wearing earlier."

"We picked up Memory's purse. It had been locked up in a drawer in George Cleaver's desk."

"The country club manager?"

"Right. He wasn't able to tell us what had happened to her sweater. It was just gone. How it wound up on Laurel, I do not know. Nor do I know when or why."

Mac and Cliff spent the next hour speculating about Laurel's movements after Mac dropped her at her place. They decided they needed to know the location of her purse and other personal items—watch, rings, earrings—none of which were found on her person, any of which might have given emergency responders a clue as to her identity.

“When did Memory notice her purse was missing?” Horsely asked finally.

“She mentioned it on our way to the motel.”

Horsely looked like he was getting an idea. “People said the sweater was the thing that confirmed Quint’s identification of the mutilated body.”

Mac and his boss looked hard at each other. Mac suggested Quint Ressler or someone else might have planted the sweater on Laurel. They theorized, but neither of them could guess why Quint or anyone else would have done such a thing.

## Chapter Six

"I cannot imagine she was killed on purpose." Memory wrapped her arms around her ribs as she paced her dad's dated living room, unable or unwilling to look Mac in the face or see the sincerity he had intentionally planted there. "She couldn't have been murdered. People like Laurel do not get murdered, do they?"

Memory suddenly stopped and stared into the adjacent foyer. She had left a can of black spray paint balanced on the Newell post at the bottom of the stairs. She had pruned peach trees the day before and sealed the open wounds with the paint. She'd forgotten it. It looked ridiculous perched like an Andy Warhol objet d'art. She really needed to put it away. She must remember to do that…later.

"Can you picture Laurel out in that rain, trudging along the side of the road getting wet and muddy voluntarily?" Mac asked, drawing her attention back to the subject under discussion. He sat in the middle of the aged camel-back sofa studying Memory's reactions to his replay of the random bits and pieces of information he'd gathered that afternoon.

"No." Memory looked woeful. "Laurel was completely repulsed by how wet and dirty I was. She'd never have gotten out of a car on the side of the highway if the choice had been hers." Memory turned a harsh stare on him as she appeared to ponder the question further. Finally, she shook her head as if she couldn't think of anything that might have induced Laurel to do something so repugnant or demeaning. "Where was her car, David?"

He wondered why Memory had reverted to calling him David instead of the more familiar Mac. "In covered parking at her apartment complex."

"Is the area gated?"

"Yes, the gate works on a keycard or by a resident buzzing a visitor in."

"Do you know where her keycard was?"

"On her key chain, in her purse. She handed it to me so I could drive through the gate when I took her home."

Memory gave him a startled look. "You did give it back to her, didn't you?"

He frowned at the implication. "Of course, otherwise she couldn't have let herself into her apartment. Her house keys were on the same key chain."

"You didn't walk her to her door?"

"No."

"Why not? The rain had stopped by then, hadn't it?"

"It wasn't the weather that kept me from taking her inside. I had something else on my mind, something I wanted to do, and I wanted to get on about doing it."

"Oh." She shot him an embarrassed look.

"Yeah." He gave her a knowing grin. "By then, you had crowded everything and everyone else right out of my head."

She plunged on, seeming to ignore the hint about his other interest that night and his displeasure at her implying he might be a suspect. “They didn’t find her purse or her keys with the body?”

He answered slowly, trying to get into step with her mental process. “I guess not, which was part of what made her so hard to identify. To make things even more confusing, she was either carrying or wearing your white sweater.”

“I thought the manager at the country club said he would look for it.”

“Yes, well, I guess we know now why he didn’t find it.”

“Was Laurel’s purse at her apartment?” she asked, pressing on.

“I don’t know. What difference does that make?”

“Where were her keys? If she has to have the keycard on the key chain to get in and out of the apartment complex, surely she would have taken them with her.”

Following her reasoning, Mac’s thoughts and theories took off in a new direction. “You don’t have to have the card to get out of the complex, only to get into it. The sensor opens the gate automatically when you drive out.”

Memory stared at the floor. “Maybe Laurel was forced to leave with someone who didn’t know they’d need the keycard to get back into the complex.”

“Or her keys to get back into her apartment?”

“Maybe the someone who picked her up didn’t care about getting back in. Maybe he wasn’t worried about returning.”

“Or maybe he wasn’t thinking either of them would be coming back,” Mac ventured.

“Laurel would never voluntarily have gone any

place with anyone without her purse. Remember how amazed she was that I had lost mine? Can you see something like that happening to her?"

"Not unless maybe she was in a hurry."

"No. Didn't you hear her when I got in your car? Nothing about my situation, even my appearance, impressed her until I said I'd misplaced my purse. She jumped right on that."

"Yes, she did." He hadn't remembered that before, but she was right.

"And since she didn't take her own car, she must have gone with someone," Memory said.

"Or walked." He glanced at Memory to see disdain in her face before he retracted. "No, you're right. No chance of that. Laurel wasn't the kind of girl who enjoyed long walks, definitely not long walks on the highway in a pouring rain."

"Right." Memory seemed to know he was trying out any plausible explanation, any theory that popped into his brain, "We're just speculating here, Mac, trying to fit the pieces together to make a picture. I didn't mean to inhibit your brainstorming by being critical."

Her change to the familiar nickname again tickled his ears and boosted his morale. He figured it indicated she had made a psychological U-turn back to trusting him. "No matter how stupid the theories sound?"

She gave him an indulgent smile. "Right. Theorizing can turn up pretty goofy scenarios sometimes."

"But we don't seem to hear any of these goofy scenarios coming from you."

"Maybe I'm more careful to screen my thoughts before allowing them to impact your tender ears."

"Why would that be?"

"Maybe because I'm more concerned about what you think of me than you are about what I think of you."

He gave her a skeptical smile. "No, I don't think that's it." Before she could respond, he added, "Speaking of tender body parts, how's your lip?"

"Who was speaking of tender body parts?"

"You mentioned my tender ears and I guess that just made me remember your busted lip."

She ran the tip of her tongue along her lower lip. "It's okay."

"The swelling's gone down. How'd you get that anyway?"

"Just clumsy, I guess."

"Did you take a tumble when you were walking out there in all that rain?"

She huffed, stiffening with what looked like indignation. "No, I did not take a tumble." Her words seemed to carry a double meaning. He waited giving her time to fill the silence with an explanation. She gave him a sidelong look. "Actually, I ran into something."

"Ran into what?"

She grimaced, touching the lip carefully with an index finger. "Quint's fist."

"He told someone at the country club you ran into a doorjamb."

"That was Quint's version."

"He hit you?" Mac stood and stepped closer, scanning her face for any other evidence of abuse. She retreated a couple of paces apparently feeling threatened by his sudden, aggressive movement.

Mac had been tough, always bigger and meaner than Quint. In fact, no one, not even upper-class teammates, messed with Mac much. He didn't have to endure the usual locker room hazing as an underclassman, particularly not after the knife incident. It was a commonly held opinion around Astrick that Mac McCann was a thug.

Quint, on the other hand, came from a prominent family. His dad was on the school board, which gave Quint preferential treatment in class and out. Even though he was plenty big enough to have played football, Quint was not inclined to endure the coaches' indifference to his discomfort during two-a-day practices on scorching August days to get toughened up for the season. He played a little tennis, but not competitively.

Memory patted Mac's arm, bringing him back. "Quint's amorous advances had just been pretty rudely rejected by someone he thought should be feeling grateful to him."

"You?"

"Yes. We sparred all through dinner. He kept coming on to me, telling risqué jokes and making sexual remarks. I never thought of Quint as attractive or charming, or even tolerable when we were growing up."

"So, why'd you take him your dad's probate?"

"Quint had drawn Daddy's will. His dad and mine sold used cars together at the Ford place years ago, before his dad opened his own used car lot and eventually married the daughter of the man who owned the Buick dealership.

"Quint was at Daddy's funeral. He said he'd cut

me a good deal on the probate. We started talking about what kind of pleadings I did and about how he was using old forms on old computers. I agreed to update his setup, if he'd get new computers. In exchange, he would do Daddy's probate for half price. I figured those touchy-feely hands the girls used to talk about in high school were safe now that he was married and had matured."

She drifted across the room into the L-shaped dining area, strategically putting the dining room table between herself and Mac. "I took a little too much for granted."

"You should have known better. You were still dealing with Quint. He's been lying and wheeling and dealing since grammar school."

"I guess so." She sounded contrite.

"Leopards don't change their spots, they just get bigger and meaner." He studied her silently for a long moment before he continued. "So, do you want to file assault charges against him?"

"No. I don't have a corroborating witness."

"Where did this happen?"

"In the country club entry when I was leaving. He manhandled me off the dance floor to get what he called a little fresh air. When I'd had more fresh than I wanted, I decided to leave. He tried to stop me. His idea of reasoning with a woman is to apply his fists. People came in right after he punched me and he pulled out a tissue and said I'd had a little too much to drink and had run smack-dab into the doorjamb. Then he rolled his eyes and said other things, which implied I was drunk. When the others went on inside, he went back to trying to reason with me again."

"And you objected to being reasoned with?"

"I objected to being mauled. He wanted to get me to his car where he would drive us to some destination of his choosing. His family has a cabin out at Astrick Lake. Even when we were in high school, girls told raunchy stories about parties out there."

"You were never invited before?"

"Quint's parties weren't for beginners."

"So you refused to get in his car?"

"He pinched my arm and forced me out into the parking lot where I hoped there would be some other people. There were none. Of course, it was raining by then. Not many people hang out in a parking lot in the rain." Suddenly she pulled up the sleeve of her shirt and twisted her arm revealing the inside of her elbow. Mac's eyes followed to the shadowy discoloration of an angry bruise.

When their eyes met, he tried to hide the malice, which took the form of bile backing up in his throat. Keeping his voice low, he said, "And that's when that happened?"

She pulled her shirtsleeve back to her wrist. "He opened the passenger door and put my arm in a hammer lock behind me. Push had come to shove. I jammed my heel into his instep and slammed the door. He caught me from behind. I whirled around and kneed him. Hard." She grimaced. "I'd never done that to anyone before. It must have hurt because he flew into this wild-eyed rage and swung a fist at my stomach. I bent to avoid the blow and it landed at my shoulder." She hesitated, regarding Mac solemnly. "I suppose it could have been an accident. Reflex. I hope it was. I'd never been hit before that night." She shrugged. "I have to say

I don't care much for it."

Mac stared, his own fists clenching. "I see why you didn't want to come back out to your dad's isolated farm house that night. Quint's always been a punitive guy. Not surprisingly, he limits his tirades to people he doesn't figure can or will hit back."

"Now you can understand why I didn't look forward to seeing him again."

Mac looked at the wall beyond her, but his anger was almost palpable. He had to concentrate to unclench his fists and wondered if his own growing rage was what made her shiver. "Are you cold?"

"No, but you're scaring the daylights out of me. What are you thinking, staring at me like that?"

He gave her a caustic little smile. "I was thinking I owe Quint a lot more than a quick pop in the chops." Imagining that forthcoming occasion, the dark mood lifted and Mac's smile became genuine. "But I can hardly pulverize a guy when his stupidity put me in a motel room with you for a night, can I?"

Although they were alone in her dad's house, Memory looked around, as if her parents' ghosts might suddenly materialize. "Don't say things like that in here."

"Like what?"

"That we spent the night in a motel room together. Not out loud."

"Why not? We both know it was perfectly innocent."

She bit her upper and lower lips together, then winced. "David?"

"I like it better when you call me Mac."

"Okay. Mac?"

"What is it?" He waited, but she hesitated. "Come on. Out with it."

"Were there undercurrents of…? I'm sure you know more about this than I do. Was the atmosphere in the motel room charged? What I mean is, was there some kind of electrical current between us Friday night?"

"Electrical current? More like lightning bolts, I'd say. Hot blasts of desire. Need. An incredible, physical yearning for long, slow, mutually gratifying sex."

In spite of the blush, she smiled. "Well, I don't know that I would have put it exactly like that but, obviously, you felt it too, that strange something?"

"That wasn't a strange something, Memory. For me it was familiar, only a hell of a lot stronger than usual, and I normally have a voracious appetite for that particular commodity we common folk refer to as casual sex."

"Are you telling me you were interested?"

"Interested? In having sex with you? Hell, yes, I was interested."

She looked surprised. He didn't want to alarm her, so he took a deep breath and lowered his voice.

"Yes, my sweet doofus, the thought crossed my mind. But it didn't pass all the way through, that is: in and out. It was more like an idea that drove up and parked right in the big middle of my thinking process." He returned her uncertain smile. "Not only that, I had the impression you were entertaining those same thoughts, only you didn't know how to…let me know."

"I tried." She hesitated and he studied her face as he waited, mesmerized all over again by her dark almond eyes and her pert chin and nose. He didn't dare touch her at that moment. He wanted and needed to give her plenty of room to think this concept to its natural…climax.

She cleared her throat before she continued. "Every time I'm around you, I wonder about something from a long time ago. It's something silly."

"What?"

She locked her eyes with his as if vitally interested in every expression, of every nuance of his response. "When we were in grade school, one day it snowed and your cheeks were rosy from the cold and it was like they had this little layer of white fuzz." She stalled.

He gave her a puzzled smile but could not, for the life of him, imagine what she was getting at; therefore, couldn't help her get there. "Okay. White fuzz. What about it?"

"Well, I thought about it for days. I couldn't help wondering if it was as soft as it looked. I wanted to touch your face to see if it was. You sat at the desk right beside me and every day I looked at that fuzz and wondered."

"Why didn't you just reach out and touch it?"

"What would you have done if I had?"

Apparently his stunned expression didn't suit her, nor the fact he couldn't come up with a quick answer, because she suddenly pivoted and walked away. He followed her down the hall and into the kitchen, then watched without comment as she pulled two saucepans from under the cabinet. "I need to think about supper."

Now what? Was she going to invite him to stay, or was she hinting it was time for him to leave? And what was the point of recalling his fuzzy, grade-school face?

Mac leaned against a counter, folded his arms over

his chest, and waited, surveying the recently remodeled kitchen, stark white with muted accents which appeared to reflect the simplicity and purity of the woman who had decorated it.

"What are we having?" he asked, tired of hoping for an invitation, which she had yet to extend.

She seemed intent on not looking at him. "You're taking a lot for granted."

He laughed. "You've been wrestling with your conscience about us all day, haven't you?" He straightened as she started to object. "It's obvious, sweetheart. You might as well admit it. You like having me around."

She shut her eyes as if trying to dismiss him from her sight and get him out of her mind at the same time. It didn't seem to work as she didn't look as if she could help returning his hopeful grin when her eyes popped open again.

"Okay, I admit I'm getting used to having you around. But if you're planning to stay for supper, you have to bring the wine."

His imperious self-confidence fled. "I…I don't have any wine. Not on me."

"You weren't as confident of being invited as you pretended then, were you?"

He laughed lightly. "How about if I go get us some wine. Red or white?"

"We're having lasagna, tossed salad, Italian bread and carrot cake for dessert, if I have some quiet time to get creative and construct all that."

"Right. How about if I come back at seven. Will that give you time?"

She glanced at the wall clock over the swinging

door. It was four-twenty. "I think so."

"I'm gone." He pushed through the swinging door, but reappeared on the return swing. "I need some..."

"Money?" She looked embarrassed to have asked him to bring something for dinner without offering to pay for it.

He laughed, gazing steadily into her eyes. "Motivation."

"I don't understand."

"A kiss." He gave her his frisky puppy grin. "To put the necessary zip in my wheels."

"I suppose I could manage one little kiss, if it's required."

He eased toward her, keeping both arms at his sides. She'd nearly gotten herself into big trouble in the motel room when he'd allowed her to take the lead in their little drama, so he planned to give her that same opportunity again...and again.

When they were within arm's length, she cupped her hands at either side of his face, re-igniting his grin. The kiss caught him mid grin and was over before he had a chance to embellish it.

"Now, go," she said, turning around.

"That wasn't my best work. How about we run that by one more time?" He gave an exaggerated pucker.

She giggled. "Maybe that will be a reward for later, if we follow through on our respective responsibilities."

He caught her hand and pressed her open palm to his face. "No more peach fuzz, see? A kid might have been satisfied with a little touchy-feely and that sisterly smack, but a man needs more."

She slanted him a sidelong glance. "So does a woman, McCann. So does a woman."

## Chapter Seven

She hadn't heard Mac's car, maybe felt the vibration. Memory was whipping cream and the old hand mixer made a lot of racket. She unplugged the beater and sat it on its heel, swiped her hands against her hair to redirect any flyaway wisps, and hurried to the front of the house to welcome her dinner guest.

The form standing in the hallway, already inside the house, was a squat, heavyset fellow who had his back to her as he gazed out through the glass in the front door. There was something crumpled on top of his head.

"Can I help you?" Memory asked, wondering what the stranger was doing inside the house. She didn't recognize him as a neighbor. Nor had she heard either the doorbell or a knock. That darn mixer must have masked more sound than she thought.

The stranger tugged at the item on his head as he turned, pulling a woman's stocking down to cover his face.

Memory sputtered a laugh thinking this was someone's idea of a joke, until he began moving toward her.

She whirled, instinct telling her to run. She darted through the house to the dining room, the man in close pursuit. On the far side of the room, he caught her arm and spun her around. Before he could snare her, she was off again, this time in the opposite direction, toward the front door. Her foot slid as she pivoted to run out the door. She flapped her arms trying to keep her balance. Grappling for the Newell post to right herself, her flailing hand bumped then grabbed the out-of-place can of spray paint. When she caught it, the unseated lid that had been perched precariously, toppled off. Neither she nor her assailant noticed. The small rug inside the door muffled the sound of the cap when it bounced.

Struggling to stay out of the reach of the man's thick hands, Memory threw him off balance when, unexpectedly, she turned around again, this time heading straight toward him. Raising the can, she pointed the nozzle on the spray paint and pressed the trigger, aiming the stream at his face, his eyes.

As paint met stocking, the man let out a high shriek and jammed both hands against his eyes, clawing, trying to rip away the improvised mask. Paint permeated the stocking's mesh and dribbled onto his shirt.

Memory had a ludicrous thought as she reacted, darting through the house again toward the back door. She always over sprayed things, made them drip and run instead of lacquering on the smooth coverage she intended. This time over spraying had given her an advantage. She exploded out the back door and leaped the three steps, discarding the can and idle thoughts as she ran.

She galloped, running as fast as she could toward the back road, a washed-out, little-used shortcut from town. She didn't take the chance of looking back to see if her attacker followed. Her legs were longer than his.

If she paid attention and didn't fall or slow down, she could make it through the foliage to the river road. Unless he knew his way around these woods, she could lose him in the dense undergrowth.

Another frantic thought: had she left anything cooking on top of the stove? No. The lasagna in the oven needed another twenty minutes. It might get overdone if she didn't get back, but there was no danger of fire.

A car. She heard a car. Had the man been able to clear his eyes, start his car, and come after her?

She ducked into the trees beside the road and tried to slow her frantic breathing. She could find her way to the river road through the trees, but it meant keeping her mind clear. That's what she needed to do: use her head. Think.

Then she realized the car she heard was coming from town rather than from the house.

When she saw Mac's Lexus making slow progress, avoiding the worst ruts, she drew a full, deep breath and stepped out into the roadway.

The car lurched to a stop. Mac turned off the engine and calmly stepped out. He paused for a heartbeat and stared at her before he began walking, approaching her slowly. His eyes never left her face.

New energy propelled Memory and she nearly knocked him down as she launched herself straight into his arms. Neither of them spoke at first as they stood locked in an embrace, both trembling but for what turned out to be entirely different reasons.

"What happened?" Mac asked, and she thanked God for his insight in knowing something significant had occurred.

"A man came in my house."

"Did you know him?"

"No."

"And that frightened you?"

"Mac, no." Breathless, she sounded exasperated, although she didn't intend to, but she had expected more from his insight. "He had a woman's stocking over his head."

"He did?" He looked and sounded skeptical.

She fanned her hand at him in an attempt to erase any wrong conclusions. "Yes, and he grabbed me—my arm." She indicated her left forearm smeared with black paint that looked like a bruise.

Mac's pleasant expression dissolved into a furious glower. "He came inside your house?"

She nodded.

"How did he get in? Did you open the door?"

"Of course not."

"Who was it?"

"I just said I didn't know him."

"Okay, what did he look like?"

"Didn't you hear me? He had a stocking over his face. I don't know what he looked like."

"What did the part of him you could see look like? Was he tall, short? Fat? Thin? What?"

"He was probably five-five or six and weighed quite a bit, like two hundred fifty pounds. He didn't look exactly fat. He was solid, sort of squatty/muscular."

"Could you tell what color his hair was?"

"Maybe sandy, but that might have been the stocking."

"How did you get away from him?"

"Oh, yeah, and that's how the police can find him. I sprayed him with black spray paint."

"What?"

"Remember? It was there on the Newell post. I meant to put it away, but I just kept forgetting to do it, which turned out to be a good thing. When he caught me, I grabbed the can. I thought it was empty and it sputtered, but then I gave it a desperate shake and it cleared and sprayed straight into his face. He screamed and let me go and he got really busy trying to remove the stocking."

A slow grin replaced concern on Mac's face and he nodded. "Good girl. Good thinking."

"Oh, no, I didn't think of it. The can was just there."

"While he was occupied trying to get the stocking off his head, you ran."

"Yes. Out the back door."

"Did you see a car?"

She puzzled a minute. No, she didn't remember seeing a car, although she could see through the windows and the open front door that the man had not parked in front of the house, as everyone—residents and visitors alike—normally did. "No. I wonder where it was," she said.

"So, are you okay?"

"Yes, but I'm really glad to see you."

"I could tell." He grinned again and she returned the appreciative look, before his happy expression dissolved. "What's wrong now?"

She looked alarmed. "Our supper may not be edible if we don't go back pretty soon."

"We're going back. First, I'm going to call the

sheriff on my handy, dandy cell phone, and I'm going to get my gun out of the trunk of my car, then we are going right back to make sure this interloper, unlike Goldilocks, doesn't help himself to our porridge."

"I didn't put the cake in the oven yet and it has to cook for an hour. My great supper is going to be a big fat flop." Under the circumstances, that sounded nonsensical, even to her.

He chuckled, put an arm around her shoulders, and gave her a series of consoling pats as he guided her to his car. "That's okay. Food was only part of what I was coming back for."

She fell into step beside him. "I'm sure glad you came back early."

"Yeah, me too."

He made the call from his car, told the sheriff's dispatcher to spread the word, look for a would-be burglar with black paint on his face or clothing. He followed with the rest of the rather sketchy description.

Mac sounded disappointed when he examined the paint can at the house moments later. "Latex," he muttered. "Washable. It would have been better if it had been an oil-base."

Her voice oozed sarcasm as she said, "I'll make a note of that for the next time I'm attacked."

Mac grinned. He didn't know Miss Perfection had a caustic side or that she could be combative when cornered. He was beginning to like Memory Smith even more than he had before, and that was saying a lot.

****

Their dinner, delayed by the sheriff's interview and cursory investigation, was delicious, but Memory seemed preoccupied, jumped at every sound. The old house creaked and groaned with the breeze which rose with the moon.

The sample kissing earlier had stimulated other appetites in Mac, ones more compelling than food. He was not overly concerned about the burglar, who appeared to have been caught in a run-of-the-mill break-in into what he mistakenly assumed was a farm house unoccupied during daylight hours. The culprit had definitely come out on the short end of the exchange. His encounter with Memory might encourage the man to go straight. Mac smiled to himself as he imagined the scenario she had described several times—to him then to the sheriff and two deputies.

Mac and Memory both had wine. He made it hard for her to tell how much she was drinking by topping off the glasses long before they needed refilling.

The carrot cake, baked during the sheriff's investigation, looked tempting, but Mac declined her first offer and said, "Later." Instead, he took her hand to escort her from her chair at the dining table into the semi-dark living room. He didn't bother turning on additional lights. There was enough diffused lighting from the hallway to provide all they would require for his planned after-dinner activity.

Music lilted from the old eight-track player, a full orchestra issuing deep, vibrant sounds that made Mac's body thrum. He relieved Memory of her wine glass and set it, with his, on a side table, then eased onto the sofa and tugged her hand, drawing her across his lap.

Lounging across him, face to face, she fidgeted. When she started to say something, he clamped a hand on the back of her neck and pulled her mouth to his. He settled back, nestling into the sofa, and allowed her to set the pace as he maneuvered her willing body, molding her chest to his, alert to her every sigh, the trembling that came with each change as his hand glided slowly around her shoulder and under her arm before his fingers came to rest at the side of her breast. She stiffened. He stopped every movement, except his mouth, which he set to gently schooling hers.

When she relaxed, he deepened the kiss. She wrapped one arm behind his neck and pressed her body more closely against his as the music rolled over them in waves, cresting and tumbling in rhythmic sweeps. He knew he'd never hear the old big band sound again without recalling these moments in Memory's arms.

Suddenly, unexpectedly, she broke the kiss and leaned away from him, peering into his face. "What are you thinking about?"

He smiled. It was a woman's question, one the female of the species often asked at times like these. It surprised him that she would ask such a traditionally female question when she was so unlike any other woman he knew. "The truth?"

She nodded.

"That I wish this sofa had been there the other night when all we were wearing was bed sheets."

She laughed, not a snicker, but a bawdy, definitely unladylike guffaw. "Not likely I would have cooperated this way then, mister."

Her noisy response made him laugh too. "What? You didn't trust me?" He hesitated, wanting to ask something that had baffled him at the time and the several times he'd thought of it since. "In the motel…?"

The smile remained on her lips and she said,

"Hmmm?" encouraging him to complete the question.

"You wanted to come in the bathroom when I was in the shower, didn't you?"

The smile evaporated from her face. He watched her closely.

"What was that about?"

She removed the arm from around his neck, laced the fingers of both her hands together and stared down at them. "I'm not exactly sure. Anyway, how did you know?"

"Answer my question first." The silence thickened while he waited.

When she finally looked at him, her eyes had narrowed and she assumed what appeared to be a meditative expression. "I wanted to get into the shower with you to see what would happen."

"Surely you knew what would happen. A man and a woman nude in a shower together? I was already in a bad way. I was in there in the first place to try to cool down a little."

Her mouth set in a pout. "I wanted to have sex with you."

He eyed her with overwhelming disbelief. "You did?"

She frowned at her hands, bobbed her head up and down, and wheezed a sigh. "That's what I said. Yes."

The look she gave him would have chilled any red-blooded male in the middle of a forest fire. Then she continued. "You made it clear you weren't interested."

It was his turn for a bawdy laugh. "Oh, honey." He choked for a minute, grappling for words, then just gave up and laughed harder. "Baby, baby, baby, I would have accommodated you in a heartbeat, if I'd had any idea you knew what you were doing. I didn't think you did. You acted like you were confused, like maybe you…hadn't been in a situation like that before. I didn't want to take advantage of you."

Suddenly she was off his lap and up. Her feet hit the floor practically in mid stride. "Look, McCann, ever since junior high I've been trying to get some guy in Astrick to hold my hand or put his arm around me or kiss me or any of that other romantic stuff." Hands on her hips, she glowered down, looming over him. "And do you know what? Not one was ever interested."

He shouted a laugh full of surprise and total disbelief. "No, no, no, sweetheart. We were interested. We were all interested. It was just that you were so…"

"What?" She looked alarmed and wiggled her fingers, palms up, beckoning him, encouraging him to finish his sentence.

He looked directly into her beautiful, puzzled face trying to determine if she were kidding, but what he saw in her expression was sincere confusion.

"Pristine," he said finally. "You were a legend, Memory. You were the town's very own angel, one that accidentally tumbled out of heaven and landed among us. Look at yourself. You were—that is, you are—perfect, so breathtakingly beautiful, not one guy felt worthy. Not even Prince Ressler, who we all figured was the closest thing to royalty we had."

Her glower became a bewildered frown. "Guys thought I was too good for them?"

"You occupied the community pedestal, baby. It's a wonder the city fathers didn't put a marble statue of you in front of the courthouse and require pedestrians to cross ourselves or genuflect as we passed."

"Are you making this up?"

"No, Memory. Scout's honor."

"You were never a Boy Scout."

"No, I wasn't."

Her eyes rounded and shimmered. Her shoulders began to shake as sputtering laughter rippled from her throat. The laughter increased in volume and accelerated each time she glanced at him until, finally, she threw her head back and the laugh became the unladylike guffaw he'd enjoyed earlier, this time punctuated with snorts.

And Mac laughed with her. He liked seeing her so at ease, giving herself up with such complete abandon. Might she be that spontaneous in bed? He'd like to check it out. And he intended to, now that he knew she felt so neglected. Yes, sir, he'd like to investigate the sexual dimensions of this woman thoroughly. And soon.

With that in mind, Mac got up off the sofa and stepped in front of her. Her giggles continued, intermittently, but she sobered fast enough as he put his open hand on the side of her face.

"What are you doing?" There was wonder in her eyes and her expression grew somber.

"Nothing much. I just want to kiss you some more."

She pretended she might turn away, but he read her face, saw the curiosity light up her eyes at the prospect.

"No, no, miracle girl, you're not going any place. You've dodged this bullet as long as you're going to."

Keeping his open hand on her face, not touching her anywhere else, he bent and brushed his mouth over hers. He couldn't help smiling as she stood perfectly still, her chin tilted to receive the chaste little kiss. Her eyes widened as he leaned away to study her. She shuffled her feet until her body moved closer and was again perfectly aligned with his.

He grinned, realizing it was his turn to shuffle. Easing forward, he planted one foot between hers, wedging his knee between her knees and squaring his hips. He couldn't help marveling at how well their bodies fit—as if they were made for joining. He could see definite possibilities—probabilities—here.

Her eyes half closed, her chin tilted, she puckered. God, if he was dreaming, he didn't want to wake up. He lowered his mouth to hers, careful not to let his own intensity alarm her. Then her arms snaked around his waist and he wrapped her shoulders, pulling her voluptuous curves into his own angular body.

This was heaven, pure and simple. Moments later, he felt lightheaded and reminded himself to breathe as he repositioned his lips without lifting them from hers. A little prodding eased hers open, only slightly. He chided himself again. *Easy, hoss. This is new to her. You are a pioneer, the first man in this uncharted territory. One small step for man; one giant leap for mankind.*

Intellectually, he had the concept, but his body was taking command of the siege, in spite of the mental restraints he tried to impose. His brain needed to resume control. To do that, he'd have to break the kiss. Just as that decision was made, her rosebud mouth opened a little more and his brain yielded control again.

She wriggled against him, snuggling. He allowed his tongue a quick sortie, only to find that explorer captured as she opened wider and inhaled, her mouth welcoming the intruder on its own.

Caught in a swirling eddy, a whirlpool pulling him down, down, he locked his arms around her and began a lover's sway, coaxing, luring her body, his knee gliding between her legs. He took slow, steady steps backward, pulling her with him until his calves made contact with the sofa. His right hand swept forward from her back and along her belt line to her midriff, then climbed cautiously. She shifted to give the rover better access, offering more, and his hand drifted to capture a full, willing breast, prompting a groan of pleasure from the throat of the conquered.

Mac had a fleeting thought: who was predator here and who the prey? Just as quickly as the question arose, he realized: he didn't care.

He broke the kiss and nibbled down her jaw to capture an earlobe between his teeth, triggering another groan. His body temperature climbed.

One hand cradling the breast, his other acquiring one well-rounded hip, he sank onto the sofa, hauling her along and arranging her on top of him. Perfect. Oh, yeah, their positions were exactly right. It would be easy to maneuver her onto her back from there.

She pulled her head up, squinting, giving him an earnest look. He saw the familiar smokiness in her eyes. She was caught in passion's web. Afraid that seeing the mounting desire in his face might frighten her, he paused for a moment, giving her the opportunity to make a choice. To his delight, she tangled the fingers of both hands into his hair and jammed his face to her chest.

He mouthed her breasts outside her clothing as his fingers twitched in a vain attempt to conquer the buttons on her shirt.

"Wait." The word came as a rasp, but was clearly distinguishable. Mac froze, obedient to her command. She wheezed, as if she'd been running. "I don't know what's happening. Something weird. What I mean is…I'm…ah…I'm not thinking very clearly."

He tilted his face enabling him to see hers as well as he could from that proximity. She touched his hand that had been working on the buttons, but she didn't push it away. "What are we doing, exactly?"

"Well," he hesitated, wondering how honest to be. "I'm trying to get a little clothing out of our way to facilitate things."

"What things?"

Complete honesty was probably the better course. "The grope."

"So you can touch me?"

"Yes."

"And am I supposed to do the same unbuttoning with you?"

His own laugh surprised him. "Yes."

"When?"

"Whenever you feel like it. Whenever you get curious."

"How about now? I'm pretty curious right now."

"Have at it." He presented his shirtfront and tightened his stomach. He might as well give her a good impression; in case she'd forgotten how good he looked in the sheet.

She remained on top of him and worked timidly at first. She breathed through her mouth as she concentrated on undoing his shirt buttons. She didn't take time to push the fabric aside as she advanced, as if she were not urgently interested in seeing what was underneath. Her breathing became erratic and her face flushed, but she persisted with a look of determination. He watched in silence, but noticed that the air around them seemed to be getting hotter as they inhaled and exhaled. The lower half of her pressed into him, tormenting him, but he didn't flinch. She concentrated as if she were in a trance.

When all his shirt buttons were free, she caught both sides of the placket between index fingers and thumbs, set her jaw in a determined expression, and lifted the fabric away from his torso. Her lower half pressed even more firmly into his and he bleated an audible "Ohhhh" that echoed with hers. Rapid breathing became gasps.

"I thought I couldn't possibly remember how you looked," she gave him an apologetic glance, "but I did. Would you mind if I touched you?"

"No. I mean, yes. What I mean is, it'd be perfectly okay for you to touch me."

She pressed the pads of her fingers against him cautiously at first as he held his breath in a heroic effort not to moan as she felt him up.

Shooting an occasional concerned glimpse at his face, she eventually flattened both of her palms against his pecs and smiled. He flexed involuntarily and she gave a nervous giggle but her eyes remained on his chest.

She pushed up to straddle him and splayed her hands, set them gliding slowly up and down and side to side over his exposed chest and stomach. As she did, she arched her back and began to sway, pushing his temperature to feverish.

Memory started when Mac shifted to free the shirttail and give her better access, but she quickly settled back to her task, bending to slide her hands around his rib cage, as if in her fascination, she wanted to touch every inch of the flesh she had exposed.

Determined to be still until she got tired or bored, he watched and tried to ignore the intimacy of her sitting astride him. She closed her eyes and her head rolled as she rocked back and forth, apparently enjoying the feel of a man's erection beneath her.

Mac fingered the buttons on her blouse again. Her eyes popped open and he whispered, "Turn about's fair play."

A tiny frown pinched her brows, but she nodded and resumed the torturous rocking.

If his reticence had been tested before, this was the ultimate measure. Scarcely able to breathe, he unfastened all the buttons on her blouse then spread the opening. The bra stood as the next obstacle, but he went with his proven technique, pulling her forward, fondling, kissing and coaxing her as he released the hooks at her back.

Her eyes round, she trembled as her breasts broke free of their lacy harness. He moved decisively at that critical moment, sweeping her shirt and bra off her shoulders and arms in one move. Then, before she realized what was happening, he removed and tossed his own shirt, to make her feel less threatened.

Then there they were, she still straddling him, both nude from the waists up.

"Are you warm enough?" she asked, brushing hot hands over his stomach and chest.

"Yeah. Are you?" His question had a double

meaning, which he doubted she had the experience to get.

Using an index finger, she wiped perspiration from her upper lip, yet he saw the telltale goose bumps in the darkened circles around her nipples. Wanting to appear sympathetic, he offered the heat of his mouth as an act of charity. She gasped as he caught one pert nub between his lips and breathed heat on it. When she remained still, watching him, he circled the tip with his tongue, then began suckling, slowly taking more and more of her until she gave a moan of pleasure and began to writhe.

In the past he had experimented to determine what moves pleased women most. Suddenly he realized the others had been training, preparation for this night. He intended to bring every bit of their past satisfaction to this effort, to provide every ounce of pleasure he knew how to give; to lay every piece of sexual treasure at the feet of this woman whom he had worshiped and adored all their lives. She was a goddess, the one woman worthy of the homage he had waited a lifetime to pay.

When he withdrew his mouth from her breast, she whined and threaded her fingers into his hair to pull him back. She needn't have worried. He wasn't through. He fully intended to lave and attend to the other breast as he had the first, to prepare her for the heat of his mouth in other, even more intimate places.

When she seemed to realize he didn't intend to stop, she rocked her head back, yielding her nakedness like a vestal virgin presenting herself for sacrifice.

Oh, God, could it be this easy?

## Chapter Eight

He knew it was too easy. Too good to be true. Still, once they were into it he hadn't expected her to call a halt so abruptly, or maybe to interrupt them at all. She became fully alert just as he began coaxing the zipper on her jeans.

"What base is this?" she asked, her voice hoarse as she worked her body off to one side of his.

"Third." He tugged the waistband of her jeans, trying to pull her back onto him, but she stiffened. "We are, sweetheart, turning toward home."

"Is that what you're going to tell people?"

The question stopped him cold and he surrendered his hold on her jeans. He didn't dare look at the perfect nakedness of her upper body right there in front of his eyes. "What? Tell people that I got to third base with the legendary Memory Smith?"

She looked so stricken that he grinned.

"Baby, first off, it's not anybody else's business." He moved his hands to settle on her thighs. "Our relationship, Memory, is strictly between you and me. Privileged." Casually, he sent his hands to her waist, and lay back flat to study her face as she continued to straddle him. "No one would believe me anyway. We're both pretty well saddled with our respective reputations. To make a claim like that stick, I would have to produce pictures or convince you to corroborate my story."

"Really? How odd."

He couldn't help enjoying her naiveté all over again. But the mood, the dreamlike momentum that had carried them to this point, had dissolved.

She groaned as he lifted his hands from her body. Not wanting to disappoint, he caught her shoulders and eased her off of him, allowing himself one more long, lascivious glance. "Maybe we can get back to this later."

He wanted her, badly, then and there, but maybe an intermission was for the best. He needed to exhibit some maturity. Some restraint. He needed to bring her along slowly, not in a frenzy. Still, he couldn't help feeling defeated as she climbed off of him and stooped to retrieve her bra and blouse. She didn't look at him.

Instinctively he knew seducing her slowly would be best. It was a hard reality to accept at that moment, but, no, he didn't want to manipulate this woman into bed. He would rather tantalize her into initiating things on her own. He figured the best way to do that was to kiss her senseless and touch her and encourage her to kiss and touch him until her own desire motivated her, until she became desperate with wanting to share herself and fully ready to share a little of him. Oh, yeah, that was definitely the program he should follow. He needed to coax her along until she was the one climbing the walls. Get her primed until she became the aggressor. A sweet plan. Now, if he just had the fortitude to follow it up.

As he entertained those thoughts, he and Memory reclaimed and replaced their respective clothing in silence. Having reached his decision, he offered her an opportunity. "I want you to come home with me tonight."

"I don't think that's a good idea." She gave him a mysterious, tolerant smile, reminiscent of the Mona Lisa.

"No?" He followed her glance to the front of his trousers where there remained substantial evidence of his earlier enthusiasm. "Aren't you afraid to stay here by yourself?"

She rolled her eyes as if she were not thrilled with that choice either, then set her jaw, squared her shoulders, and pursed her lips. "What kind of person would I be to let some jerk run me out of my own home? This is my house. This has always been my safe hole. My briar patch."

"Until tonight. When there's a break-in, most people feel violated, like when the security was breached, their homes were contaminated."

"Yeah, well, I've been thinking about that. He probably didn't expect me to be home."

"But your car was here."

She dismissed him with a wave. "For all he knew, I could have been out with someone else, who drove their car. Besides, the sheriff probably has him sacked up by now. How many short, squatty guys do you think are running around with black spray-painted faces?"

Mac was not nearly as confident about the efficiency of local law enforcement as she was. No one from the sheriff's office had called back to say they had nabbed her bad guy. Also, a burglar who doesn't expect to find anyone at home doesn't have the convenient stocking poised on the top of his head to pull down to hide his face.

Watching and listening he realized she was trying to bolster her own courage. He thought it better not to share his negative thoughts. “Your car is still here,” he pointed out, then gently tried to show her the fallacy in her logic. “When I leave, your burglar might get the impression you've left with me and try again.”

“I’ll leave some lights on downstairs. Besides, surely he saw there was nothing of any real value here. I doubt he’ll be back.” She shot Mac a quick look. “Don’t you think I’m right?”

Mac noted that she hadn’t asked for his opinion until she’d mulled her own thoughts around pretty thoroughly. It might be better if he didn’t give her the benefit of his thinking at the moment. If she were going to stay in her home, he didn’t want her feeling any more threatened than she did already.

She waited for his answer, staring at his face.

“Where do you sleep?” he asked. “Downstairs?”

“No. All three bedrooms are upstairs.”

“Maybe you could sack out on the couch here. That would make it easy to get out of the house in a hurry, if you needed to.” He eyed their recent playground.

“Um, I don’t think I could sleep here tonight.” She looked embarrassed. “It will be hard enough to fall asleep in my own bedroom, with so many new…sensations…to think about. I’m sure I couldn’t get any rest there,” she indicated the sofa, “where those stimulating sensations came to life.”

Mac laughed lightly. “Do you mind if I go upstairs then? Have a look around?”

“Sure, if it will make you feel better.” She cast him a skeptical glance. “You’re not thinking of initiating any new games up there, are you?”

He tried to look judicious. "No, ma'am." He thought a moment. "I could stay over, you know. Bunk down here myself."

"You could sleep there, on that sofa, and not think of our…ah…previous activities?"

"Oh, I'd probably think of them, all right, but that'd be okay with me." He gave her a lazy grin.

"What if the memory of those sensations motivated you right up the stairs?"

The grin waned. "I guess that could happen, but I guarantee it wouldn't unless you—in no uncertain terms—invited me. You can trust me, Memory. I'm not some crazed animal so hot for your bod that I'd attack you uninvited. I'd have thought you would have realized that by now."

Worry lined her face. "The truth is, I don't think I trust either one of us, especially not under the same roof…at night. Our main problem could be me. We probably could resist temptation better by putting five or six miles between us."

"Why bother resisting?"

She studied him for several heartbeats before she spoke, her voice low. "Because neither one of us believes I'm psychologically ready to tag all the bases yet, do we?"

He smiled. "That's true, at least for the moment. How about more practice?"

"Okay. When?" She sputtered an embarrassed little laugh.

"Tomorrow?"

"I'll make myself available."

"You're going to stay around town for a while then, I take it?"

Her expression fell. “I’d like to stay a couple more days, at least to see if they can find who did that awful thing.”

“Will your boss be okay with your staying?”

“Yes.” She didn’t offer more and he was reluctant to ask.

Not wanting to leave on a down note, Mac strode into the kitchen where he began rinsing supper dishes. The sight of his domesticity seemed to brighten her.

“Hey, you don’t have to do that.”

“Sure, I do. Little Tommy Tucker sang for his supper, but, at the risk of embarrassing myself, I’d rather rinse dishes for mine. I can carry a tune, but not very far.”

She giggled and began loading the dishwasher. In the ten minutes it took them to return the kitchen to proper order, she was effervescing again, restored to her earlier bright self. He latched the back screen and secured the door—wishing she had a dead bolt on that one—before they turned out the kitchen lights.

Ambling, working his way through the house, he double checked the locks on the windows. She needed to install a security system, but he thought it better not to mention that just before he left her alone for the night.

“Walk me to my car?” he asked.

She slid her slender hand into his thick one. “Okay.”

Outside in the moonlight, his reaching for the car door was a ruse. He used the motion to tug her around in front of him and pinion her between his body and his vehicle. She looked up at him boldly, playfully. “What now?”

"Now, I leave." He scrutinized her face a moment. "Unless, of course, you want me to tuck you in and say your prayers."

Her wicked little laugh cascaded like wind chimes. "No, thanks. I've put myself to bed with no assistance for several years now."

"Right."

He lingered too long over what he intended to be a chaste little kiss goodnight. She seemed malleable, responding to his hands, his arms, his body. She pressed herself into him as if she wanted to be closer, then closer still. The innocuous gesture deepened into a physical joining which had him whispering sweet breathless words in her ear. "You are an angel," he wheezed. "My own sweet heavenly being."

Listening intently, locked in his arms, she didn't seem at all eager to be rid of him. Her reluctance gave him the strength he needed to catch her shoulders firmly in both hands and lever himself away. "Good night, my sleepy princess."

She looked tipsy and her eyes crossed slightly as she grinned. "And you would be?"

"Prince Charming."

"Of course. Good night, sweet prince."

He watched her walk back toward the house a little unsteadily, weave up the steps onto the porch, and open the screen door. Just before she stepped inside, he whispered her name.

"Memory?"

She turned. "What?"

His voice sounded reverent. "I love you."

The Mona Lisa smile was back as she took and held a deep breath. "Good."

He had progressed that far and he wanted to finish. "I've wanted to tell you that ever since second grade. I thought as long as things seemed so clear between us right now, I'd go ahead and mention it."

"I'm glad."

"That I love you or that I mentioned it?"

"Both."

"And what do you have to say about that?"

"I already said I'm glad."

He tried not to let his disappointment show as he ducked into his car muttering, "Yeah. Well, thanks a lot."

****

Before Mac's taillights disappeared, Memory closed and locked the front door, left the porch lights burning, then snapped off the inside lights, except for the one in the entry hall, and climbed the stairs. She felt physically drained but raging hormones had her recalling the warmth of Mac's body.

She changed into her favorite, well-worn cotton nightgown and was in the bathroom brushing her teeth when she heard a tinkling that sounded like glass breaking. She listened a long moment, heard the dead bolt snick open, and the front door creak its familiar objections. Silently, she closed the bathroom door and locked herself inside with the turn of the skeleton key, then removed the key from the keyhole.

Memory had always loved the smaller upstairs bathroom. Unlike the large one, it had no window, which gave her a feeling of total privacy. At the moment, however, no window provided no alternate way of escape. The only way out was the door.

Trembling, she shoved the key back in the keyhole,

trying to quell the panic rising in her chest like reflux. She desperately needed to keep her mind clear and think, but footfalls on the stairs paralyzed her. Someone was coming.

She needed to think and move, but reason came slowly. The noise had sounded like glass being broken out of the front door. Neither Mac nor any of her neighbors would have broken glass out of a window or a door to gain entrance. Not unless the house were on fire. She sniffed. She didn't smell smoke.

The stairs creaked. Whoever was coming was heavy as evidenced by the depth of the wood's complaints. Memory found the familiar sound oddly reassuring. It sounded like only one person. One person. She could defend herself and her home against one person. This was her home. Her turf. Earlier she had proved she could put an intruder to flight, proved it to herself, if not to anyone else. Apparently she was going to have to do it again, this time without the convenient spray paint.

She scanned the small room for a weapon, considered the potential in each item she saw. Toothbrush? Safety razor? Toilet brush with the flimsy plastic handle? All possibilities. The intruder was advancing steadily. She needed a plan.

Along with the regular creaking of the stairs and the heavy footfalls, she could also hear him wheeze. She imagined the short round fellow with the stocking over his head. Was he back? If so, the guy certainly was persistent. What could he want? There was nothing of any value in the house. She would be glad to give him anything on the place. All he had to do was ask. By breaking in, however, he had turned himself from a needy stranger into an adversary spoiling for a fight. Not her area of expertise, but she could handle it. She hoped.

Desperate, Memory opened the medicine cabinet. Aspirin, mouthwash, cosmetics. Nothing inspired her. Another familiar squawk indicated the intruder had stepped onto the landing. He was nine stairs and a dozen steps away.

Memory spun in a circle before her brain recorded hairspray right there, on the back of the toilet. An aerosol spray had given her an advantage before. She checked directions on the side of the canister. "Shake well before using." She usually disregarded instructions, but this time she needed all the holding power she could get. She grimaced at the pun. A note on the can warned that the contents should be rinsed immediately if inadvertently sprayed into the eyes. Right.

The guy was wheezing already. Winded from the climb, maybe he wouldn't be in condition to put up much of a fight.

She uncapped the can and snapped off the bathroom light. The bead inside the can rattled as she shook it. Darkness might give her some advantage. Also the intruder probably would expect to find her cowering, not getting all up in his face.

She jumped when he hit the door. It held. It was solid oak, not some composition door or hollow core. Her dad had been frugal, but he felt strongly enough about wood to pay extra for the genuine article.

"Thanks, Daddy," she whispered and shook the can more frantically.

With a second blow, the door held but wood

splintered midway down the doorjamb, near the latch. The hairspray percolated and began to sizzle out the nozzle. Good. Over shaking might give the contents more thrust to carry extra distance.

The doorjamb gave with the third strike and a short, stout form, his face hidden within a new, unblemished stocking, hurtled forward. Silhouetted in the light from the hallway, he lost his balance and stumbled. The delay gave him time to see the spray can. He shouted, "Not again," and threw up an arm to shield his face, but, teetering he couldn't keep the protective appendage in place.

Memory pressed the button and the hairspray spewed noisily directly into the man's face. She soaked him: his nose and eyes. He ducked and dodged trying to avoid the fizzing spray, but she followed, maintaining her attack. When her index finger weakened, she released, gave the can half-a-dozen new shakes, and pressed the nozzle with her thumb.

Instead of grabbing her, reflexively the intruder snatched the stocking off his head and began to convulse, overcome by alternating fits of coughs and wheezing.

How much could he take? Was she permanently blinding the poor soul? Memory rudely brought herself back to the here and now. The man obviously had allergies. Maybe even asthma. But he was her enemy, and she wondered again: Why?

He dropped to his knees then toppled sideways on the floor clawing at his eyes with both hands and shrieking. Again, she noticed that his cries were high. He sounded like a girl and she wondered if he might be in the wrong business. A man who assaults people for a living probably should get in shape, see a doctor about those allergies, and control his voice so he sounded more like a threat than a victim.

He writhed on the floor directly in front of the lavatory. If she got out of his way and he calmed down a little, he could rinse his eyes and maybe get beyond all this hysteria. With no hesitation, she leaped over his anguishing frame, dropped the hairspray can and bolted for the stairs.

What if he had an accomplice? She whipped around and ran back to retrieve her trusty sidearm—the hairspray—and stole another quick glance at the man who was curled into a ball and sobbing.

No mercy, Memory chided, prodding her resolve. And no prisoners. In spite of her rationalizing, she had a hard time subduing her conscience as she ran. Her parents had raised her to help people. Concern for others was part of her genetic make-up as well as her upbringing. It was hard to overcome.

The front door stood wide open, convenient as she leaped the broken glass in her bare feet and darted into the open air and freedom, still clutching the spray can. Shoeless and in her nightgown, she broke into a full run, around the house and out the back. By the time she reached the river road, she had a stitch in her side and slowed to ease it.

"He shouldn't have inhaled," she muttered, exonerating herself. "Everybody knows that stuff's not good for you, especially when you get a straight shot in the face—in the eyes—like he did. He sure shouldn't have sucked it into his lungs that way."

She did not hear any sounds from the house as she ran, only the pounding of her own heart and the gasps of her ragged breathing while she gulped air and fought the pain in her side. When she slowed and listened closely, she heard high, eerie wails carrying north on the south wind. She identified the familiar cries punctuated by shouted obscenities and threats. Obviously he had no idea which way she had gone. Possibly, he didn't care.

Memory slowed her pace, deferring to the stitch in her side, and thought back over the past twenty-four hours: the astonishing, exotic new experiences—not all of them unpleasant—here she was, completely exhausted and ready for bed, traipsing the river road barefooted, wearing her favorite—and fortunately, her most modest—cotton nightie.

Swell.

It could be worse. The road could actually carry traffic, which this one, fortunately, did not. Where could she go to be safe? People considered her eccentric. She had hoped eventually to overcome her reputation for being out of step. Tonight's activities, out in her nightie, would hardly quell anyone's thoughts regarding her peculiarities.

She needed to call Mac. She had no other real choice. She'd had only two close girlfriends in high school. They had both moved away. Her parents were gone. Friends in Metcalf were two hours down the turnpike. Who could she turn to? She had no one. Sudden tears blurred her vision.

"Stop that," she said out loud. "Don't get maudlin." She squared her shoulders and picked up her feet, making herself march, trying for militant. Modern women didn't dissolve into tears at the first sign of trouble. No, ma'am. Women were Marines and participated in combat these days. Real women were no longer sissies. Her chin quivered and she shoved it forward, annoyed at herself for being such a wuss.

At the end of the river road, where it merged with a county highway, Charlie's station was locked up tight for the night. A phone booth stood at the corner, beyond the gas pumps. Of course, she had no money. Old pay phones hardly ever worked anyway. She picked up the receiver and got a dial tone. She punched in Mac's cell phone number, but it didn't ring.

"Please deposit twenty-five cents," an ancient recording advised.

Memory hung up and studied the ground around the booth, raking her bare toes over what appeared to be shining possibilities, a paperclip and tabs off pop and beer cans. There were no coins, not even a slug.

The breeze which she had scarcely noticed earlier suddenly had a bite to it. She could keep walking and hope that if anyone drove by and noticed her, it would be some kindhearted, close-mouthed individual with a quarter or a cell phone. As a last resort, she checked the coin changer on the phone.

She would rather have seen that quarter in that little metal chamber at that moment than a hundred-dollar bill. It winked up at her in the muted light of the phone booth.

Memory read the instruction on the front of the phone, then deposited the quarter and dialed, slowly and carefully. It rang three times before Mac answered. "Hello."

"The little man came back and broke into my house again." Her voice sounded hollow in the enclosure. "He had a new stocking mask."

Not for the first time, Memory appreciated the fact that Mac was a quick study. It only took him a heartbeat to get the picture. "Are you all right?"

"Yes."

"Are you still at the house?"

"No. I'm in the phone booth at Charlie's out on River Road."

"I'll be right there."

"Mac?"

"What?"

"I need something to wear."

"We'll worry about that after I pick you up."

She clutched the receiver with both hands, waiting for him to break the connection. But he spoke again.

"What do you have on?"

"My nightie."

"In that case, I'll be there double quick." Then he hung up. He was on his cell. He could have stayed on the line. His voice could have kept her company while he drove. She guessed he hadn't wanted to do that. Or maybe he hadn't thought of it. Maybe he would think of it and call back. Either way, she should stay right where she was.

Unexpectedly, her quarter dropped back into the change bin. Memory smiled and left it there for anyone else who might be in need. She opened the door to douse the light, and remained in the phone booth. Her shivering accelerated some ten minutes later when car lights approached. August was holding onto Indian summer, but that nip in the nighttime breeze might be contributing to her nervousness. Or maybe her nervousness was making her cold. Or maybe the chill came with the anticipation of seeing Mac again.

Rather than just cruising close and letting her jump into the car, Mac slammed the vehicle into park and got out, leaving the engine running and the car lights on, pointing directly at her.

He had taken only a step or two forward when Memory darted from the phone booth and, running, threw herself into his open arms. He wrapped her in a tight embrace, one arm around her waist, the other clamped to the back of her head. They stood like that, holding one another, without exchanging a word, for several therapeutic seconds. Even when he did speak, Mac didn't change his position. "Are you all right?"

"Hmmm," she said, making an affirmative hum before she could find her voice. "Better every minute."

"Do you feel okay? Do you feel safe now?"

"Safe? With you? Yes. I feel safer in your arms right this minute than I would feel anywhere else in the world."

His satisfied feeling changed to one of determination. "This time it's not up to you. You're going home with me."

"Okay."

He had rehearsed his sales pitch, but she short-circuited it. He could save the cajoling and sound reasoning for another time. With her, he figured he probably would need some of those same arguments again, sooner or later.

# Chapter Nine

He had already called the sheriff. That call was one of the reasons he had for not staying on the phone with her. They heard the wail of sirens on the highway moments later as Memory wrapped herself in her long terrycloth robe.

Broken glass in the entrance hall and the battered door of the upstairs bathroom were mute evidence of the intruder's work, but the guy himself was gone. Recalling the incident for law enforcement people, Memory said the man had worn, not only the stocking mask, but gloves. Deflated by his absence, she doubted they would find his fingerprints.

After a battery of questions, the sheriff suggested Memory go along with McCann.

"Bath or shower?" Mac asked when they walked into his apartment.

Without answering, Memory toured the place, which didn't take long. It was a one-bedroom. He had lived there long enough for it to reflect him and his habits, which was precisely what he noticed as he looked around, assessing the place as if seeing it for the first time.

Neither of them spoke for several heartbeats. Mac was first to break the silence.

"Let's take a load off—sit—while you tell me exactly what occurred at your house after I left tonight.

I'd like for you to tell me chronologically and in detail." He directed her into the recliner and he sat on the sofa, putting distance between them. It definitely was better for his concentration that they not be within touching range. He lifted a legal pad and pen from the side table drawer and began jotting notes.

When she finished describing her latest encounter with the stocky intruder, Mac shook his head and swallowed a smile.

"It's not funny," she protested.

"No, I know it's not, but I can just imagine how the guy felt, you know, about the time he said 'Not again,' and saw you drawing a bead on him with another aerosol can. You're going to give this guy a complex if you don't quit thwarting him every time he tries to assault you. He may develop permanent psychological damage from your always outmaneuvering him with your assorted sprays."

She could see the humor in his interpretation. "I sure hope so. What I can't figure out is what he wants. He comes and goes with impunity, but he doesn't make any demands or ask any questions. He never seems interested in taking anything."

"Personally, he's paying a hefty toll every time." Mac didn't seem able to contain the grin. "He's bound to be after something."

"Why doesn't he just tell me what he wants? Or take whatever he's after as soon as I'm out of his way, and go? Why keep forcing these confrontations? His behavior is weird and weirder."

Mac's tentative grin fell to a scowl, and he again grew serious contemplating her very pertinent questions.

"Either he doesn't know what he's after and needs you to identify it and hand it over, or you are the item. Maybe he thinks you know something and he wants to guarantee your silence. But it doesn't look to me like he means you any permanent harm."

"Right. If he were going to murder me, he could have done it by now. I figure masking his features so I can't recognize him indicates I'm supposed to survive." She paused. "Of course, the mask may not be enough. I'd recognize his physique in a minute if I saw him at the grocery store or on the street."

Mac looked at her curiously, as if she had said something important. "Memory, maybe, subconsciously, you have an idea about what he wants. Let's brainstorm. Loosen up, and let yourself go. What do you imagine you have that he needs?"

"That's the part I can't figure out. All he's done with his cloak and dagger routines so far is pique my curiosity…and yours, too, of course. His behavior makes me think I should leave here and never come back." She cast him a tight frown. "But, darn it, this is my home. I don't want to be forced to leave."

"I don't want you to go, either."

"Okay." She gave him a tender glance. "I'm sure he doesn't like your hanging around. Drawing the attention of an assistant district attorney can't be good for his plan, can't possibly be of any benefit to him, can it?"

"None that I can see." His kinder expression was back, but it was forced. Suddenly he needed to lift the dour mood that had settled in the room.

"Coffee, tea, or me?" he asked.

Memory smiled vaguely without looking at him.

She glanced at the assortment of reading materials on his side table. Political commentaries, a tattletale insider's new book, news magazines, two or three issues of Sports Illustrated—including the swimsuit issue. All of the periodicals were open to various articles, as if his reading had been interrupted or his interest had waned…repeatedly.

He followed as she stood and strolled into the kitchen. She walked to the refrigerator, opened the door and picked up a pizza box. Before she could discover its petrified remains, Mac snatched the box from her. He tossed it into the trash, leaving her to examine the appliance's remaining contents: condiments, a couple of dimpled apples, a bag of aged carrots and one package of pale limp celery. There was part of an onion, four eggs in the egg-keeper, a variety of cheeses, all in zippered bags, a quart of two-percent milk, a carton of orange juice, four cans of Coors Light, a nearly empty bottle of V-8 Juice, and a water-stained box of Girl Scout cookies.

"What's funny?" he asked, studying her face. "What do the contents of my refrigerator reveal that has you grinning?"

She didn't meet his gaze. "That the resident here is generous and diverse. Flexible. Given to bursts of spontaneity and charity."

"Do you approve of generous, diverse, flexible, spontaneous…ah…

"Charitable."

"Yeah, charitable people?"

"You bet."

He grinned. "Well, all right then."

She laughed lightly, finally allowing her eyes to

engage his. “It may be even better than all right.”

He lost the grin. “So what does this mean? That you are now confident I will not let you starve, or something more significant?”

Passing him, she patted his face and shook her head, maintaining the pleasant look. “I was not the least concerned that you would let anything bad happen to me, much less let me starve.”

“Then what did concern you?”

“Around you, I get a little…”

“What?”

“Edgy. Have you noticed that when we’re together I become what some people might consider erratic?”

“I guess. I’ve never actually thought of you as predictable, but I don’t consider you exactly impulsive either.”

It was her turn to sober. “No. But every time we’re together, circumstances tend to become…precarious.”

“I wonder if it bodes better or worse for us that I know what you mean.” He looked at her a moment, then set his jaws, clenched his fists, and turned to stride purposefully to his bedroom. He returned almost immediately with an unopened package of pajamas.

“Tell you what,” he said. “We’re both tired. We’ll think better when our brains are rested. Let’s sleep on it.”

Hairs prickled a warning along the back of her neck and she shot him a wry glance. “Maybe you’d better take me to Flanagan’s.”

“No way.”

“Yes, way. Neither of us would be able to sleep soundly here…in the same place…together.”

He arched his eyebrows. “Oh, yeah, we can sleep,

and we'll sleep real well, if you'll let me teach you this little sleep aid I know that insures consenting adults will slumber like babies."

"Thanks. Maybe another time." She didn't dare look directly at him. He was entirely too beautiful—tall and strong and...getting better looking the closer friends they became. Now, too, she knew something about the pleasure his hands could arouse in her. She warmed just remembering and risked a glance at his face.

A seductive smile lazily commandeered his expression, giving him an enchanted look. "But you are entertaining the idea, aren't you?"

"No." Her breath caught as she studied his handsome face. His eyes had a glitter that made her look away. "Maybe," she muttered. "What I mean is, I might have thought about it." She shot him another glance to find him grinning. "Once or twice."

****

Mac persuaded Memory to take the pajamas and a pair of his house shoes. They picked up her car, which he insisted on driving to misdirect anyone who might recognize it as hers. In his Lexus, she followed him to Flanagan's where he again went inside to get her a room.

"Is Memory here again?" Mrs. Flanagan inquired when Mac walked through the office door.

He signed the register. "Yes, but it's strictly hush-hush, Mrs. Flanagan. It looks like someone is after her."

"A squatty little man, built like a fireplug?"

Suddenly the older woman had his attention. "Yes, ma'am. How'd you know that?"

"He stayed here his first night in town."

"Do you know his name?"

"The one he signed was Steam. Dicky Steam."

"When was that?"

"Early last week. Monday, maybe."

"Where did he stay after that? Do you know?"

"No, but he hasn't been at the hotel or the Holiday or the Sunset. He could be sleeping in his car, I suppose, but I doubt it. He's a snappy dresser. He doesn't look wrinkled or unkempt enough to be sleeping in his car."

"When have you seen him since he stayed here?"

"At the cafe." She gestured toward the south.

"Milo's?"

"Yes. They tell me he's there three meals a day. If you ask me, he might try getting by on two. He's straining his seams."

"Yeah, well, maybe they'll cut back on his calories in prison, which will be his new residence, as soon as I get my hands on him."

Mrs. Flanagan followed him out the door. "I'm coming with you. I need to talk to Memory a minute."

Mac didn't object. A chaperone might be a good idea.

In the room, Memory sat in a chair, Mac perched on the side of the bed and Mrs. Flanagan fussed over the fall of the drapes as she pulled them closed.

"I heard today that Quint Ressler and his wife separated." She spoke as the drapery cord played through her hands. "Both of them want to be first to the courthouse in the morning. I've heard there's some advantage to being first to file." She looked at Mac, who nodded but obviously did not want to follow that conversational detour, so she continued.

"They say Doris Ressler is nearly insane over being so jealous. You probably don't remember, but Doris was not Quint's first choice. Or even his second, push come to shove."

That sidebar ignited Mac's curiosity. "I remembered that he and Laurel were hot and heavy in high school," he said. "Was she his first choice?"

"Probably," Mrs. Flanagan said, frowning as if straining to recall. "But he married that Helen Mouser person, don't you remember?"

"Mouser? Oh, yeah, the car dealer's daughter. I do remember that. Didn't something odd happen to her?"

Mrs. Flanagan's eyebrows shot up. "She disappeared. Went to the grocery store one afternoon and never made it home. Her car was found two weeks later in Chattanooga, Tennessee, six hundred miles from here. In months and months of diligent searching, they didn't find any sign of her. Some speculated Quinton murdered her and buried her around here, at least that was her daddy's thinking on the matter.

"Years later, she was declared dead. By then, Quint and Laurel were a hot item again. Then he up and married Doris, for what reason I will never know. Doris was quite a bit older than Quint and not nearly as pretty as Laurel. There've been whispers that she blackmailed him. Has evidence against him; that she keeps it in a safe deposit box that belongs to her by herself. Odd thing was, marrying Doris didn't stop him and Laurel from going out with each other."

Memory nodded. "Whatever Doris had against him must not have been too bad."

Mrs. Flanagan didn't appear to agree. "I'm here to tell you, there's nothing harder on a woman than a man who cheats. It was plain to everybody from the outset. Poor Doris married the wrong feller if she was looking for someone tried and true. Quint never had much character to speak about. Nothing like this man right here." A quick nod indicated Mac.

Memory bowed her head, trying to ignore the obvious recommendation, and attempted to redirect the conversation. "If she's jealous, it's probably because she loves him very much."

"Don't imagine she does. Sometimes what a woman feels for her man more resembles pride of ownership than love. There's talk Doris finally might have had a belly full of his philandering and ran over his girlfriend to punish him, or maybe hired it done. A bunch of people knew Quint and Laurel was going out. Have been off an' on ever since high school, according to my church circle. Of course, that old saying isn't usually true, about the wife being the last to know."

When no one else spoke, Mrs. Flanagan settled herself on the foot of the bed and stared at Memory. "Others' been speculating for some time that Quint had a new girlfriend. Some say you're her. They say the word divorce never came up between Quint and Doris until you came back for your daddy's funeral and started flitting in and out of Ressler's office." Suddenly Mrs. Flanagan stopped all other movement and looked directly at Memory. "Any truth to that?"

"To what? That I was flitting in and out of his office? Yes, that's true. I don't know anything about his marriage. I've never even met his wife. I was in his office strictly on business. I was always there during office hours with other people around, either updating computers or reading and signing papers in my dad's probate. I am definitely not interested in romance with Quinton Ressler." She gave Mac a furtive glance. He nodded, indicating he caught her drift.

Taking advantage of the momentary silence, Mrs. Flanagan transferred her focus to Mac.

"Of course, David, you're getting your share of talk too. Gossip has it that Laurel was telling folks you and her planned to get married, that you got wind of her affair with Quint, accused her, beat her up, threw her out on the side of the road, then came back around and ran her over."

"What?" Mac looked like he'd been slapped and started to stand.

Mrs. Flanagan waved him down but, instead of sitting, he stood anyway and paced to the draped window as she continued. "You was a wild boy, David McCann. Lots of folks around here remember it. You had a fiery bad temper, given the fact you were reared by a sweet, patient woman like your grandma. No one that thinks you did it thinks it was premeditated, of course, which should be in your favor if it goes to court."

Mac groaned and looked from one woman to the other.

Memory frowned.

Mrs. Flanagan got up from the bed, crossed the room and sat in the chair across the small table from Memory.

"Someone else, I think maybe it was the police chief, speculated that someone might have hired a gunslinger—say, that fireplug fellow—to get rid of you, and they're thinking maybe he ran over the wrong party. A case of mistaken identity. Or maybe he's still around 'cause he needs to straighten things out by finishing the job he was paid to do in the first place."

Memory shivered, but didn't offer an alternative to Mrs. Flanagan's theories.

"There's some that think Quint himself might have run over the woman on the road that night thinking it was Memory and, being drunk, thought to get even for her embarrassing him at the country club like she did. The man's got an awful ego. He might not want other ladies to find out there was a woman around who didn't consider him worth considering."

Mac cleared his throat, interrupting, although Mrs. Flanagan seemed to be running down anyway. "So tell me your list of suspects who might have done the deed."

"Well, there's Doris Ressler, Quint Ressler, the fireplug fellow, and you and..." She waved a hand. "Also, there's one other theory." She glanced at Memory. "It's that this one here saw something in Quint's office when she was working on the computers, some shenanigans going on with the bookkeeping over there. That might have provoked some employee into wanting to keep her quiet, permanently."

## Chapter Ten

After Mac and Mrs. Flanagan left, Memory spent a restless night.

In the light of day, her fear of staying alone at home seemed foolish. What she wanted most was to clean up and change clothes at her own house. Disregarding her arguments over the telephone, Mac insisted on following her to the farm and waiting.

While she showered and dressed, he swept up the glass in front of the door, finishing just as Mr. Judkins, a local carpenter he had called, arrived with a new, solid oak, six-paneled door for the upstairs bathroom. Judkins replaced the missing pane in the front door, and said hello to Memory as she came downstairs and he went up. It was mid-morning by the time he finished replacing the doorjamb and fitting the new door to the upstairs bathroom. By then Memory had convinced Mac she could drive her own car and run her own errands in town in broad daylight without his escort.

That accomplished, she headed straight for Quint Ressler's office. She pulled into the lot marked: "Reserved for Ressler Law Offices. Unauthorized vehicles will be towed."

Because she was acquainted with the office routine, Memory knew Quint wouldn't be there before ten on a weekday. Only one of the legal assistants might be working. The only person in the office for the next hour or so would be the receptionist, a sweet, vacuous girl named Karen who answered the phones. Thirty minutes would be plenty of time for Memory to pick up her instructional CDs and leave thank-you/good-bye notes. She wasn't ready for a face-to-face with Quinton. Not yet.

Karen looked up and gave Memory a broad smile. "Hi."

"Good morning. How are you?" Memory returned the smile and tried to act as if she had not been assaulted twice, but she couldn't help wondering if Karen had seen the squat little man around their offices, or if she knew what his assignment might be. Studying the girl, however, Memory was comforted by Karen's usual offhanded manner.

"I'm fine," Karen said. "There's some coffee in the break room."

"Thanks, but I'll just be in and out." Memory walked straight to the hallway and down to the office she used when she worked on the computers. She ignored the telephone, which rang two or three times, until Karen popped into the area where Memory was working.

"Gotta go out for a minute. Will you catch the phones for me?" Before Memory could respond, Karen added, "I'll be right back. Honest."

"Okay. Sure." She had some time before she needed to vacate.

She heard the bell over the front door sound as Karen left. A few minutes later, sorting through CDs, separating the ones she might need from those she planned to leave for Ressler's use, Memory heard the bell again. When Karen didn't call out, Memory did.

"Hey, is that you?"

There was no response. Memory's heart leaped. Good grief. She was getting completely paranoid. Karen had just forgotten Memory was there or had mumbled, which she sometimes did.

One of the CDs she needed was missing. Maybe it was in Quint's office. Memory walked from her temporary office through a connecting door into Quinton's suite. His office had its own small washroom and a minuscule insert fireplace beneath a lavish mahogany mantel. Petite as it was, the fireplace was the focal point in a wall dominated by bookshelves. The man had a dart board on the adjacent wall. Taken altogether, his private office had the look and feel of an English pub. The atmosphere impressed the clients, exactly as it was designed to do.

Memory glanced at the dart board. As if the man needed any more distractions. Still, the clients weren't the only ones impressed. After that last look around, Memory turned to leave.

Movement in the doorway to the hall drew her attention. There, looking at her through his usual pantyhose disguise, was her short, determined nemesis. She had a fleeting thought: the man must have a truckload of stockings. He shredded the things faster than any female she knew.

He held a weapon in his right hand, aimed directly at her. It looked like a gun, but not exactly. It was clunky looking, more closely resembled a kid's rubber band pistol. He positioned himself just outside the door to the hallway , where he could keep an eye on the door to her temporary office, the only other exit. If she tried to make a break for either of them, she'd be right in his line of fire.

While options tap-danced through her mind, Memory instinctively reached for the dart board.

Quinton, the all-wise advisor, had cautioned her about the darts. They were very sharp and perfectly weighted. He didn't like for novices to practice in here and risk damaging the furnishings or the highly polished mahogany walls rimming the target.

But Memory didn't plan to practice on that target. She had something more substantial in mind, a target rubbing his eyes at the moment, as if his eyesight were hindered by the stocking.

She took aim at his head. He made no effort to duck or dodge as she hurled the first dart. It didn't have enough momentum behind it and was only part way to its destination when it nose-dived. The man's head bent as he tried to keep his eyes on the dart, but the effort slowed his reflexes. He didn't move quickly enough and the dying swan missile struck, sinking into his meaty thigh.

His anguished howl probably was heard for blocks. His head jerked up and he aligned the dark circles beneath his red-rimmed eyes directly with Memory's face. She didn't know why he always looked so astonished. He should be accustomed to the idea by now that she would use any means available—spray cans, darts, any weapon at hand—to defend herself.

The man's jaw jutted as he bent from the waist and grabbed the dart with his left hand. He screamed again as he yanked it out of his leg and threw it, with some force, at the floor. That was when Memory realized he could have thrown it right back at her. She thanked God he hadn't.

In the next moment, however, she saw why, as he raised his weapon, pointed it at her, and fired. She stepped left and the projectile stuck in the wall a good four inches right of her shoulder. This guy was in for a world of hurt when Quinton Ressler found out he had put a dart in that heretofore-unblemished mahogany wall.

Memory had never seen a movie where a criminal worth his salt lined up at pointblank range and missed. She whirled to regard the dart which vibrated, widening the pinprick in Ressler's precious mahogany before it shook loose and dropped to the floor.

The peculiar gun—obviously a dart gun—appeared to be a single-shot device. The man fumbled in his coat pocket to produce new ammunition and brought the weapon close to his face, tilting his head, trying to see through the mesh covering his eyes to reload. Memory began peppering him with darts. Two, three, four, five. She supposed her emotions affected her aim. The first dart hit the wall to his right. If this guy didn't kill her, Quinton probably would for the damage she was inflicting on this room.

Disregarding that, she threw Number Six. The short man hunkered in his effort to reload his own weapon and her shot twanged into the hall wall directly over his head. Another fistful of darts did more damage to Quint's walls than to the man and, suddenly, she was out of ammo.

Scanning for something else to throw, she chose first a stapler, then a hole punch, both of which the man neatly sidestepped. A low, gloating little laugh emerged from behind the stocking. She threw the paper clip holder, showering him with the contents, prompting another low laugh.

"Sticks and stones may break my bones, but paper clips will never hurt me." He continued in a singsong falsetto voice. "Tranquilize this."

Apparently his gun shot tranquilizers.

Keeping her eyes on him, she ran a hand over the desk and grabbed a fountain pen from the desk set. She hurled it, point first. Adrenaline put more force behind the throw than she realized. The intruder's dart gun pointed directly at her. The man's hand fisted on the handle as the pen hit its mark, knifing neatly between two knuckles just as he fired.

His shot went wild, hit and bounced off the wall behind Memory's shoulder. The events that followed seemed surreal.

The pen lodged between his knuckles vibrated wildly but stayed. He dropped his dart gun and stared at his injured hand for a moment, then, startling them both, he gave a banshee shriek. Squalling, he plucked the pen from his hand, threw it on the floor and stomped it, shattering it into a hundred slivers. Without a glance at Memory, he grabbed the dart gun, turned his back to her and bent, apparently reloading. His shirt pulled out of his trousers and provided a broad expanse of bared backside. Memory didn't hesitate. She grabbed the two darts he had fired at her and hummed them, one at a time, aiming for the exposed skin. He raised up just as the first tiny missile hit and sank to its hilt in gelatinous flesh. He twisted left, then right, clawing, trying to grab and remove the missile without dropping the newly loaded dart gun in his hand. He yowled like a stuck pig and whirled around. Opening and closing his hands ineffectively, he dropped the pistol then spun, grappling impotently at the offending darts. He looked like some whirling dervish cartoon character. Then like a punctured balloon, he wilted. His legs wobbled crazily as they crumpled beneath him.

Miraculously the second dart she threw had hit within an inch of the first. Memory jabbed her doubled fists into the air. Hers were not great shots, but she had hit meat and that was all that mattered. She had triumphed again. A person who rarely participated in physical competitions, Memory grinned. She really seemed to be getting the hang of this hand-to-hand combat stuff.

She scooted back into her temporary office and exited the area to race down the hall and out, leaving her assailant's bulky form slumped in the doorway to Quint's office.

## Chapter Eleven

"It didn't occur to you to call Nine-One-One?" Mac asked, his tone over the telephone incredulous.

"Well, gee, no, not at that moment, actually, it didn't."

With that one question, he erased nearly all of her confidence.

"I don't suppose you bothered to take the stocking off the guy's face so you could describe him later either."

Memory wasn't in the mood for hindsight advice and non-constructive criticism.

"Listen, pal, this is the guy who has been trying to kill or maim me for days. I didn't really care what he looked like. All that mattered in those moments was stopping him and saving my skin."

"I thought by now you knew a man who intends to kill someone does not hide his face or use a tranquilizer gun."

"So, if the chief has the gun, he has the guy, right? If he has the guy, it hardly matters whether I can describe him, does it? There weren't a whole herd of short, stocky guys running around Ressler's office this morning with stockings over their heads."

"It wouldn't matter," his voice dropped, "if the guy had still been there. By the time Karen called for help, the bad guy was gone."

"I did not abandon Karen. I waited in the parking lot until she got back so I could keep an eye on the exit to make sure he didn't take off. He didn't. I told her what happened. Then, she called the police on her cell while I was standing right there beside her, shaking. She thought I was going to pass out or something. She's the one who said I didn't need to hang around. She'd keep an eye on things. The police were on their way. I heard the sirens. I didn't want to have to face Quinton after the damage we'd done to his office. What happened?"

"The police didn't get there in time. They found evidence of a struggle, but you and your guy were gone."

"Gone? Someone must have moved the body. Maybe Quint…"

"Memory, there was no body."

Her sigh sounded pathetic, even to her, like a mix of relief and a sob. "I was pretty sure I finished him this time."

"Apparently not."

She was quiet for several seconds. "I guess that's probably a good thing, my not killing him? I mean, at least I'm not a murderess."

"I suppose that could be considered a good thing. Whatever possessed you to go to Quint's office this morning anyway?"

"I went to pick up some CDs and instruction books I'd left. I went early to avoid any unpleasantness."

"That makes sense."

"Mac, under normal circumstances, I am a very sensible person."

When he pointedly didn't confirm her claim, she

swallowed. "I can tell you one thing, McCann, I'm going to load up and go back to Metcalf today, back where I'll be safe."

****

As the day and the questions continued, Memory felt less and less sure of herself. She didn't finish the debriefing until late afternoon. She knew she'd told Mac she was going back to Metcalf, but she desperately needed a nap. Just an hour or so of rest before tackling the drive.

She slipped out of her shoes inside the front door and climbed the stairs to her room. She stretched out on top of the bed and closed her eyes. The house creaked. Was the short guy back? Had she locked the front door? She always did. It was a habit.

She got up and hurried soundlessly to the head of the stairs. The door was closed, the deadbolt in the horizontal position—locked.

Maybe if she brushed her teeth.

"Who can sleep in the daytime?" she muttered. She needed to pack and get back to the city, to her apartment, her job, a life where individuals behaved rationally. Her nerves jangled.

She called Mac on his cell phone and caught him at the sheriff's office.

"It's too late to start back tonight," Mac said. She heard the sheriff's voice in the background agree. "You're overtired. Stay one more night."

She gritted her teeth. "If I do stay, I'm darn well staying here in my own home."

She heard the two men's voices as they considered her request as if she were a lost child and they were trying to appease her until a responsible adult arrived.

"I'll keep the cordless phone in my hand the whole time," she said, sweetening the deal. "This will give me a chance to go through the papers in Dad's desk and the photo albums. After a little nap, I'll probably be up all night, which means no one's going to sneak up on me this time."

"Memory, that's a dumb idea."

"Mr. McCann, you have no authority to keep a woman from staying in her own home."

"Sheriff," Mac said, speaking away from the phone, "will you put a deputy out there to keep an eye on the house?" He hesitated a moment. "Never mind, I'll do it myself."

The sheriff's voice followed. "I can send my evidence officer over for a while. You and he can split the shift."

"She's not your responsibility," Mac said.

"No more than she is yours," the sheriff countered.

Memory felt like she was eavesdropping on a private conversation, as if the two men had forgotten she was there.

"Hey," she shouted into the phone.

"We've got it worked out," Mac said. "I'll call you later."

As she hung up the phone, she heard the sheriff end his conversation with Mac with, "Call if you need to and we'll relieve you."

She smiled. Knowing someone would be on duty felt reassuring.

****

It was nearly two a.m. when Memory, sitting cross-legged on the living room floor, heard a car. She stirred but didn't bother moving from behind the box of records she was sorting when the driver cut the engine some distance down the driveway. Although no one had come to the door, she knew Mac and the sheriff were having her watched. The new arrival probably signaled a change of shifts.

She was not alarmed to hear a heavy footfall on the porch and a man sneeze. Probably Mac coming to check on her. She sat straighter and smiled.

Reading over the deed on the farm from the previous owners to her mother and dad, it took her a moment to react when her visitor violently rattled the doorknob. She looked up through the newly installed window pane in the door, to see a man's head concealed beneath the familiar suntan stocking.

"Not again." She sat motionless as he cocked his head, apparently eying the newly replaced pane that stood between him and direct access to the dead bolt and knob. She stared a moment, stunned, before the sound of the glass breaking ignited her. She didn't think to grab the cordless phone at her elbow or her cell on the coffee table. She dropped the paper document, leaped to her feet, ran to the stairs, and up.

Shoot. Wrong way. The dead bolt clicked and the door opened. It was too late to double back. Upstairs, of course, she only had the bathroom.

She flipped on the light, slammed the newly installed door, and threw the brand new bolt. She was really glad Mac had called the carpenter to do the repairs and had insisted on the more secure lock which, he said, seemed to be a necessity in her house. They had both laughed then, as if he were kidding.

She pressed her ear against the door, listening as the intruder moved around downstairs.

Suddenly, the six-by-ten room went dark. Someone had thrown the switch in the breaker box in the kitchen. The darkness did not frighten her. Even pitch black, the room was familiar.

Remembering the book of matches on top of the small gas wall stove near the bathtub, Memory fumbled around, found it, and struck one, thinking she would light the decorative candle on the vanity. But the candle was gone, along with everything else. The vanity itself, had been stripped bare. There were only three matches left in the book.

She threw open the medicine cabinet and held the match close. It was empty.

Spinning, scanning the room, she realized whoever had stripped the vanity had taken everything, had not even left residue in the soap dishes, nor soap dishes themselves. The culprit had done a thorough job. Not so much as a toothbrush remained.

Lucky for her, he had missed the book of matches on the stove. The match burned her finger. She blew it out.

Think. Surely there was something she could use to defend herself. She lit a second match—which left two—and directed the light all around, examining every nook and cranny. Nothing. Not a toilet paper roll or even the spool remained. He must have guessed she would choose that little room for her hidey-hole. It had worked for her before.

There had to be something.

She heard a footfall on the stairs. “Mac?” she called, hoping she had mistaken his dark, chestnut-colored hair for a stocking and that he had bent over, to pick up something, maybe. No response. Reason returned. Mac would never have broken the window pane.

As the footsteps came relentlessly up the stairs, their creaking reported his progress. The man's high-pitched voice called to her, the sound maybe exaggerated by excitement.

"I took everything out of there this time, sister. You're going to pay for what you done to me. Oh, yeah, things are gonna go my way this time."

Frightened almost to the point of not being able to think, Memory struck a third match and scanned the tiny room again. Both towel bars were gone. She glanced up. He had even unscrewed and removed the shower rod and its brackets. She turned round and round. Her subconscious had noticed something, but fear clouded her mind. She needed to think. Just as she blew out the third match, she saw a potential weapon. Of course.

Moving quietly in the darkness, she lifted the lid from the toilet tank. Whoa. It was heavier than she expected. She left it in place and, guiding by touch, closed the toilet seat. She took hold of one end of the tank lid and lifted. She jerked up to keep the far end from hitting the floor. Gently, she eased one end to the tile and rested the other against the bathtub. She lit the last match to get her bearings, then extinguished the light, and lifted the tank top to balance it on the toilet seat. The darn thing was too heavy for her to raise and swing down with much control. But if she stood on the toilet seat, she might be able to swing it like a pendulum, slam it into the little man.

She doubted she'd have more than one strike. She had to hit that first one out of the park. And in the dark.

She allowed a weak, wavering sigh as she imagined her little scenario. In the dark, standing on the toilet seat, she definitely would have an element-of-surprise advantage, at least for a few seconds. She lifted the tank lid again. It would take every bit of muscle she had to swing through, and a monumental back swing for her to do any damage.

He rattled the knob. Adrenaline renewed. Suddenly the heavy lid felt lighter.

Gritting her teeth, she lifted one end of the tank lid with both hands, but was unable to step onto the toilet seat hoisting the extra weight. Silently, as her would-be assailant continued rattling the knob—psyching her out, she supposed—she laid the tank lid across the lavatory, climbed onto the toilet, clamped one end of the tank lid with both hands and lifted.

"Come on, girlie, don't make me break down another door. I got bruises from before. I didn't leave you nothing in there to hurt me with this time. You can't even squirt me with a tube of toothpaste." His giggle sounded adolescent.

Memory teetered onto her toes for a moment as the heavy tank lid pulled her off balance. She set her jaw and leaned backward to compensate for the weight, pulling the lid against her body. There she stood, feeling ridiculous, poised atop the toilet seat holding a tank lid in front of her. Her back and shoulders ached. The muscles in her forearms burned. She wouldn't be able to hold the position long.

He hit the door and the noise startled her, but the door held. He cursed.

She would hold off on the back swing until he broke through, then she hoped his reflexes would be stymied in the dark. Concentrating, visualizing her move, Memory took long, deep breaths. Still, she started when he slammed against the door again, hitting it with either his foot or a shoulder. The door quivered in the jamb, but held. After several more poundings, each more violent than the last, the door remained intact, but the jamb began to splinter. With the sixth blow, the battered door exploded inward.

As anticipated, the little man stumbled into the room waving his arms, doing a jig in the struggle to keep his feet. Light from the hallway silhouetted him and outlined the dart gun in his hand. Memory didn't remember ordering her burning arms to launch the back swing, but she saw the little man's stark surprise as she began her forward thrust, a look that dissolved to alarm as she followed through.

He emptied both hands trying to shield his face. The gun clattered to the floor. The heavy tank lid collided with a hand first. Memory heard the awful crunch of bones shattering and the man's earsplitting, now familiar shriek.

The heft of the lid carried it through its pendulum stroke, ricocheting off the side of the guy's face. She released the lid. Its momentum drove the near end into his stomach before the other end dropped, knifing across his feet. The man's shrieking stopped as he doubled over with a howl.

As he crumpled, the dart gun, on the floor out of his reach, fired. The explosion echoed off walls in the confined space, muffling the thud as the tank lid slid to the floor beside the man's prone form. One of his legs twitched. Then the darkened bathroom was quiet except for wheezing that oddly comforted Memory. She felt relieved that he wasn't dead…again.

Propelled by adrenaline and instinct, she leaped over the intruder's unmoving body and ran.

Clamoring down the stairs, she flew out the front door and scrambled into her car. She would get him medical attention as soon as she was safely beyond his reach.

She pulled into the phone booth at Charlie's Station, got a quarter intentionally stashed in her car ash tray, and called Mac's cell. When he answered, she hadn't planned what to say and only stammered. "Mac? Mac?" Unable to create a sentence, she kept repeating his name.

"Not again," he said, correctly interpreting her babble.

"Yes. Yes. David…I mean Mac, oh, yes."

"What about the deputy outside your house?"

"I…I don't know about a deputy."

"Where are you?"

"At Charlie's Station."

"Stay there. Do not move."

She hung up without responding and dialed Nine-One-One.

"I need to report a break-in, and an injured man."

The female dispatcher took the address. "Stay on the line," the woman said. "Emergency assistance is on the way. You are at the pay phone on Highway Two-thirty-one. That's Charlie's, right?"

"Right."

"Could you not call from the Smith home?"

"No, I could not."

"Is there a fire or other emergency there?"

"No." When she said that, Memory suddenly and

quite unexpectedly giggled. She was always calling for help after the emergency was over, which was ridiculous. She needed to call before the emergency happened. If she'd known ahead of time, she would have done it. But Memory hadn't noticed his tampering with her bathroom, because she'd been downstairs all afternoon and evening and used the half bath down there.

"That little worm," she said, as she realized his plan…and how easily it could have been thwarted, if she had noticed earlier. "He could have saved himself a concussion."

On the other end of the phone line, the dispatcher said, "Ma'am? Ma'am? Speak into the phone, Ma'am, I can't understand what you're saying."

Memory totally lost it as she gave in to loud, unladylike, snorting laughter.

That's the way Mac found her, crumpled in a cross-legged heap in the phone booth, the door open, the receiver dangling at her side. When he drove up, she swiped at her mouth trying to mop the drool, still hawking and spewing unrepentant laughter.

****

Maybe she was hysterical. He could slap her, but she probably needed to vent that unreleased stress at the moment more than she needed to provide a sensible explanation. There would be time for explanations later.

"Is he in the house?" he tried as her laughter subsided.

She nodded. "In the b-b-bathroom. Up-upstairs." She began giggling and choked. "Again."

Eventually, when the shouts of unbridled merriment waned, Mac offered her a hand. She took it and he pulled her to her feet. He didn't ask any questions, afraid of setting her off again.

Enjoying the silence, he put her in his car and drove her back to her house in time to see the paramedics load a figure on a stretcher into an ambulance before they leaped into the vehicle and took off, sirens wailing.

His arm around Memory's shoulders, Mac didn't attempt to ask either the retreating medics nor the deputies milling around inside and outside the house, about the identity of the man or inquire about his condition. Nor did he make any inquiries about the "crime scene." He didn't really care. Memory was okay. The bad guy finally was in custody. Assistant District Attorney David McCann could wait for answers to other, less significant questions.

****

Without any prodding, Memory led him into the house and up the stairs.

"He must have come in earlier, sometime during the day," she said, her voice and manner subdued. "He cleaned out the bathroom. Took everything I might have used as a weapon: towel bars, toothbrushes, soap, combs, my hairbrush, everything."

"Even with you unarmed, the guy didn't stand a chance. What did you use?"

She stopped at the bathroom door. A splash of blood marred the white ceramic tile floor. The lid to the toilet tank lay unbroken, on the floor beside the toilet. Splintered bits of oak from the battered doorjamb lay scattered over the floor.

Mac eyed the tank lid a long time. "That was your weapon of choice?"

"I didn't have anything else."

"Hot water, maybe?"

"I didn't have anything to put it in."

"So you thought of using water?"

She sighed. "No, honestly, I don't think I did."

"So, what did you do?"

"Well, the light was out. He must have flipped the breaker for this room, because there was light behind him from the hallway when he exploded through the door."

Mac glanced at the overhead light, which was burning brightly.

"Obviously, someone has flipped it back on," she said, countering his look.

"Okay."

"I found a book of matches where we've always kept them, by the stove handle. I guess he overlooked them when he took everything else. There were only four matches. I struck one and looked around trying to find something to use to fend him off." She shrugged, hoping Mac would understand. "By the time I struck the last match, the tank lid was the only thing I could think of."

"So you hit him with it?"

"Yes. I had to stand on the toilet seat for leverage. It was too heavy for me to swing flat-footed and get it any higher than his shins."

"So you stood on the toilet seat and when he broke in, you busted him."

"Right."

He fingered the splintered doorjamb. "You do play hell with doors, woman."

"I'm not the one who keeps doing that."

Mac regarded her silently long enough to pique her curiosity.

"What?"

He chuckled. "I just wonder what he thought when he came barreling through that door and found you, weapon in hand, standing on the toilet."

Memory both smiled and frowned at the same time. "In the dark. That was totally his fault, not mine."

"You caught him by surprise."

"Yes."

"He didn't react?"

"Not quickly enough."

"And you let him have it with the tank lid?"

"Yes."

A low, rolling laugh burbled up from Mac's chest and he didn't bother to stifle it. The woman of his dreams, a kindly, timid soul, the most feminine, gentlewoman he'd ever known, had the ingenuity and the guts to use a toilet tank lid to foil an attacker, to whop an assailant upside the head when he backed her into a corner. Mac made a mental note to be very careful about backing this sweet thing into any corners. Her gentle appearance and demeanor were deceiving.

"You've humiliated the poor, dumb schmuck every time he thought he had you."

"I really wish he would quit. I don't like hurting him any more than he likes getting hurt."

Mac nodded, smiling. "I think his plan this time was to remove every possible weapon so that maybe you wouldn't be able to beat him." He smiled into her eyes. "You know if these stories get out, he's not only going to have physical scars, he'll be emotionally damaged, maybe for life. He'll be the laughing stock of the prison system. No self-respecting criminal is going to give him the time of day."

Memory frowned. "Destroying the man's self-esteem or his reputation among his peers is not my intention, or my fault."

Mac looked up at the ceiling and crossed his arms over his chest in what looked like an effort to squelch the laughter, but just when he thought he had it under control, he looked at the tank lid on the floor or into Memory's glower and the laugh erupted.

Watching him, she relented. After all, hadn't that been her first reaction when she was safe and collapsed in the phone booth, when she couldn't get it out of her mind how ridiculous the whole thing looked?

Mac finally sobered. "All I know is, you've stymied him every time. Maybe you didn't follow standard law enforcement procedures or use proper legal maneuvers, but, by golly, you've stopped him."

Memory said, "I guess." Only one unanswered question niggled in the back of her mind. "I don't know him and I still don't know what he's after. How could I have made a stranger so mad that he just keeps coming like this?"

Mac's expression darkened. "Yeah, there is that."

"So, what are you thinking?"

"That he was hired."

"Who in the world would pay someone to come after me?"

"A disgruntled lover?"

Her scowl deepened. "I told you before. I don't do boyfriends. There are no disgruntled guys."

"You mean none that you know about."

"I mean none, period. I don't date that much. I

mean, men do ask me out. With some I explain beforehand that I don't…ah…you know."

Curious, he wanted her to finish that sentence. "No, I don't know. What do you tell them beforehand?"

"I tell them I am not promiscuous."

"You didn't tell me that."

Okay, he was teasing. "So far, you are the only man—make that person—outside my immediate family, that I have ever spent the night with in a motel."

"Quite a distinction. I think I may take that as a compliment, even though I had to wheedle myself into your dire circumstances to get there." He regarded her soberly. "Besides that, nothing happened."

"Not because I wasn't willing."

"No? Well, I'm thinking nothing happened because you weren't ready."

"Mac, I am twenty-eight years old and I am the only…ah…amateur…my age in this hemisphere."

"That may be true, but we have only our independent research to verify that. I've only been studying the matter since I was twelve. I haven't checked everyone."

"What's that supposed to mean? More research?"

He grinned wickedly.

# Chapter Twelve

"How were you able to get out of the house?" the police department's evidence officer and assistant chief, Mitch Wyatt, asked, questioning Memory in the district attorney's office an hour later.

In spite of David's contention that she needed a good night's sleep, the officer wanted to debrief her while the incident was fresh in her mind.

"I ran outside, got in my car, and drove to Charlie's station."

"You had the presence of mind to locate your purse and car keys?"

She looked at the man as if she could read her answers from a Teleprompter on his forehead. It was a nice forehead, a familiar one. Mitch had been a senior in high school when Memory was in the eighth grade and she'd had a crush on him. He had five o'clock shadow now, of course, in the wee small hours of the morning, and his clothes were wrinkled, but he still had the dark brown trustworthy eyes that reminded her of her dad's.

"No. I didn't take my purse. Didn't even think of it. The car keys were in the car. Dad was typical. Country people usually leave the keys in their vehicles. It's convenient and the vehicles are perfectly safe from neighbors, unless they need one in an emergency, which makes it okay to borrow. Of course, a thief doesn't have to bother coming inside, troubling anyone for the keys."

Sitting directly across from her at the table, Wyatt bowed his head and smiled toward his lap. "Makes sense. Did your dad lose a lot of vehicles?"

"Not one in my lifetime."

During the hour of questioning, Memory and her interrogator developed a rapport. She supposed that was why, when they finished, he suggested she leave her car out at Charlie's and let him give her a ride home.

He studied her. "That is, if you want to go home. Would you rather stay with friends?"

His instincts were good. She didn't exactly want to go home. Things had been too strange there lately. Even though they had the squatty little perpetrator in custody, she felt uneasy about Mac's suggestion that the guy might be someone's hireling. If that were the case, what would prevent his employer from hiring someone else, or from coming after her himself?

Flanagan's might be an answer, but somehow that didn't feel right either.

Mac would know what to do. He lived in the Timber Terrace Apartments. She could drive by and see if he was at home.

"I'd like to get my car, if you'll run me out to Charlie's to pick it up," she said. Wyatt looked disappointed. She tried to make it up to him. "Thanks very much for the offer."

In her own car, Memory cruised Main Street, which was nearly deserted. Mac's car wasn't at Timber Terrace. The clock on her dash said it was nearly four a.m. Was he staying overnight with someone? A girlfriend? The idea rankled. She didn't really care to know about his personal relationships, yet she felt a sudden, urgent need to find him, to see his face, to draw strength and reassurance from his voice and his smile. She wouldn't be able to rest—wouldn't know where to rest—until she found him. Where could he be?

Memory drove aimlessly, wound through residential areas, past the bowling alley and the convenience store, the only two places she could think of that stayed open all night. A run out the highway, by Flanagan's and the loop back downtown was wasted fuel and effort. For no reason, she circled the courthouse, supposing it was because that was where she had last seen him. Miraculously, his car was there, in its assigned spot. It was nearly sunup. The building looked ominous in the silent stillness. Memory pulled into the area in front marked, "Law Officers Parking Only," darted up the stairs and was surprised to find the massive courthouse doors unlocked. Who locked up courthouses at night and opened them in the morning, and how were people supposed to know the hours? They weren't posted. There were no "Open" or "Closed" signs.

She pulled the door open and hesitated a minute, waiting for fear or caution to bristle the little warning hairs on the back of her neck. The hairs remained quiet. Feeling more assured by the inactivity, Memory crept into the heavy silence that hung like a fog in the lobby of the great, grim building. She felt comforted by the familiar smell of floor polish and the muted security lighting.

The District Attorney's offices were on the third floor. Not normally claustrophobic, Memory nevertheless disregarded the elevators and took the stairs two at a time to the second floor. From there she climbed more slowly, one step at a time. Anxiety helped make her winded. To catch her breath, she hesitated before taking the final step that put her in the expansive corridor of the third floor.

Someone was whistling and the sound echoed down the hallway. Maybe it was a janitor. Maybe not. She paused. Her mind was a little fuzzy, a usual result of an all nighter. Or maybe it was the anticipation of seeing Mac. At that thought, she straightened. Renewed confidence propelled her, quickening her steps until her heels clattered, the noise reverberating through the quiet halls.

The whistling stopped. A door opened, and a familiar figure stepped into the half-light of the corridor. Memory froze, uncertain of his mood until he grinned and began walking toward her, slowly at first, then double-time.

She hesitated only a minute before hurrying to meet him. Her steps quickened until she flew, ratcheting the distance between them until he swept her into his arms, gathering her close into the safest haven she knew. He dusted welcoming kisses over her cheek, her forehead, her eyes as she tilted her head, mutely requesting more. Just as she was settling in for a long siege, he caught her upper arms in a firm grip and set her away from him. "Where the hell have you been?"

"Driving all over looking for you."

"I went down to check on you about three. They said you'd left. I couldn't believe you took off without talking to me. I'd been hanging around all night waiting for you. I'm guessing you're over your mad."

"So now are you mad at me?"

"I guess not." He paused as what at first appeared to be a forced pleasant expression dissolved into anger. "Hell, yes, I'm mad at you. What were you thinking? I drove out to the house, by Flanagan's, even swung by my apartment and Quint's office. I couldn't figure out where you'd gone."

"As I said, I was driving around looking for you, of course." The repeat stilled him and he searched her face as if looking for an indication she was joking. She gave him her most sincere, trustworthy look and his vise-like grip on her upper arms relaxed.

"Well that's…"

"What? Go ahead. What were you going to say?"

"I was going to say that's good. I mean, that's…nice. Actually, very nice." He grinned and tugged, pulling her close to wrap his arms around her tightly. "I'd say it was very, very nice. The word is: if people know where you are, I'm easy to find. All they have to do is look behind and there I'll be, heeling like a trained pup."

Her laugh was muffled by his shirtfront and he grew very still. "Wanna go home with me and fool around?" His voice had that singsong quality she didn't quite trust. When she didn't answer, he eased a step back. "Are you okay? Were you scared when you couldn't find me?" He lifted her chin and rocked his head back to scan her face.

Suddenly she couldn't breathe, much less speak. Maybe she was having an anxiety attack. She felt tears boiling up as the events of the last few days came crashing down on her all at once.

"Are you hurt?" he asked.

She waggled her head from side to side. "I just

feel…out of control.” A keening little cry escaped her clamped lips, but she couldn’t seem to form any more words, either in her head or with her voice.

Draping one arm around her shoulders, he ushered her through the door marked “Cliff Horsely, District Attorney” into a reception room. He didn’t bother to snap on the overheads as a lamp already bathed the room in soft, incandescent light. He prodded her through another door whose letters read: “First Assistant, David McCann.”

The overhead fluorescent lights made her forget the time as Mac settled her in a chair, one which felt sturdy and dependable, like the man. It smelled like him, too. Leathery. He produced a paper cup of water and two tablets, but she turned her head. “I don’t take pills.”

“These aren’t pills, goofy. They’re aspirin.”

She took the tablets and chased them with the full cup of water. Looking satisfied, he pulled the second client’s chair closer to hers. “Okay, tell me what’s got you in a tizzy this time.”

She strained to smile, then made the mistake of looking directly into his earnest expression. Unable to get her mercurial mood swings under control, she began snickering. “I…don’t…know.” Her shoulders shook as she tried to control the silly giggling which effervesced through her nose and out her eyes. “I do not have a clue.” It wasn’t that funny. There wasn’t actually anything funny at all, but she exploded with snorts of wheezing laughter.

Leaning back in his chair, Mac regarded her oddly. The puzzled look on his face only made her laugh harder.

****

He wondered if she were going into shock. Maybe harrowing events had finally caught up with her and she'd snapped. Maybe she was hysterical. Again he entertained the thought of slapping her, but he couldn't make himself do it. She wasn't hurting anything. Okay, maybe his pride. A little. Even at that, he couldn't do anything abusive. Not to her. No, he could allow her to let off a little steam, maybe release some of the tension built up inside.

As the outburst became sporadic fits, the giggling was interrupted by tears. Still studying her, he risked a question. "When was the last time you slept?"

She grew quiet and frowned at him as if something important depended on her answer. "I don't know." She slumped, looking contrite, as if she were ashamed of the response.

"Think you can drive a couple of blocks?" he asked.

"Your apartment's not that close."

"No. We're going to leave your car in Jim Bigger's car lot. If someone's looking for you and sees it, the location won't provide any clue as to your whereabouts. Come on." He stood and gave her a hand up. "Let's go before people get out on the road, taking kids to school and going to work."

Docile as a lamb, she trailed him to the courthouse parking lot, then followed as he drove the three blocks to Bigger's lot. Mac put a note under the windshield wiper. "Jim, change the oil and detail this when you have time. Mac."

Memory didn't ask questions, simply followed orders as Mac put her in his car.

A Beemer came roaring around them on a quiet

residential street, just before they got to the boulevard, ran through a right-turn-on-red, and nearly rear-ended a parked car. Mac turned the same way, trailing the erratic driver.

"You'd better watch her," Memory said. "She had a cell phone in her ear."

"He."

"He? He has a ponytail."

"And an earring."

"Oh, yeah?"

"Yeah, but your she is still a he."

"If it's the tattoo on his forearm, lots of women have those now, too, you know."

"Better not let one of those women be you."

"Don't be ridiculous."

"You're saying you don't have a tattoo?"

"Of course not." She was quiet for a moment, watching the taillights of the driver ahead of them grow smaller. "Have you?"

"What?"

"Don't be evasive. Have you got a tattoo?"

"I'll take the fifth on that."

She looked surprised. "You do have one? Where?"

He slanted her a slow grin. "Maybe, if you're real sweet, I'll show it to you sometime."

The Beemer pulled into the curb and sat, its lights on as they cruised by. In a moment, it passed them again and, this time, cut short in front of the Lexus forcing Mac to hit the brakes and drawing Memory's attention back to their debate about the driver being male or female.

"What makes you so sure that's a man? A lot of women drive aggressively."

He grinned. "The real tell is the mustache. I saw it when he passed us the first time."

Lacing her fingers together, Memory smiled at her lap. "Yeah, well I suppose that's convincing, all right. A mustache. I missed that."

"A mustache may still be a giveaway today, but the way things are going, maybe not for long. Dykes are coming up with some unusual sex toys."

Covering her mouth, Memory smiled. She would like to pursue that, find out exactly what sex toys he'd seen and the extent of his knowledge about unusual sexual proclivities, but she might wait until another time. She was just getting extraneous volatile emotions under control. No use getting goofy again. That was his term, but she thought it fit.

As they pulled into apartment parking, Memory straightened in the seat. "David McCann, I cannot stay at your place." He didn't answer. "What I mean is, I'm too unstable right now. Emotionally. You and I can't sleep in the same…place."

"No? Well, I guess we can argue about that some other time. Right now, that's not my plan."

"Good. Will you take me back to Flanagan's?"

"No. You're staying here."

"David, no."

"I'm staying at Flanagan's."

"That's ridiculous. There's no need for you to be booted out of your own bed. The little guy is locked up. He won't be a problem anymore." She clasped her hands together to stop the shaking. "David, it's silly for me to stay anywhere else. I should just go home."

****

It did not escape his notice that she was calling him

David again. Did that indicate new estrangement? He would worry about that later. "No. Your stalker might be locked down, but the guy who hired him isn't."

"Or gal."

"What?" He cut the engine and turned toward her.

"I've been thinking about it. A man who wanted to injure me or get something from me probably wouldn't risk involving someone else: someone who would be able to testify against him if they got caught. He would do the dirty deeds himself. On the other hand, a woman might not feel like she had the muscle or the nerve to accomplish the job. She might feel more compelled to hire someone."

Now there was a possibility he hadn't considered. "Either way, if you're at my place and your car is not, neither he nor she will be able to find you, and you can get some real rest."

****

She must be addled from lack of sleep and the crazy things that happened because his logic made perfect sense.

Memory followed along quietly as he handed her out of his car and led her up the outside stairs to his apartment.

This time the apartment appeared neat and clean, but not excessively so. He bolted the front door, then left her standing beside it as he disappeared into his bedroom to return in a moment with a man's pajama shirt.

"I put clean sheets on the bed yesterday and I didn't have a chance to use them last night. As you can see, I've closed all the blinds and drapes. The windows are locked. I also looked under the bed and in the closets. We are alone." He crossed the room. "See this? The door has a lock in the knob, a dead bolt and a substantial security chain. Use all three. Take a shower or, no, take a long, hot soak in the tub, put on these clean jammies," he handed her the soft cotton pajama top, "and get in bed. If you're hungry, there's cereal and the milk is good. I just bought it."

"This is so unfair to you."

"No, it's not. The only injustice is that you'll be in my bed, which is exactly what I've had in mind, but I won't be, which is not the way I imagined it." He grinned self consciously.

"Do you want to stay here with me, then?" she asked.

He trailed his eyes all the way down to her toes and back. His expression was an odd mix of approval and determination. "I really can't, sweet thing. We're both tired. Not at our best. When we finally take quality time for each other, I want us well rested and in top form."

She wasn't sure exactly what he was talking about, but it obviously made sense to him. She would sooner trust his instincts about their relationship than her own, at the moment.

Memory followed as he walked into the bathroom where he loaded toiletries into a dopp kit. "There's a brand new toothbrush in the medicine cabinet," he said, pointing at the mirror over the lavatory.

"David, you don't have to keep providing me toothbrushes."

"I don't know, it feels good, like we've got this intimate, personal thing going on."

She wasn't sure what that meant either. She seemed to be having trouble following his line of thought. Maybe he was right. Maybe she needed serious sleep.

She trailed him through the apartment to the front door where he turned around and paused, studying her face. When he finished looking, he stepped close, placed a hand on her neck, to steady her, she supposed, while he kissed her forehead, like a Dutch uncle. "Bolt the door behind me," he whispered, then he was gone.

She doubted she could sleep in this strange place with its strange noises, but it wasn't long before it became familiar: the sound of ice dropping from the maker into the box and the gurgling as the tray refilled, the air pump cycling off and on, the bump of the hot water tank heating a new supply after she filled the bathtub to its brim.

In the soft pajama shirt, brushing her teeth, she laughed behind the foam. David McCann truly was unusual. Oddly, she couldn't remember the first time they met. It seemed like she had known David—Mac—forever; as if fate had inexorably entwined their lives, like a braid, woven together, then separated, only to be plaited again. Reminiscing about their growing up years, recalling him and events and experiences they had shared—teachers and classmates and townspeople—gave her a warm fuzzy feeling. She shivered with satisfaction.

David McCann was a troubled kid, suspended from high school more than once, she thought, for fighting. Coaches and teachers tried to channel his inner anger into sports. That worked some, she supposed. She remembered his name and pictures of him in the newspaper after sporting events. He and some buddies of his derailed a freight train once, stacking iron on the tracks, fooling around, like unsupervised kids did. Something identifying McCann was found at the scene. He was expelled from school because he wouldn't give up the names of the other guys involved. He wasn't bad, just mischievous. He was always good-looking, even when his hair was too long. She thought he might have gotten expelled once for that, too.

Now, this great-looking, former bad boy liked her. Did a man provide multiple toothbrushes for a woman unless he felt sexually attracted to her? He said it. A toothbrush definitely could be considered an intimate thing going on.

Feeling safer than she had in days, Memory developed an unexpected apprehension as she walked to the bedroom door and thought about sleeping in Mac's bed. It seemed too brazen. The intimacy of toothbrushes was one thing, sharing a man's sheets, even when he was absent, seemed entirely too—as her grandmother might have said—unseemly.

Rather than pull back the covers, which somehow symbolized exposing a very personal part of the man, Memory rummaged in the linen closet in the hallway where she turned up a lovely old handmade quilt. Mac didn't seem the type of man to have that kind of keepsake. His hidden sensitivities just kept surprising her. She wondered about his depth as she snapped off the lights, wrapped herself in the quilt and stretched out on the living room sofa. Although the room had an expanse of windows, the predawn view was hidden behind the pulled drapes.

Snuggling against the back of the couch, pulling her feet up into the warmth of the quilt, Memory wondered what time it was, but fell asleep before she could bother looking for a clock.

****

She was aware of sunlight through the bank of windows behind the draperies late in the morning. Other than pulling the quilt up to cover her eyes, Memory did not stir.

When she roused to go to the bathroom, the digital clock read 2:32. Light outside meant it had to be afternoon. She probably should get up and dressed, however, the phone hadn't rung and no one had come to the door. Except for occasional car noises outside, it was as if the world were taking a day off. Pulling the quilt tightly around her, she shuffled into the bedroom where she eased her cocooned body across Mac's bed, no longer concerned about imagined intimacy.

Late afternoon sunlight glittered through a seam in the bedroom's blind-covered windows directly into her face and Memory blinked, disoriented. Like a bear must feel coming out of hibernation, she awoke stiff and aware of a voracious hunger.

Luxuriously, she stretched, one-by-one freeing arms and legs from her cocoon. Dying rays streaked across the bed through seams between blinds, warming her, and she smiled. No one in the world at that moment felt richer, better rested, or more content than she did.

Now, if she could rustle up something to eat, life would be perfect. He'd mentioned cereal. That would ward off starvation. She was about to get up when she heard a noise. She scrambled to her feet, pulled the quilt tightly around her, and scurried into the living room.

The lock in the doorknob clicked. The dead bolt turned. The security chain, however, held, as Mac's voice called quietly. "If you're hungry, you'd better come open this door."

The man was clairvoyant. Not only that, he had perfect timing.

She relaxed her grip on the quilt and ran on tiptoes to free the chain, the smell of warm bread prodding her. He carried a bag of sweet rolls, a pizza box, and two steaming cups of coffee. The man was…perfect.

## Chapter Thirteen

Memory called her office in Metcalf to ask for a couple more days leave the next week to allow her to be present for the arraignment of the man who had attacked her. She mentioned she might need more time off later to testify as a witness in what could be a murder trial.

Determined to stay at the farm, Memory had the glass in the front door replaced, again, added new dead bolts there and on the back door and had a security system installed, one that included motion detectors around the exterior of the house and the outbuildings closest to it.

Mac took her to the movies Sunday night. They held hands and later necked in the car when he took her home, but when she overcame her misgivings and asked him in, he studied her face a long moment before he declined.

"You won't have to marry me, or anything," she assured, guessing at the reason for his concern. "I'm not like Laurel, David."

David again. He wasn't able to control the flinch. "I'm not worried. Your dad's not going to be coming after me with a shotgun."

"McCann, I'm not totally without potential spouses. Several guys have expressed interest in attempting marital bliss with me. I am the one who hasn't been interested."

She didn't care for the smug look he flashed before he said, "For the record, no one has turned me down yet, either."

"How many women have you asked to marry you?"

"None."

"So how do you know they wouldn't have turned you down?"

"Gossip gave me a heads-up, which is probably why I didn't ask. Also, of course, because I haven't met anyone I consider…long term."

"Do you mean no woman worthy of being the wife of Astrick's legendary bad boy?"

He laughed lightly. "Not my word, but no woman worthy of being the wife of the district attorney's right-hand man and, I add modestly, this burg's most eligible bachelor."

"Your record's safe with me."

"So, why invite me in? Do you plan to use my body then toss me aside?"

It was her turn to giggle softly. "Maybe I'm tantalized by thoughts of your tattoo. Maybe I want to see it. What are the odds?"

"Of getting me into bed?"

"No. I've already done that. What are the odds of my getting to see your tattoo?"

He arched his eyebrows. "I'd say they're…good."

"How about getting a little action on the side?"

"Also good." He sounded receptive, then ruined the moment by taking a step back. "But not tonight."

"No?" She felt and sounded genuinely disappointed.

"No, not tonight. We need to keep you focused on the mission."

"What about you?"

"There's an old saying about love in a man's life being but a thing apart, 'tis a woman's whole creation.'"

"Do you believe that?"

"I do."

"You think I am not capable of thinking of anything but romance?"

"Sure, I think you're capable of thinking of other things. You are exceptionally bright, for a female."

"What a sexist thing to say."

"What I mean is, I believe women are capable of doing most things, but that their nesting instincts are better developed than a man's." He retreated a step as her expression darkened. "That's not criticism, Memory. It's a compliment. The nesting instinct is probably responsible for keeping world populations growing since Adam and Eve."

"Yeah, well, I've got a bulletin for you, McCann: the population just took another hit from a self-centered, egotistical, bureaucratic male."

He threw up his hands, surrendering, but Memory whirled and shot through the newly refurbished front door into her house and summarily slammed that door in his face.

David McCann pivoted on his heel and marched to his car. Sometimes trying to be gallant wasn't worth shit. Again Memory had lulled him into thinking she wasn't like other women. Hah! How stupid was he not to have seen it?

Memory Smith might look like an angel, but she

could tempt a man to do things contrary to his own best interests. Now that he had her pegged, he might exercise some manly restraint and keep some distance between himself and that little temptress.

Oh, yeah, he could definitely see that happening.

Not!

****

Because she had seen District Attorney Cliff Horsely half-a-dozen times around the courthouse and downtown, Memory knew who he was when he greeted her in the reception room of his offices on Monday morning, grabbed her hand, and introduced himself. Horsely had invited her for ten o'clock saying Mac would be tied up all morning in court supervising the weekend's criminal arraignments.

Horsely escorted his visitor from the reception room through the door to his private office.

"Woman of the year," he said, grinning affably and pointing her toward a client's chair, "at least to hear David McCann tell it. I'd have recognized you anywhere."

She tried to control the blush, annoyed by the schoolgirl reaction to his flattery. "Thank you, Mr. Horsely. I hear good things about you, too, from Mac…ah, David…Mr. McCann."

Horsely arched his eyebrows. "I don't imagine it matters what name you call him, Ms. Smith. You have definitely tamed one of the orneriest, tomcatting-est rowdies I've ever known."

Although she was still annoyed with David McCann, she didn't like Horsely's description. She shrugged off the negative vibes. She was probably being overly sensitive. Most likely the district attorney was just trying to be funny.

"Mr. McCann and I have known each other almost all our lives, Mr. Horsely. Obviously I have a different opinion of him than you do."

"Listen, little lady, my description was a compliment. It's McCann's junkyard-dog attitude that makes him so valuable around here."

Again, she ruffled at the man's terminology. With a straight face, he returned her look as if daring her to defend her old classmate. Knowing Mac much better than she knew this supercilious man, Memory wondered again if the district attorney intended to demean his first assistant. She had the distinct impression he did. She might nibble at the bait and try to discern a little more of the man's intent.

"To hear your description, a person might think you don't admire your first assistant, Mr. Horsely. Creating a bad image of him doesn't reflect very well on the office, or on you personally, does it?"

"A Doberman has his place, Ms. Smith, as long as he's muzzled and a wise handler keeps a firm hold on his leash."

The man's expression was benign enough, but his eyes glittered with what looked like malice. At that moment, the district attorney took a nose-dive in her estimation. Obviously he was not nearly as loyal to Mac as Mac was to him. That rankled.

The man's face, even his posture, changed markedly when they heard Mac say, "Good morning" to the receptionist. The maligned assistant was coming.

Mac stepped into the doorway. Horsely, still on his feet, beamed innocent good humor, walked forward, and clapped an arm around Mac's shoulder, as if the new arrival were his dearest friend. Memory didn't have much use for hypocrites. She struggled to keep her disapproval from showing on her face.

"What's happening, buddy?" Horsely asked. "I didn't expect you to finish nearly this soon."

Mac gave his boss a glance before he flashed Memory a puzzled grin. "Short docket." He continued looking at Memory. "What are you doing here?"

"Mr. Horsely asked me to come by this morning." She glanced at the D.A. and intentionally didn't smile. "I'm not sure yet why."

"Details." Horsely cleared his throat. "About Laurel's death, of course."

"Which is exactly why I'm here," Mac said. "I've been chewing it over and keep running across things about the hit-and-run theory that don't make sense."

"Like what, boy?"

"Like who picked Laurel up from her apartment Friday night after I took her home, and why."

Horsely shrugged. "Well, it had quit raining, but there was a lot of mud and mess. She was awfully fussy about that car of hers."

"The Mazda?"

Memory started to remind Mac that Laurel had a new car, then realized he was the one who told her about it. So, what was he up to?

Horsely quickly corrected his subordinate's error. "No, she was driving that little yellow Camry she'd just bought. Guess you didn't know about that. It was an end-of-the-year model. She wheedled and whined and got a really good deal out of them." Horsely paused and his eyes shot from Mac to Memory. "That was the scuttlebutt, anyway."

Mac puckered, emphasizing the fullness of his lips, momentarily distracting Memory. She thought he was incredibly sexy. She was getting distracted, exactly what Mac had cautioned her about. But her thoughts didn't have anything to do with some theoretical nesting instinct.

She shouldn't enjoy looking at him, particularly admiring his straight nose and the way his skin fit so tightly over his prominent jaw and cheek bones. Bummer.

"I'd forgotten she had a new car," Mac said, but Memory wasn't buying that. "You're right. She was awfully fussy about her possessions. I guess that's why she wasn't driving it that night. So how did she get back to the country club?"

Horsely shrugged and goose bumps popped out on Memory's forearms. She wasn't cold, but a stray bit of information tucked back in her subconscious put her on alert and gave her a chill. She would have to dig deeper to figure out what was happening here. There was something suspicious about Mac's boss, and Mac seemed to know it.

Oddly enough, Horsely appeared to relax when neither she nor Mac questioned his intimate knowledge of Laurel's business. He looked thoughtful for a minute, then continued. "She wasn't supposed to drive. She'd just had her wisdom teeth pulled. All four of them. She wasn't supposed to get behind the wheel for a couple of days because of the anesthetic or the pain killers, or something."

There. He'd done it again. Where did he keep coming up with details of Laurel's personal life? The D.A.'s information may have come from the woman's father, but did two men share all that in casual conversation on the golf course? Memory added those questions to a growing mental list of items she would consider later, and maybe get Mac's opinion, too.

She cast a look at Mac to find him studying her. He gave her a slight smile. Apparently he had noticed and wondered, too, about the district attorney's wealth of particulars.

Of course, the man might have picked all that up during his investigation…except Mac had said the D.A.'s evidence officer was—as usual—the one gathering information about Laurel. So why had Horsely invited Memory to come here?

## Chapter Fourteen

In the courtroom at his arraignment that afternoon, Dicky Steam looked like a woebegone character in a comic strip as he sat on a hard bench in the audience behind the bar awaiting his turn to plead. One arm was in a cast cradled in a sling, his jaw was wired, and an angry red splotch marked the knot in the bridge of his nose. He also sported a number of bruises, and one black eye outlined in putrid green.

After having spoken to her gently and with some formality, Mac walked Memory into the courtroom through the back doors rather than through the judge's office that opened onto the front of the chamber. He directed her to a bench in the back. Limited as his movements were, Steam did not attempt to turn around to see who was coming and going.

Another assistant district attorney, a woman, sat alone at the prosecutor's table.

When he had her settled, Mac pointed to her would-be assailant. She trembled and started to stand, glancing toward the exit, but Mac kept a staying hand on her shoulder.

"I don't think I can identify him," she said.

"Not right now, maybe. That's because you haven't seen him from the back before, or without his mask." Regarding the suspect, Mac tilted his head like an artist eying his subject. "And, of course, the guy has looked better."

"No, I mean I don't think I would recognize him unless he were standing and had the stocking over his face."

"Trust me. That's him."

As she studied the man's profile, she frowned. "What's happened to him? Did the police beat him up, or other inmates?"

"You're what happened to him."

"I couldn't possibly have done all that."

"It took you four tries, but every bit of the damage that shows is your work."

"Oh, no."

"Memory, it's not like you went looking for him or you were the one spoiling for a fight."

Her voice caught. "That's true."

"He's the one who wouldn't let it go. Isn't that right?"

"Well…yeah…I suppose." She turned a hard look on Mac. "Did anyone ask him about that? About why he kept attacking me or why he tried to tranquilize me?"

"He hasn't been inclined to discuss it."

"Did anyone ask him who he was working for?"

"Yes, but his lawyer's angling for a deal, so mum's the word until we're ready to offer him a break."

"Your office isn't ready to do that? Why not?" She gave him an accusing glance.

"Not quite."

The clerk called the next case. "Dicky Steam. Attempted murder and four counts of attempted armed robbery."

Memory gasped. "Murder?"

"We can't very well negotiate up, so we file the worst charges from the outset to give us wiggle room."

As Memory and Mac watched, the attorney beside Memory's assailant stood. "Your Honor, the defendant is severely injured and asks to plead from where he sits."

The judge looked curious. "Can the defendant stand up?"

"He can, Your Honor, if you insist."

"No, I guess we'll let him stay where he is. Tell me, was this defendant injured before, during, or after the events that resulted in his appearance here?"

"During, Your Honor."

"Then you don't deny he was involved in the crimes alleged?"

"We don't deny that he was present on those occasions. We are prepared to offer a plea for arraignment purposes today, however, we are not prepared to make a statement at this time."

"So, how do you plead, Mr. Steam?"

A low voice muttered something.

"What's that?" the judge called, increasing his volume.

The attorney spoke up. "He pleads 'Not Guilty,' Your Honor."

"Now there's a shocker." The judge nodded at the prosecutor's table. "What says the state as to bail?"

"Fifty thousand dollars, Your Honor," the woman representing the D.A. said.

"On attempted murder and robbery charges? Isn't that cutting him a mighty big break?"

"We consider the defendant not a flight risk at this time, Your Honor. He's going back to the hospital when we're through here this morning and will undergo six weeks of rehabilitation therapy when he's able. It appears he will be a resident of our medical center for quite a while. We'll have people keeping an eye on him."

"Whatever." The judge looked skeptical, but signed the order and waved to the clerk, indicating he was ready for the next case.

Later that afternoon, when Memory Smith didn't answer the phone at the farmhouse, Mac went looking for her. He found her car in front of the hardware store. Inside, she was exchanging the pulls she had purchased for the kitchen in her parents' home. She had been cool toward him at Steam's arraignment. Something was eating her. She might be miffed about his not sleeping with her. Or maybe it was something he'd said. He didn't know how she might react to seeing him in the hardware store; didn't want her to think he was stalking her. Maybe he was. Hell, he wasn't sure what was going on inside him so, satisfied that she was all right, he did an about-face and marched out of the store before she saw him. Maybe he'd give her a day to cool off.

Just after dark, the policeman on duty at Steam's hospital room called the assistant D.A.'s cell phone as Mac drove home from the courthouse.

"Steam's gone," he said.

"How did he get out?" Bile rose in Mac's throat and he made a U-turn to aim his car toward the Smith farm.

"The window in his room."

"What floor did you have him on?"

"Ground level to make it easier to get him to and

from physical therapy."

"Damn it to bloody hell, don't you people have any sense?" Mac ended the call without waiting for an answer. He didn't know how to explain this to Memory, but there would be no fooling around this time. He would find her and stick to her like glue. The motion detector lights came on as he parked at her house. As he was exiting his car, his cell rang again.

"We've got him."

"Where was he?"

"Hobbling down the sidewalk not six blocks from the hospital."

"Did he put up a fight?"

"No. I think he was glad to see us. He wasn't feeling so hot."

"I want him in restraints. Leg irons and lock the son-of-a-bitch to his bed."

"That's being done as we speak."

Ending the call, Mac felt like a fool and a cowardly one at that. Nevertheless, he walked up on the porch and rang the doorbell, like a civilized person might do. To her credit, when she saw him through the pane in the front door, Memory didn't hesitate. She opened the door, but the look she gave him might have wilted a less determined man.

"Can I help you?" she asked, her voice as cool as her look.

Great opener, if the circumstances had been different. "Steam escaped and I came out to tell you and sit on you myself, but they got him back. He's shackled now, under lock and key. You don't have to worry."

"I wasn't worried." She stood a moment, giving him a chance to say anything else on his mind. For the first time in his adult life, Mac let a golden opportunity slide right by.

Memory, however, did not. "Do you want to come in?"

"I guess I could, as long as I'm here." He sounded to himself like some simpering sister.

She backed up and opened the door a little wider. He stepped inside, then waited for her to secure the door and lead the way. He followed as she walked down the hallway.

"The security system seems to be working. It's bright as day out there." He needed to break the ice.

"Yes, it's very efficient."

"What were you doing?"

"Changing the knobs out on the cabinets."

"What was wrong with the first ones you bought?"

"Too small."

He coughed a little laugh and trailed her through the swinging door into the kitchen just as the doorbell rang.

"Please, God, not again." Memory's icy facade melted as her almond eyes widened into globes. She scanned the room, then yanked open the utensil drawer, grabbed a butcher knife, and turned toward the swinging door, which had swung shut.

"Hold on a minute, tiger." Mac moved slowly, unsure about how rational she was. He slid an arm around her shoulders, lifted the butcher knife from her hand, and dropped it back in the open drawer.

"Remember, I just told you Dicky is grounded. Obviously, this is someone else. Besides that, when was the last time Steam used the doorbell?"

He felt the tension leach from her shoulders and he

tugged her close to him.

"Now, let's answer the door like a normal civilized couple."

She grabbed a fistful of his shirt and her eyes locked on his face. "Together?"

"Certainly."

The man visible through the oval pane in the center of the front door, wore slacks and a dress shirt and tie, but no coat. He looked like a college kid. Memory shrugged out from under Mac's arm and opened the door.

"Ms. Smith?" the young man asked. "Ms. Memory Smith?"

"Yes."

"Here." From behind his back he produced a packet of papers in a blue manuscript cover folded in thirds, an official looking document.

The young man pivoted, trotted off the porch, got into a dark sedan, and drove away. The delivery was in her hands only a moment before Mac relieved her of it.

"What is that?" she asked, squinting into Mac's face.

"Oh, this is rich." As Mac read the file-stamped documents, he chuckled, frowned, then laughed again. "You are being sued for five hundred thousand dollars in medical bills and pain and suffering for injuries received in your assaults and batteries upon the person of one Dicky Steam."

Memory's jaw dropped. "What? My assaults? Is he crazy? You're kidding, right? That's outrageous. Can he do that?"

"Sure he can. It's the American way. Anyone who can come up with a couple of hundred dollars for court costs can file a lawsuit."

"Doesn't he have to pay an attorney to do that for him?"

"Not if the lawyer is willing to take it on a contingency—to bet on the outcome."

Memory took the papers from Mac's hands and scanned them. "He wants me to pay him eighty thousand dollars for his medical bills?"

"That's not all."

She read on. "Four hundred twenty thousand for his pain and suffering?" She glowered at Mac. "He expects to get that from me? Is he kidding? I don't have that kind of money. Besides that, he's the one who kept coming after me. His pain and suffering was his own darn fault. Can he do this? Would anyone on a jury believe it?"

Shaking his head, Mac smiled at the ceiling. "I don't imagine Steam or his lawyer plan on this going to trial." Mac's humor ebbed. "He'd be laughed out of a courtroom, even if it got tried to a judge. Obviously, his lawyer is an idiot or doesn't know the facts behind his client's injuries." Mac held up a second finger to join the first emphasizing his points. "Or he doesn't know about the criminal case," a third finger, "or he doesn't realize you are familiar with the workings of the legal system," and a fourth, "or he doesn't care."

"Well, sure, I'm familiar with legitimate claims, not some trumped up thing like this. Where am I going to get five hundred thousand dollars? What in the world am I going to do?"

Mac put a comforting arm around her shoulders and guided her into the living room. "Yours is exactly the reaction Steam and his lawyer are counting on.

They expect to stampede you into offering something to appease them. They are depending on the nuisance value to shake you down. They know there's no way they can get half a million dollars, but they think you might cough up a lesser amount to make this go away. Maybe fifty thousand, or a hundred."

"I don't have anything like that kind of money." She squirmed, freeing herself from the protective arm, and flopped onto the edge of her dad's old overstuffed arm chair.

Following her lead, Mac settled on the front edge of the sofa, bringing their faces to the same level.

"Ah, but you have collateral. You own a house and a car. You have a whole potful of assets to use to get a loan."

Gaping at him, she stammered. "Oh…of course…I see." Suddenly her eyes narrowed and she clamped her mouth closed and squared her shoulders. "Well, extortion isn't going to work here. I'm not giving into him this time either, not even if this new assault is done up in a blue-back with official seals and filing stamps. No, sir, Dicky boy, you've got the wrong mark again."

Mac grinned. "Steam's lawyer may not realize his client's level of participation in the events, or, as I said before, he might not care. Look at this deal from a lawyer's point of view. A man summons you to his hospital room. He's battered and bruised. His broken jaw is wired so he has a hard time telling his story. One arm is in a cast. You feel sorry for the poor schmuck, regardless of how he got in that condition. He has stitches and abrasions that move you without his having to go into a lot of boring detail. He tells you some strange woman unexpectedly beat the shit out of him."

"Four times? Wouldn't the lawyer wonder about that? When did Steam tell this wild tale?"

"Check the date on the papers."

She looked where he pointed, then glanced back at him. "It was filed yesterday."

"Steam no doubt visited with the lawyer early in the week, apparently before he was arrested."

"Will people believe I hunted this guy down and brutally attacked him four times?"

"He might not have mentioned the circumstances. At least it's not here in the petition. His story, substantiated as it is with convincing physical evidence, probably was extensively edited. He does have authentic medical bills out the wazoo. It'd be easy for a lawyer to believe the miserable guy has been brutalized. His story is he's the victim. The attorney's sense of justice comes alive as he feels the rush of the righteous cause. This poor man before him deserves compensation and the lawyer, by God, vows to get Dicky baby everything he deserves."

"Swell." Still sitting stiffly at attention, Memory crossed her arms over her chest and frowned.

"Do you know this attorney?"

Mac looked at the document again. "I've heard about him. Ambulance chaser." Clearly beginning to enjoy himself, Mac continued. "So as Steam's attorney, he'll sign this poor schmuck on the dotted line. He'll front all the costs, which will come off the top of whatever he gets out of you, the vicious female, and forty percent of the rest. If he has to take this to court and is out the expense of issuing summons and taking depositions, he'll take fifty percent of the net.

"Mac—"

He held up a hand. “He’ll grab a camera, or maybe call in a professional photographer who will know how to record every detail of Steam’s pain and suffering to back up his case. On second thought, maybe he won’t be so greedy. Maybe he’ll limit his share to only thirty-five percent of the recovery, if the losers on the other side will settle without forcing the matter to court.”

Mac nodded and pursed his lips, obviously getting into his story. “At first blush, of course, the greedy attorney will have no way of knowing this client cannot afford to get within a hundred feet of a witness stand. In fact, his only real hope for a payday depends on the other side caving. But he starts out bold, gives the appearance of being ready to fight to the finish, maybe frightening the other side into mortgaging homes and hocking heirlooms to come up with cash to satisfy them. If the brutish female on the other side complies, as he is certain she will, he and his client will laugh all the way to the bank.”

Memory slumped back against the cushy overstuffed chair.

“But that ain’t gonna happen,” Mac said, watching her face.

Her expression flickered as it lifted from sad to reflect a spark of hope. “It ain’t?”

He chuckled at her mimicking, admiring her all over again. “No way, sweetheart.

“First, my office is going to file additional criminal felony charges against Mr. Steam. Also, the minute he gets out of the hospital, we’re going to throw his butt in jail where he will be under lock and key and not able to wander off.

“We are going to take his fingerprints and a sample

of his DNA and check into what I anticipate will be his long and checkered criminal background. Hey, are you paying attention? You didn't pick up on 'check' his 'checkered background?'"

Beginning to relax, Memory rewarded the pun with a feeble smile. She did love looking at his wonderfully rugged features. When had he become so handsome? When, so important?

Obviously drawing encouragement from her steady gaze, Mac rubbed his hands together like the villain in a melodrama. "Then we are going to turn Mr. Steam's mediocre existence into an exceptional nightmare. Eventually, in his struggle to get us off his back, he's going to tell stories district attorneys all over the country are going to stand in line to hear. Oh, yeah, Mr. Steam is going to sing like a bird. When we find out who hired him to come after you, we are going to nail that yokel harder than we do Steam.

"By the way, his filing this lawsuit is a good thing; a very good thing. It's got my juices flowing. I find it downright invigorating."

Although Memory couldn't fathom exactly why her being sued for half a million dollars made his day, she basked in the pleasure she derived from it having made Chief Deputy D.A. Mac McCann a happy man.

****

Mac sprang for dinner at Spuds, the nicest restaurant in town, then drove her home, at her insistence. Despite the earlier incident with the butcher knife, she was fairly convincing that she felt safe staying there by herself. As they walked from his car to her house, the new motion detector flooded the area with light. Mac felt a modicum of comfort as Memory fumbled in her purse to find the remote control and douse the blinding illumination. At least she'd have plenty of warning if Steam dared to show up again.

"Will you have breakfast with me?" he asked, once the front porch was suitably dim again.

"How about lunch, instead?"

He hid his disappointment at not being first on her mind. "Okay. Where?"

"I'll meet you outside your office, at noon."

He shrugged and accepted the alternative graciously. She kissed him good night, then upped his morale when she asked him inside. "We could sit on the sofa and talk a little while, if you've got time. Or…"

"Or, what?"

"Mac, remember the night at Flanagan's? Wrapped in sheets?"

"I do."

"Could we do that again? Here?"

"Tonight?"

He noticed that she didn't give him a straight yes or no. "I keep remembering how you looked with that sheet wrapped around your waist, with your bare chest and stomach, and, well, I've seen men without their shirts, of course, but I've never seen a grown man…nude.''

Never?"

"…But I've thought about it quite a bit."

"I have, too, Memory, thought about us in our bedsheets that night."

"Do you want to come in for a while?"

"I would love to, but it's late. How about we save the toga party for tomorrow night, and start early, like in the afternoon. Right after lunch."

She looked so disappointed that he nudged her backward through the door. She snapped on a light, which he promptly snapped off, leaving them in the dark hallway. He led her through to the living room where one small lamp provided a night light.

"Memory, we are not a one-night-stand couple." He kissed the hollow at her throat. "I love you. I adore you. I want you, but I want you for keeps. His hands traced her long arms, then pulled her snugly against him. His hands roved her back and down to fondle her hips.

She gasped and he felt her heart suddenly pound like a trip hammer. Was it his hands or words that excited her?

"Tomorrow, we'll come here early, lock the doors, take off all our clothes and put on our sheets, then we'll see where things go from there. What do you say?"

Her eyes narrowed. "I say yes, but you don't have to say you love me. It's not required."

Mac laughed without commenting. So it was the words. He patted her backside as he planted a thorough good-night kiss. Standing on the porch a long moment later, he waited for her to lock and bolt the door.

****

Early Tuesday morning Memory received a call from her boss in Metcalf. He needed her back. Could she plan to be in the office the next morning?

Having taken advantage of his good nature for a full week already, she reluctantly agreed.

She arrived at the courthouse parking lot outside Mac's office on time, refreshed, wondering what he would say to her impending departure, if he'd ask her to stay. She waited twenty minutes, but there was no sign of Mac. Wondering if something was wrong, she went inside and ran up the stairs and there he was, just coming down the corridor. Anticipation prompted her to move toward him and open her arms as he approached. It took her a moment to realize he was accompanied by a disheveled-looking group of people. As she did, he bypassed her, allowing only a stiff, formal nod—as if he didn't even know her! She pivoted, watching his back as he walked away from her, leading his ramshackle group of followers to his office.

What the devil? How could the man touch her so intimately, whisper such loving words, at night when they were alone, then turn into a cold fish in the daylight, in front of other people? Witnesses? Maybe he didn't want anyone else to think they were a couple.

Why not?

Maybe he had a reputation to protect.

She approached the doorway to his outer office uncertainly. Was that why he'd wanted her to meet him outside? He wanted their liaison to be a secret?

In that moment, he glanced back at her, frowned, hesitated, then somewhat forcefully shut the door to his inner office. Memory felt stunned, as if he'd just summarily closed her out of his office—and, most likely—out of his life.

Clearly, he'd had time to rethink his position, and had decided he preferred the status quo.

Well! A building didn't have to fall on her.

Disappointment, shame, and humiliation washed over her in one huge wave. How could she have been so stupid? So gullible? She was just another one of David McCann's many conquests, and apparently not one he was particularly proud of.

The secretary spoke. Memory smiled wanly at the girl, but that was all she could manage. Her emotions were running so high, she couldn't trust herself to speak. She needed to get out of there. Tears threatening, Memory left as she had arrived, without saying a word.

She had a life to get back to in Metcalf.

****

"She left? Just like that?"

Mac had gotten his motley crew settled, made his excuses, and stepped out of his office to talk to Memory, but the secretary said she'd left.

"What did she say? Did she leave a message?"

"No, sir. In fact, I don't believe she spoke at all."

"Do you mean she walked out? Just like that? No note, no explanation?"

"Apparently so."

He rolled his eyes in exasperation, then returned to the people in his office, wondering at Memory's abrupt departure. Several hours later, Mac paced his office alone, struggling to comprehend. He'd called Memory's house and her cell phone all afternoon, began as soon as he got rid of the last witnesses in the armed robbery of a local bar downtown. Seemed everybody had a story to tell, and none of them matched.

Mid-afternoon, he drove out to Memory's house.

The place was locked up tight. She was gone.

The sheriff's deputy he called said Memory had packed, loaded her car, and left town right after noon.

Clearly, she'd come to tell him she'd changed her mind and was going back to Metcalf. Mac didn't know why her abandonment came as a surprise. Story of his life. That was what women did. He knew that. What did he expect? Shit. Here he was, a seasoned campaigner with women, yet he'd fallen hook, line, and sinker for Memory Smith's wide-eyed innocent act.

As an assistant D.A. he dealt with con artists, grifters, accomplished liars, and criminals every day. His upbringing had prepared him well to see through subterfuge. Other law enforcement people admired his insights, trusted him to see beyond the teary eyes, quivering chins, palsied shakes, and other feigned signs of distress. But this one, the miracle child, had fooled him as completely as if he were some fresh-faced kid.

Memory.

She was gone, just like the first most important woman in his life.

Mac slammed his fist into the wall, needing physical pain to mask the sudden wave of self-hatred washing up from his insides. His throat ached. If he were still young and stupid, he'd have gone looking to beat the hell out of someone to vent his frustration. But he wasn't that kid any more. He couldn't indulge himself in a teenage tantrum. He was an adult now, with enough rage and frustration building inside him to have him clamping his hands over his ears and clawing at his hair.

How could he have been so stupid?

He slumped into the chair behind his desk, propped his elbows on the surface, and rested his forehead in the palms of his hands.

What was he supposed to do now?

## Chapter Fifteen

Struggling for indifference, Mac didn't want to ask about her. He was able to glean some information from conversations around the office. District Attorney Cliff Horsely had met with Memory at the police station early the afternoon she left town. Apparently she hadn't felt comfortable coming back to the office and Horsely had accommodated her.

She didn't bother to call Mac with an explanation for her disappearance. He certainly saw no reason to call her. She was the one who needed to apologize. Teasing him the way she had, and then, vanishing.

Horsely excused her from attending Steam's preliminary hearing two weeks later, saying they had enough evidence and testimony to bind the man over for trial without her.

Although he did not welcome the awkwardness of seeing Memory again, Mac was disappointed.

"How's the Steam case coming along?" Mac asked the D.A.'s legal assistant a week later as he casually thumbed through the mail.

"Cliff met with that Smith woman yesterday at city hall. He said the case is airtight."

Mac's heart skipped. "Met with Memory Smith? At city hall? Here in Astrick?"

"Yes, why?" She did a double take and studied his face. He schooled his expression to nonchalant, hard to do at that moment.

"It was my case. Do you know why they met at city hall?"

"No. Is it important?"

Mac turned his attention back to the mail. "No." Damn the D.A. and damn Memory. Why were they being so secretive?

That week, his grandmother mentioned she had seen Memory at the diner on Saturday.

Again, the woman had been right there in town and hadn't called or made any effort to see him. Her lack of interest galled him. In return he made no further effort to contact her.

Clearly, she'd changed her mind about him.

Finally, early the next Friday afternoon, after a fourth full week of sleepless, soul-searching nights, Mac drove to Metcalf…on business. He wasn't going there to see Memory. He needed a new suit for court.

Yeah, right. A soon as it was bought, he left the city's rush-hour traffic and threaded his way over to Church Street, an historical drive at the edge of the downtown business district. Instead of becoming more nervous, his intensity eased as Mac turned onto Church. She was nearby. The thought that he was getting closer, that he might even see her, actually soothed him.

Slowing, he cruised to the two-hundred block. It was an old part of town, once an area of stately mansions and massive live oaks. He held his Lexus to a crawl, finally pulling to the curb across the street from a sprawling old place which bore the number "Two Forty-seven."

Her house.

Not the bungalow he had imagined, it was quite the

opposite, four stories, at least thirty rooms. He noticed a small, neatly hand-lettered sign in the corner of a front window. "Apartment for Rent."

His mouth got a familiar tinny taste and he could scarcely contain his excitement. This was where she rented.

He couldn't say why, but that made him happy. Probably because it implied her situation was temporary. She could leave at any time.

He could work with that.

Assuming she would still speak to him.

Seriously, he could see her point. He'd been an ass.

He shifted uncomfortably in the car. Okay, so he had put himself in a bad spot. Now what? There had to be a way out.

He tried replaying what had happened between them from her perspective. He had ignored her when she came to meet him at the courthouse. He had turned his back, and she'd probably felt the way he had been feeling these past four weeks…like he had somehow abandoned her. He probably needed to apologize.

Apologize, hell. He needed to grovel. Groveling wasn't his style, but if it took groveling to get them back where they were, he needed to step up…or down.

What did a person do when he injured another person? A courageous man swallowed his pride and offered to do penance. He'd never done that before with a woman. It wouldn't be pretty. After all, she was partially to blame…

Then again, if their relationship meant anything to her, would she have let him toss her aside so easily?

Yes. She would. Memory Smith did not impose herself on others. She was non aggressive, which was one of the things he admired most about her. She took the offensive only when she was forced to. However, she stood firm in the face of attack—physical, verbal, emotional—whether it came from a thug in a stocking mask or a longtime admirer.

"Oh, God," Mac whispered. "How do I make this right?"

Finally, drawing a deep breath, he picked his cell phone out of the car's ashtray and punched in Memory's number. As it rang, he stepped out of his car and walked to the passenger side.

"Hello?" The breathless quality of her voice jarred him. He had assumed she wouldn't be home from work. He had planned to say something wickedly clever to her answering machine; had it scripted in his mind. He was not prepared to converse with a human being.

"Hello?" she repeated.

"Hey."

He thought he heard her inhale during the delay before she responded. "Hey."

"Do you know who this is?"

"Yes."

"Are you sure? I could be an obscene caller."

"I suppose you could be, considering the frame of mind you were in the last time I saw you."

"Meaning you aren't sure I'm not? You shouldn't talk to strangers who fail to identify themselves."

"David, is there a reason for this call?"

"Probably."

"Okay."

He held silent. This wasn't going well. Plus, she was calling him David again. He needed to choose his next words carefully. So far, he only seemed to be antagonizing her.

"McCann, what do you want?"

It could hardly get any worse. "I want to see you."

"I'll be back in a couple of weeks."

"How about if I see you in Metcalf?"

"Why?"

"We could have dinner and maybe take in a movie or something."

"When?"

"The sooner the better, as far as I'm concerned."

He heard the smile in her voice. "Tonight's it for this week and probably the next couple of weeks. I have a devastatingly busy schedule."

He couldn't help a smile of his own. "It's only five-twenty, a little early for dinner."

"I need to put on my shoes and comb my hair. I can be ready in the two hours it will take you to get here."

"I am here."

"Where?"

"Standing by my car in front of two forty-seven Church Street."

Mini blinds in a floor-to-ceiling dormer window on the third floor crawled up the sill and there she stood in a T-shirt and jogging shorts, looking out at him.

Leaning his hip on the front fender of his car, feet crossed at the ankles, he smiled and waved with his free hand. Her answering smile was tentative, but she waved back.

"My shoes are already on," he said absorbing the smile that slowly warmed her face.

"I'll be down in a minute," she said and hung up. After a moment, time for second thoughts, the mini blinds abruptly dropped, covering the window.

Mac chuckled quietly, anticipating, and genuinely happy for the first time in weeks.

It took longer than he expected for her to appear at the front door, a vision in a broomstick skirt, a cap-sleeved sweater, and sandals. She stopped and gave him a hard look as if bracing herself before she hurried across the broad porch and negotiated the steps without taking her eyes off of him. Her facial expression changed from skeptical to eager as she got closer, which he considered a good sign; definitely promising.

He didn't realize he was walking forward until she broke into a trot, her long, gorgeous legs outlined by the swirling skirt, her full breasts rocking with the rhythm of her quickening steps.

With no plan, he opened his arms, bent a little from the waist, and advanced, closing on her. Her long arms flew all the way around his neck, her nose smushed into the side of his face and her feet came off the ground as he caught her. He lifted, clamping her tightly against him, and swung her in a full circle as if she were a child. In those moments his world, until then bleak and completely out of whack, righted. He didn't care if the earth continued turning on its axis or not. He was happy holding onto the one most joyous thought: Memory was in his arms. He was whole.

## Chapter Sixteen

The world did revolve and time did advance, however, defying Mac's wishes. When Memory squirmed, he lowered her feet back to the ground. He didn't want her to be embarrassed by her own exuberance. No words, no other response, could have expressed her feelings more eloquently. He was forgiven.

David McCann had always prided himself on being tough. Having survived his mother's abandonment, he grew up knowing he could endure anything—any physical difficulty, any emotional challenge. He didn't need anyone, their approval or their good will. Not until now. If he had hung around Memory back then, she would have owned his soul as surely as she owned it now. He probably would have been even less successful defending himself against her then—her charm, her scent, her laughter, her secret glances…her.

"Are you hungry?" he asked, to divert their attention from the embarrassment of disentangling themselves.

She smoothed her skirt, then raised her incredible eyes to his. "Sure, if you are."

It was still daylight, although the sun was crawling toward the horizon. "We'll go get something to eat, then maybe a movie."

Her quick frown surprised him as he opened the

passenger door and put her in the car. After he got in the driver's side, he took her hand. He wanted to investigate the thought that had produced her frown. "Did you have other plans tonight?"

She stared at their hands linked over the console between them. "Personally, and if it's all right with you, I'd like to go some place and park. You have some explaining to do. We could talk for a while, then maybe…make out."

The laugh started somewhere deep in his chest and bubbled up through his throat like a geyser—unstoppable. "I see," he managed, barely able to suppress his giddy relief. "How about a nice motel?" he suggested. Might as well come right out with it.

"That would be too…" She didn't finish.

"Okay, now you suggest something."

"Dove's Creek."

"What's that?"

"Lover's lane."

"You really want to park?"

"I haven't ever done it before. I've always wanted to."

"So, we are going to rewind ourselves back to high school?"

"If that's okay with you."

"Certainly, it's okay with me. Do you think we should wait until dark?"

"Dark? Oh. Sure. I wasn't familiar with the protocol."

"That's when lover's lanes are really at their best, after dark."

"I suppose." She looked and sounded disappointed.

"Of course, we are old enough and independent

enough to set our own rules. If you want to go now, it's a little unorthodox, but it'll probably be less crowded now than later."

Her expression brightened and she looked at him as if he were again her hero. "Let's do."

He started the engine. "Which way?"

****

"Okay, explain why you invited me to come meet you for lunch, then acted like you'd never seen me before?"

"That's in the past and forgotten now."

"Not by me, it's not. When we have problems, we need to communicate. I've never been around anyone who snubbed me so completely. What was that about?"

"I was trying to work out a really ugly case with some uncooperative folks. I didn't want you tainted by breathing in the same air they did."

"You could have given me a sign, excused yourself from them long enough to let me know you could see me."

"I probably should have, and I did, a few minutes later, but all's forgiven now, right?"

"Not until you explain."

Mac looked away, over the dashboard, and into the valley, and finally came to a conclusion. "Okay, but I don't want to upset you all over again."

"I'll probably get over it. Let's hear it."

"I don't know where to begin."

"At the beginning."

"Okay." He drew a deep breath. "When I was six, my mother took me to the department of human services and told the lady behind the desk she didn't want me anymore."

"What?"

He held up a hand. "She left. Eventually, they called my grandmother. She came and picked me up. My grandmother raised me. She felt sorry for me, so she overindulged me. Growing up, I ran with a wild crowd, smoked, sniffed, huffed, and shot-up every substance we could get our hands on. We boosted cars and drank and smoked weed. None of us ever had any money, so we stole stuff. I was in and out of trouble all the time. I shop-lifted, jimmied vending machines, helped myself to displays. I had quick hands. A buddy and I found a car with the keys inside and went joy-riding when I was fourteen. There was the knife incident in metal shop, fights at school. People got under my skin talking about how I didn't have parents.

"When I was seventeen, a buddy and I got caught burglarizing Winn's Sporting Goods. My grandmother was about ready to give up on me by then. The district attorney spelled it out: the army or jail."

Memory stared out the windshield. When she didn't say anything, he continued.

"That's why I didn't graduate with the rest of you. The last semester of your senior year, I was in boot camp learning to be a soldier.

"The army became my family, a family with tough, unforgiving rules they expected me to learn and obey."

"Was it awful?"

He smiled at her sympathetic look.

"No. It was great. For the first time in my life, things were clear: black or white. Right or wrong. I loved the clarity.

"Sergeant Jarmin was my first mama in the army. He was a wiry little black man, all knifelike creases and spit and polish. He told me I was a worthwhile human being and he planned to make a productive citizen out of me. He kept a foot in my butt making me prove he was right. That little guy drove me hard. He'd gotten his G.E.D. and got me on the road to graduation. When I got that, he made me sign up for college. I went nights and weekends.

"I got out of the army, and out from under Mama Jarmin, to find the G.I. bill available. So, I went to law school."

Memory laughed. "Do you stay in contact with the sergeant?"

"He sends me a Christmas card every year. Funny thing was, Memory, he reminded me of you, in a way."

She sobered. "What do you mean by that?"

Mac wound his index finger into a loose curl dangling in front of her ear. "He always thought I was a better person than I thought I was. You were like that, too, all the time we were kids."

"You didn't know I existed when we were kids. Admit it."

"From kindergarten up, I was always aware of you."

"In junior high, you were totally indifferent."

"Not so. I always knew your locker number—even your combination. I knew which lunch period you had, and I watched out for your reputation. Nobody said anything raw about you when I was around."

"Really?"

"Really."

"Now, can we get to the fun part of your plan?" He rolled onto his right hip, putting his mouth close to hers, then squirmed. "Bucket seats are cool, but I'd give a lot to be driving an old pickup truck with a broad bench seat tonight."

He turned away from her, opened the door, and stepped out of the car. After helping her out the passenger side, he turned her around to pull the back of her snugly against the front of him, and wrapped his arms around her waist, then duck-walked them to a cluster of pine trees marking the overlook.

The sunset was spectacular, maybe enhanced by the sweet-smelling woman nestled in his arms. Neither of them said anything significant, whispering about the weather and his drive from Astrick to Metcalf, traffic, etc.

It was obvious to him that they had another touchy subject to cover.

"Memory, I didn't understand why you took off without saying anything."

She remained mute for several heartbeats before she cleared her throat.

"You said you loved me." Her words came out as a whisper. "You probably say that to every girl you like, but no one has ever told me that before. Maybe it was foolish of me, but your saying you love me was important to me, a first-in-a-lifetime moment."

Mac tightened his arms. "Memory, I do love you."

"When you turned away from me in the courthouse the very next day, I knew the words didn't mean anything special to you. I was just too naive to realize it was standard dating talk."

"No, no, Sugar. I've never told any other woman—except my mother and grandmother—that I loved her.

Memory remained still, gazing at the darkening sky, giving no indication she wanted to escape. "I didn't know that. I thought you were embarrassed for me to be there, in your work environment. I really did not intend to be an embarrassment."

"That was ridiculous."

She stiffened. "Ridiculous? You're kidding, right? There in the corridor of a public building with you surrounded by those people, I was supposed to know you still liked me, still wanted me, in the light of day? My boss had called that morning practically ordering me back to my office. Work was backing up. They needed me. I needed to leave, especially if you were tired of me. I figured if I was just another one of your conquests. You'd find someone else and forget me."

"Good idea, but it didn't work."

"Sure it did. When you didn't call, I knew I was right."

"Thinking that was…not intelligent."

"How was I to know that?" Her words were blunt, but her tone was conciliatory.

"I have trust issues with females."

"I realize that now."

Memory pivoted in his arms and stood on tiptoe to kiss his chin. Mac lowered his mouth. He'd take her pity or anything else this woman offered. A moment later, she took his hand and turned them toward a path along the ridge.

"So you grew up, in spite of the difficulties, to become a success," she said quietly, prodding him.

"Not exactly. In fact, I've never been willing to…well…invest myself in anyone—except Gram, of course—until you popped back into my life, wet, bedraggled, and plodding along beside a highway in a thunderstorm."

There was a long silence as they strolled together in the deepening shadows on the path.

"I'm sorry," they said, almost in unison. She glanced up and they laughed into each other's eyes. Mac cleared his throat, signaling he wanted to speak.

"I'm not usually possessive."

"Hmm." Her hum indicated she understood, but she didn't offer anything else.

They stood studying each other for a heartbeat before he scooped her into his arms. His momentum carried them roughly against the side of the car. She wriggled and squirmed until their bodies flattened into each other. When she lifted her eyes to his, he saw enchantment there. She might be naive, but the wisdom of women since Eve in the Garden of Eden sparked in her. Leaning against the car, Memory raised her mouth, summoning Mac's, almost against his will. He was stronger than she, taller, heavier, faster, and more experienced in the world, yet he was hers to command. Did that make sense?

Her mouth opened to consume his.

Mac didn't care much for most females beyond a basic need. This woman was the exception. She writhed as he pressed against her. He couldn't get enough. She was his woman. She had all the standard equipment, but unique value. Having her would be to win a contest he had never felt qualified to enter. He had never wanted a woman the way he wanted her.

Their mouths sealed, he realigned his body with hers, then raised his head to see how she was taking it, not that he planned to give her a choice. To his delight, she seemed swept up on the same wave carrying him.

Resuming the kiss, he slipped a foot between her

two and bent his knee, establishing his presence. Instead of resisting or pretending to be coy, she widened her stance, the expanding broomstick skirt giving access. The fabric rode up as Mac deftly shifted his other foot to position himself fully between her legs. Once there, he flexed, pressing the most intimate part of him to the open invitation. To his surprise, a whispery little moan vibrated from her mouth into his. The sound was like the purr of a contented cat.

Her arms circled his neck and she pulled, fitting herself more closely to him. He captured her tight, round bottom—still clothed—in his hands and lifted, positioning the V between her legs perfectly to his erection. She stilled for a moment, then relaxed against him, and he wondered if she were surprised by her own willing responses. Moments later, she loosened her hold on his neck and began rubbing her chest against his in a time-honored grind of seduction.

Fighting himself and her, he struggled to breathe. "I don't think you know what you're doing."

She slammed her mouth hard into his and sucked his tongue inside, forcing him to deepen the kiss. He did a little grind of his own and she gasped. He grinned. She flexed her arms, pulling herself up to put her mouth against his ear. "Mac?" Her voice was a purr of promise. "Take me to third base. Please. Ever since that night at Flanagan's, being with you is all I think about, awake or sleeping. I imagine being in that room again, wrapped in bedsheets. I imagine you touching me. Please. Touch me like you did that night. Give me new memories."

He lifted her, situating her hips on the car, maintaining his post between her legs. She relaxed her arms and propped her hands on his shoulders. He caught her forearms and wrapped them again tightly around his neck, then put his hands under her arms and pulled them forward. She took a deep breath and thrust her breasts up, giving him better access. God, things didn't get any better than this. He fondled her, kneading her breasts thoroughly before he brought his thumbs and index fingers forward to tweak the hard nipples, ripened, pronounced even under her sweater and bra.

She was studying his face, her eyes glazed, as if she had fallen into a hypnotic trance. That secret Mona Lisa smile lifted her mouth. He recognized the expression, one that had fascinated men for centuries.

Twilight settled around them and they were totally alone in a rose-colored setting which appealed to every sense. The fragrances of her made his mind swirl. The two of them became Adam and Eve in the Garden.

Established as he was between her legs, he kissed and caressed, all the while working his way into her clothing. He pushed her sweater up, revealing smooth, unblemished flesh as he skimmed the shell over her head and off. He popped the front fasteners on her bra while she studied his face mesmerized. Like the original couple in that original Garden, neither he nor she were concerned about anyone else intruding into this very private world created for two.

Memory held absolutely still, watching Mac lower his mouth to a bare breast. Her breath caught and her hips began to writhe, tormenting them both. Lacing her fingers into the thick hair on the back of his head, she raised her breasts, begging for more. Her skin tightened against her ribs and she inhaled until her midriff became concave. Mac's body responded with no conscious instruction from his brain.

He continued kissing her breasts, distracting her, as he settled both hands, light as butterflies, on her thighs. He worked those hands under the wispy fullness of her skirt. They crawled to the edge of her panties, then retreated as she groaned what might have been an objection. She squirmed and moaned as he ran his hands up and down her long thighs, schooling her, soothing, relaxing, preparing her. Gradually, he splayed his hands, opening them to allow his thumbs to skim the insides of her thighs. Slowly, hypnotically, as he continued mouthing her breasts, he increased the intimacy of his hands, sliding his fingers over her panties, positioning them, stroking her mound carefully while she twisted and groaned with pleasure. He liked pleasing her.

She squirmed beneath his hands, encouraging his thumbs. Finally, he slid one finger inside her panties to tease the warm, moist entry. At her gasp, he rested the accompanying hand, letting it cover and warm her mound as he waited.

When she moved again, he took it as a signal to resume.

Tonguing a nipple, his mind centered on that one finger and its mission. She was so easy to please. Maybe because it was new. She didn't let him know what she wanted. He hoped that was because she didn't know and enjoyed anything he did.

His hand slipped inside the waistband of her panties and down over the mound until his probing finger again worked into her entry. He wanted to remove her panties, the one remaining obstacle to his objective. When he pulled at the waistband, she yipped.

It was a tiny sound which sounded more like surprise than objection. Again, he waited, holding what he had, his mouth mindlessly teasing a breast, his thoughts centered on keeping the probing finger on task below.

She didn't speak as he waited a series of heartbeats. Twilight was gone and they were shrouded in the coming darkness. They might not have the place to themselves much longer. He needed to think of another more private setting in which to continue this tutoring.

Memory drew a long breath, maybe thinking the same thing for, although she didn't speak, she pushed her legs a little further apart, making the thatch all the more accessible.

Mac took her mouth fully with his own, caught a breast in one hand, gently pinching its nipple, and pushed the other hand down, slipping that long finger deep into the damp cavern. She splayed wide, open to him, creamed and welcoming. A gasp intensified his erection. His pleasure swelled with each whimper. Her muffled moan filled his mouth before she caught his invading hand with both of hers and bucked against it once, then again and again, panting.

Moments later, when she stilled, he raised his mouth from hers, withdrew the hand from inside her panties and stopped fondling her breast, although he could not make himself surrender his position between her legs.

"We have now rounded third." The huskiness in his voice surprised him. "We have to find some place more private if we are going for home, because doing it right is going to take us a while—maybe the rest of the night—and I don't want any interruptions."

His resolve wavered as Memory gazed at him through passion-veiled eyes.

****

Memory knew she should care where they were or who might see them, but, at that moment, she didn't. She was oblivious to everything but the heat of Mac's body and his mouth, those wicked, knowing hands, and the way they drove her toward fevered heights. There was more beyond where he had taken her. Mac knew the way. He could take them there. She felt safe, though not quite certain whether the intensity arcing between them came from sexual excitement or love. She must not get confused. She mustn't be silly enough to think this behavior was as important to him as it was to her.

The stunning thing was the fire—her own desire—burned hotter than she imagined lust could. She had never known a sensation like this mind-numbing need. Other men had tried to whet her sexual appetite. Some of those were prettier than Mac, but none of them had his unique appeal. None seemed as strong, as capable, as perfect. None had his character, or that romantic scar that marred his eyebrow, or his square jaw, or his humor, or his passion, or any of the thousand other things that made him so irresistibly sexy.

She also found the element of danger in him thrilling. This man would never be totally domesticated. She liked that wildness about him, the certainty of his physical domination mitigated by the innate gentleness that not everybody was able to see but which glowed from his soul like a beacon pulling her.

"Can you recommend a hotel?" Mac's voice again sounded husky. "I need a room for tonight anyway."

Her illusions nose-dived. He was ready to get rid of

her. He wanted to get on about the business that had brought him here.

"I…ah…guess you're right." She struggled not to let her disappointment show. "I need to be getting home myself."

His gaze roved slowly over her bare torso, her throat, her face and, finally, lifted to her eyes. "I was thinking you might stay with me."

"Oh." She brightened. "Like at Flanagan's?"

"Not exactly. This time I was thinking we would be more, ah, physically involved."

"Oh."

He yielded as she pushed him back a step. She grabbed her bra and sweater, tossed onto the windshield, and put them on.

Her expression had become businesslike and he couldn't fathom her thoughts. She looked sad, almost as if she were ready to cry, and then he saw tears winking in the corners of her eyes reflecting the moonlight as they welled. He stared dumbfounded. Why tears? Why was she sad? She didn't need to be. This wasn't the end. They weren't through. Hell, they were just getting started. They didn't need to separate. Not for a night, or a week, or anytime at all, as far as he was concerned. The night was still young. It was barely dark, probably not yet eight o'clock, though he didn't dare look at his watch.

"Memory?"

"Yes, David?"

He might have suspected another woman of angling, to elicit promises women wanted to hear, even when they knew a man didn't mean them. Not this woman. Not here. Not now. No, Memory was barely cognizant of what was happening between them, overwhelmed maybe by foreign emotions taking root inside her. How could he wield his expertise against her tonight, in her weakened condition?

Mac had always prided himself on being a man who took advantage of opportunities, who never missed a chance or shrank from a challenge. Should he let this golden opportunity pass, hoping there would be another? He ventured another look into her flushed, trusting face.

"Are we going to the hotel?"

"No, we're going to dinner."

A man's conscience could be a damned nuisance.

## Chapter Seventeen

He took her to Jubalee's for a candlelight dinner, then to a new movie, a musical that was also a love story—a chick flick. She didn't talk much and he followed her lead, keeping their limited conversations to safe topics. When he took her hand during the film, she snuggled close. Her signals confused him until he decided she might be confused, too. She talked like she was ready to take the plunge. He wanted her too much to judge.

He drove her back to Church Street before eleven and was assailed with second thoughts as he kissed her good night, maneuvering around the console. He helped her out of the car, then turned to trap her between his body and the vehicle. Then he couldn't quit kissing her. Assuming the role as teacher and mature one, she took his hand and led him to the front door of the historic old apartment house. Once there, however, she lost her aloof demeanor, grabbed the front of his shirt, and twisted her hands around the placket. It repaired his pride that she didn't seem willing or able to separate herself from him either.

He kissed her soundly, then wrapped her in his arms and kissed her again, holding nothing back. She returned his ardor.

"Motel?" he whispered, his mouth against her ear.

"Rain check?" She sounded less than certain.

"You can bet the farm on it, and I mean that in the most literal sense."

Her easy laugh broke the spell enough to allow them to release one another. Before they could relapse, the porch light came on. Someone inside blinked it twice more.

"Landlady." Memory pushed his shoulder and he yielded, pivoting until she had him facing the street.

"Mac?"

He didn't turn back around.

"Thank you."

"Any time, baby, and I do mean any time."

****

"Damn, damn, and damn," Mac muttered as he walked back to the Lexus. Once inside his car, he sat there waiting, and studied the third floor window where she had appeared before. Suddenly, light filled the windows. A moment later, the shades crawled up the opening and there she stood, looking out at him. He doubted she could see him skulking in the car's darkened interior, but she could damn well see the car hadn't moved.

What was she thinking? That he was totally gone on her? That he was some kind of loser sitting there hoping for one last glimpse?

She turned off the light and returned to stand at the window. What was she doing? Tugging on her sweater? Yes. He couldn't actually see her, but he thought he saw movement as she pulled the garment up and off over her head. He definitely saw the white as she removed her bra, yet he couldn't see her, not even the outline of her shape. Boy, what he wouldn't give for a night scope.

He glanced around uneasily, making sure there was no one else lurking nearby unable to see what he couldn't see either. This was a private performance, for his eyes only.

A dark bulkiness slid down her hips and he thought he could see the outline of skimpy white panties, the ones that might appear delicate but which had stubbornly withstood his halfhearted attempts to get them off her.

Slowly, the slender line of white also slid down. He strained but wasn't able to see, merely to imagine her, standing there in front of that window, nude, taunting him. He smiled, a wicked grin. A closet tease, was she? Well, two could play that game.

He stepped out of the car. Of course, he didn't have the benefit of full darkness. A streetlight on the corner illuminated the area. He removed his shirt and tossed it inside the car, then he stretched his arms along the roof line and flexed. He rubbed a hand over his abs and down, allowing his fingers to rove into the waistline of his trousers.

Headlights on a car cruising onto the quiet street exposed him and he turned to lean against the car.

"Trouble?" The man's voice sounded crisp in the nighttime stillness.

"No." Mac turned back to find the questioner was in uniform, riding shotgun in a cruising cop car. "No, sir," Mac reiterated.

"Do you live around here?"

"No, I don't."

The cop flashed his light into Mac's car. "You got business here this time of night?"

"I was just leaving."

"Which way are you headed?"

"On my way home to Astrick."

"Getting kind of a late start, aren't you?"

"Yeah. I need to be on my way."

"Well, have a good evening. You wide awake?"

"Yeah, wide awake."

"Have you been drinking?"

"Not a drop."

The patrolmen regarded him closely, probably evaluating his speech and movements long enough to assure he was not under the influence. The uniform seemed satisfied that Mac was telling the truth, although his body language and bare torso probably struck the man as odd. The policeman looked as if he weren't going to allow idle curiosity to make him ask for explanations he did not particularly want or need, so he finished up with a hospitable, "Have a good trip."

"Thank you, officer. Good night."

With a last quick glance at the darkened third floor, Mac got into his car, started the engine and rolled slowly down Church Street. He left his window open and didn't bother to put on his shirt. He intended to enjoy the night air and maybe let it cool him down a little. Maybe it would clear his head enough to make room for some kind of epiphany about who was after Memory Smith and why.

## Chapter Eighteen

On the way home from Metcalf, Mac made a few decisions. There were some people in town he needed to talk to.

The next morning, first thing, Mac went to the jail on the fourth floor of the county courthouse and asked the jailer to bring Dicky Steam to an interview room.

"You ain't supposed to talk to him without his lawyer, are you?" the jailer asked.

"Sharp of you to catch that, Skeet," Mac said. "You're right. I absolutely cannot talk to him about his upcoming trial, but that's not why I want to see him."

"Okay, then."

A belligerent expression looked set in cement on Dicky's face. He gave Mac a glance, then angled his eyes at the floor as he walked to the interview table and sat.

"Dicky, I have only one question for you."

Steam didn't speak.

"Who hired you to go after Memory Smith?"

The man looked up from under heavy eyebrows. "I don't believe I caught her name. Truth is, I don't believe she threw it."

"It was a woman?"

"I didn't say that," but Dicky's face indicated he hadn't intended to disclose that information.

"What did she ask you to do, exactly?"

"Asked me to discourage a new female from staying in Astrick."

"Did she identify the woman by name?"

"Yep."

"Did she give you any specifics about how far to take your discouraging?"

"Not 'til later. Later she said I was to do the job without hurting the woman, you know, no rough stuff."

"I see. Okay, thanks for your help."

"Thanks for my help?" Steam's face again became belligerent. "What's helping you going to get me?"

"My gratitude."

"What's that worth?"

"It depends on how you behave in court. If you embarrass certain people, I might forget we had this little talk. If, however, you are respectful, my gratitude might get you transferred so you'll do your time in county lockup."

"You can do that?"

"Can and will, if things go well in court. That'll be up to you. See?"

"Yeah, chief, I got you."

****

Mac caught up with Quint Ressler on Monday, poker night at the country club. Quint was the last man out of the shower, emerging just as the stragglers took the stairs up to the grill. Drying his hair, Quint did not look pleased to see Mac. His annoyance turned to concern when he glanced around to find they were alone.

"Look here, McCann, what do you want?"

"I want to know why you hired a thug like Dicky Steam to go after Memory."

"I didn't do that. How would I know where to find a guy like him? Thugs aren't listed in the yellow pages, you know."

Mac coughed a little laugh, intended more to disarm Ressler than to praise his sense of humor.

"Besides that, why would I? I was the one who got her back to town, encouraged her to stay around. Why would I have done that if I wanted her gone?"

"You might have thought you'd persuade her to sell her dad's place to you. When that didn't work, you tried to intimidate her by hiring Steam."

"Listen, I wouldn't have to hire anyone to beat up on a woman."

Mac took a threatening step closer. "Because you could handle that yourself?" Quint glanced down at his towel-wrapped body and withdrew several paces before Mac shot the gap and positioned himself between Quint and the lockers.

"I want to know how you were involved, Ressler."

"My wife is a jealous woman. She comes from a family of toughs. She might be the one you need to question."

"So, you're thinking your wife hired Steam?"

"I don't know that she did, but I don't know that she didn't. I don't know either way. All I'm saying is you could ask her."

"Right." If Quint were trying to send him down a garden path, Mac knew the way back well enough. He nearly always knew where to find Quint Ressler. "Don't make me come looking for you again, Ressler. If I want to talk again, I'll phone you with the when and where and I'll expect you to show up. Are we clear about that?"

"I've been threatened before."

"I'll bet you've never been threatened by anyone who was as eager to do you bodily harm as I am." Mac turned and walked away, cutting through the pro shop to the parking lot.

****

The next day, Mac approached Doris Ressler in a professional manner, calling first to arrange an interview, then arriving at her doorstep at the appointed time.

She answered the door chime herself, although Mac saw a uniformed black maid dusting in the dining room as his hostess led him into a tasteful study.

Doris Ressler's trim figure complimented the conservative gray silk slacks and coordinated sweater. She wore stockings with her shoes, disregarding the barelegged look younger women made fashionable. He thought her not following the fad made her appear more genteel. She spoke and moved with cool detachment. Mac had to remind himself more than once that she had been a bartender at one time, and before that a waitress and always an easy date. There were no lingering vestiges of her former occupations or past life of deprivation.

"Please, sit down, Mr. McCann. Would you like something cool to drink?"

"No, ma'am, thank you. This shouldn't take long. There's no need to put yourself out."

She didn't insist.

He sat at one end of a long, leather sofa and studied his subject. Straightforward with no-nonsense appeared to be the best approach with her, so he launched the interview bluntly.

"Did you pay Dicky Steam to come to Astrick?"

She looked directly into his face with something that resembled a smirk, but, to her credit, she didn't contemplate the question long. "No, I didn't."

She didn't add "but," but her inflection indicated she might have something else to say.

"If you had hired him, what would you have asked him to do for you, Mrs. Ressler?"

"Like several other women, I might have asked him to make Memory Smith disappear." She looked alarmed, reading Mac's expression, and she waved off what she inferred he was thinking. "Not disappear from the face of the earth. I wouldn't have wanted him to go to extremes. I'd have wanted him to make her nervous, hopefully uncomfortable enough to sell her family farm to my husband and return to her life in Metcalf."

"How would you have suggested he go about that?"

"The newspaper said he advertised in some men's magazine that he was a professional intimidator. I might have instructed him to stalk her, but I would have emphasized that she not be injured, just frightened."

"Why would anyone else have wanted to frighten her?"

She looked surprised and maybe a little disappointed that he asked such an obvious question. "Why? To get her out of town, of course."

"Why would anyone want her out of town?"

"I don't know the woman, personally. She grew up here, behaving for years like everybody's princess. She's never done anything to refute that ridiculous reputation that she is some kind of saint. I've competed with Goody-Two-Shoes types all my life. They can be annoying."

"Why would you feel you had to compete with Ms. Smith?"

"Don't pretend you don't know." She gave him a jaundiced look. "Quint and I have an open marriage, which includes candid communication. We are brutally honest with one another. I think that's important in a good marriage. I can tell the minute Quint takes an interest in another woman. It wouldn't do him any good to try to hide it, even if he wanted to."

"Then you knew about his ongoing interest in Laurel Dubois?"

She gave him a deprecating look. "Mr. McCann, a woman doesn't need a college degree to have common sense. I insisted right from the first that he be completely honest with me. He described every move he and Laurel shared in the bedroom. She had rather limited tastes. I helped him design and perfect some of the toys and games she came to enjoy. My husband and I had some entertaining discussions about Laurel's affectations. She was a cold fish between the sheets and it took the best of both of us to improve her performance. I contributed for Quint's sake and his enjoyment. We experimented with some of my ideas before he tried them on her."

Mac didn't argue with the woman's assessment of Laurel's sexual expertise.

"Memory Smith was an entirely different matter. Quint got positively nauseating when he spoke of her. He actually thought he might have a chance with her, if he could get free of me, which was wrong. I've made a lifelong study of people raised in privilege. Most of them are born with average intelligence and enjoy their advantages, but as often as not, they lack the common sense God gave a goose."

"You thought Memory was different?"

"I was referring to Quint. Certainly, Ms. Smith has common sense."

"So you didn't think he had a chance with her?"

Her eyes narrowed. "My husband is weak, Mr. McCann; a garden variety alcoholic. He has a hard time getting it up, even with flattery and encouragement."

"So, why did you want Memory to leave town?"

"As I said, I did not hire that person who hassled her. Her threat to me was not caused by any reality, but by the romantic fantasies in Quint's mind. She made him feel young again. I didn't want my high-mileage husband making a fool of himself pretending to be a young stud. He was no stud when he was twenty and trying to look as if he is one now…well, he would have wound up looking comical."

"You thought you could keep his image unscathed, if Memory were elsewhere?"

"Not unscathed, but at least decent. As a bonus, I was hoping she would sell Quint her farm, while she was winding things up."

"Do you know who did hire Dicky Steam?"

"No." She paused and he let the silence stretch until she filled it. "I can tell you Laurel Dubois called here one night. Quint was out, which she knew. She called to speak with me. She asked if I knew of someone who would be willing to bedevil a person. I gave her a name."

"Dicky Steam?"

"No. I assume Mr. Steam is an associate of the man I suggested."

"One more question: why do you want Quint to have the Smith farm?"

She looked surprised for a moment, like he was kidding, then she swallowed her incredulity and came up with an explanation on the fly.

"Land is a much better investment than stocks and bonds, Mr. McCann. You put money in the hands of bankers and brokers, or most businessmen, and they'll rob you. I consider land, real property, the most reliable investment a person can make."

Watching her expressions, Mac decided Doris Ressler probably was an excellent liar, but he felt certain she was not responsible for crimes against Memory Smith, or any actions which might have resulted in the murder of Laurel Dubois.

He thanked her for the visit and asked if he had other questions, if she might allow future interviews.

Maintaining her role as the gracious hostess, she said, "Certainly."

****

Mac didn't look forward to doing his last interview. It wasn't with a thug or a sleazy lawyer, or a wealthy matron. He was going for a serious talk with his boss, Cliff Horsely. He had thought about it for days and realized this conversation was long overdue. Things Cliff had said popped in and out of Mac's mind at odd times. For one thing, his boss knew far too much about Laurel Dubois' private life. He had inadvertently or intentionally revealed a significant amount of intimate knowledge. Even Memory had noticed it. Tossing those details around, it appeared that good old Cliff had been inordinately interested in Laurel. Had he done anything about it? Had she known?

Granted, Laurel was attractive, in a spoiled, pouty little girl way. That might have appealed to a man ten years older than she was.

Horsely whistled as he stepped into the front office. Mac stood, either out of deference to his boss or out of a sense of self preservation. He needed to be tactful and approach the man cautiously.

"Mac, what are you doing in here?" Horsely said as he burst through the door of his private office.

"Were you having an affair with Laurel Dubois?" Not exactly the circumspect route he had planned, but the question did suck the suspense out of the room.

Horsely took a step back to close the door but the expression on his face was one of a man scrambling to come up with an appropriate response.

"Were you?" Mac was glad the urgency had left his voice.

"I might have been interested in her at one time."

Mac wondered if Horsely were as relieved as he looked.

"Would you have been interested enough to discuss marriage?"

The D.A.'s eyes shifted to his desk, shot to the window, and returned, for a fleeting moment, to Mac. "She may have expressed some interest in the subject."

"You weren't receptive?"

Horsely puckered his lips as he did when he drifted into deep thought. A moment later, he drew a long breath, as if he had reached a major decision.

"Mac, I'm going to move to Metcalf when this term is up." The D.A. dropped that bombshell like it was old news. It wasn't. "I'm going to hang out a shingle, go into a solo criminal practice, and start fresh."

Mac's next question caught in his throat as he contemplated the significance of the statement. "Why?"

"Extenuating circumstances."

"What are you talking about?"

"My fortieth birthday is looming on the horizon." He paused, but Mac waited. "To tell you God's honest truth, for the first time in my life, Mac, I'm in love."

Mac felt like someone had rabbit punched him, not a crippling blow, but a discomforting one. "Not with Laurel, I take it."

"Right." Cliff heaved a heavy sigh. "I might as well come clean, but I need you to keep this information to yourself for a while."

"Okay. Who's the lucky girl?"

"Truth is, she's a he."

Mac took one step back and lowered himself into the closest chair, which happened to be the one behind Horsely's desk.

"That chair looks good on you, Mac," Horsely said.

Mac glanced down, scarcely aware of his boss's words, then up to give him an uncertain smile. "How long…have you known?"

"I never knew it exactly. I liked ladies, I just never felt an urge to marry one of them. Then, recently, I discovered I preferred…other action."

"Did Laurel know?"

"How could she have? I didn't know myself. I just happened to run into this old classmate, a guy I played football with. Funny, how something like that—a seed planted years ago—can suddenly take root. He's a big guy like me, though he's kept himself in much better shape. Truth is, Mac, he looks a little like you."

Mac didn't know whether to thank his boss or take a swing at him. Instead, he said, "So, I guess you've got no vested interest in Dicky Steam or his relationship with Memory or Laurel's untimely death or any of that?"

"None whatsoever, except for a professional interest, of course."

Without saying anything else, Mac pulled himself to his feet and headed for the closed door.

Cliff said, "I've got some campaign money left over from my war chest. I am willing to leave it to you, along with my endorsement. Coupled with your track record in the courtroom, you might be able to step right into my shoes. I would, of course, expect you to keep the confidence I shared with you just now."

Mac didn't turn around, but acknowledged Cliff's statement with a wave. "I told you I would." He didn't sound or feel exactly chipper about it at the moment. Something else was going on with Cliff Horsely; coming out, if that was what he had just done, was a smokescreen.

****

Mac went up to the club to have a drink and try to digest the things he'd learned. Memory had been stalked and Laurel murdered. Could the two matters not be related? They had to be. All this time he had assumed the crimes were linked, the stalker and the murderer the same person with the same motivation. Cliff's revelation added a twist. Sometimes prying uncovered things a man really didn't care to know.

"I was sorry to hear about Ms. Dubois," the bartender said as he served up Mac's usual bourbon and branch. Mac grunted a non response, not wanting to get into another maudlin rehash of Laurel's death.

"Yes, sir, there must have been a full moon that night to send women walking along the side of that highway."

Something about the comment registered and Mac looked at Joe the bartender. "What?"

"Both them women out on the highway afoot on the same night, and in a thunderstorm, too."

"What do you know about it, Joe?"

"First, Ms. Memory. She was up here for a while that night. Had dinner with that Ressler guy, maybe a couple of drinks, then gone, poof, on her own two feet."

"Yeah?"

"Then Ms. Dubois did the same damn thing, not an hour later."

"I was here that night, Joe. Don't you remember? I gave Ms. Dubois a ride home."

"Sure do, the first time she left."

"You knew she came back?"

"Yeah. That's how she came to be wearing Ms. Memory's sweater."

Mac set his drink down, nerves alert. "Who did she come in with, Joe? More importantly, who did she leave with, the second time? Do you remember?"

"Nobody. Didn't come in with no one and left the same way. By herself. Wasn't much of anyone around by then. She came in late—about midnight—and ordered a whiskey sour. She made a big deal about finding Ms. Memory's sweater, carried it in from the dining room. She put it around her shoulders. In a little while, she said she was going home."

"How'd she get home? She didn't have a car."

"I didn't know that. She just had the one drink,

wasn't tight or anything, so I didn't have a thought about her driving."

Mac knew Laurel hadn't taken her own car. Someone had picked her up at her apartment and brought her back to the country club. That person apparently hadn't come inside with her. Hadn't stayed. Or maybe the person had stayed, but had waited in the car. Did Laurel come back intentionally to pick up Memory's sweater, and did she do that for herself, or did someone else want it?

It was hard for Mac to believe there was no connection between the attacks on Memory, and Laurel's death. If there were no connection, he didn't know why he expected events to make sense. He felt like he was trying to force pieces of a jigsaw puzzle into wrong openings. If that were true, what else might he be mistaken about?

## Chapter Nineteen

Memory returned to Astrick after work on Friday. The first thing she did, much to Mac's surprise, was find him, still in his office, working overtime. This time, he welcomed her right inside. Good to know, but she still had questions regarding their earlier "miscommunication".

"Why did you drive to Metcalf, show up at my house a couple of weeks later?" she asked, after she was settled in a client's chair in his office. He remained standing.

Apparently he wasn't the only one curious about that. "It was four weeks later, and it was the most miserable four weeks of my life."

"So what took you so long?"

"I don't know." He paced, then circled back to stand in front of her. "Personal pride. Male ego. I was confused. I thought I knew you. I'd known you a long time. Somewhere deep inside, a part of me trusted you."

"Well, at least there's something to understand in that."

"Besides that, I felt actual physical pain from missing you, I don't know, like someone probably feels missing a phantom limb. I drove to Metcalf that night, to your house, to spy, to see if you looked happy there. After I'd gotten that far, the next step was natural enough. I wanted to hear your voice, which is why I phoned you."

"From across the street."

He cleared his throat, giving her time to say more, but she didn't, so he did. "Instead of cussing me and hanging up, like I half expected, you sounded calm, maybe even glad to hear from me. I considered that promising." He allowed another pregnant pause which she again did not offer to fill. "So I took a chance you might want to see me, too." He looked away. "Not as badly as I wanted to see you, of course, but you sounded receptive."

She finally smiled, rose to her feet in front of him, stretched to her tiptoes, and began kissing his collar bone, nuzzling under his chin. He rocked his head back to allow her access and closed his eyes. "Oh, yeah, you definitely wanted to see me."

She groaned. "Receptive is a polite term for how I feel every time I'm around you."

He began to return the nuzzling kisses along the side of her face, his lips working their way toward, then capturing hers. When he finally came up for air, he murmured against the corner of her mouth. "What would be an impolite term?"

She kissed his chin. "Huh?"

"You're not paying attention."

"Yes, I am."

"Other than receptive, the polite word, what would be an impolite word for how you feel around me?"

Her eyes opened to slits as she regarded him solemnly. "Horny."

His bawdy laugh rocked the room. "Memory Smith, the people of Astrick would never believe that word came from your delectable lips."

"Well, then, maybe you'd better apply that old southern remedy, sir, and shut my mouth."

He laughed as his lips closed on hers. Moving cautiously to make sure she knew where he was going, he cupped the round globes of her compact bottom in both hands and pulled her hard against him, aligning their bodies, which fit in all the best places. She wriggled, not an effort at escape, as he first feared, but to situate herself more snugly against him.

*God, she is hot.* That was his last lucid thought before he was lost in a long, drugging, pleasure-inducing kissing, touching, fondling, and groping.

There was no telling what might have happened, if a loud clanging in the hall hadn't signaled the cleaning crew was on its way.

"Can you leave?" she asked. "It's late."

He looked around, still in a sweet fog before he got his wits together. "No, I can't. I've got a difficult deposition first thing in the morning. The people are here from out-of-town. Only here for the day, Saturday. I'm not prepared." Seeing her disappointment, he shook his head. "But, if you're only here for the night…"

"No, no. I'm staying until Monday. Will you be available tomorrow afternoon?"

"Probably before noon. How about brunch at the hotel? You could even stay there tonight."

"Oh, no. I'm going out to the house." She hesitated. "That is, if Dicky Steam has other accommodations."

"He's still in lock-up."

"Then brunch at the hotel sounds great. I'll stop in there for coffee late in the morning. Join me when you can."

"The minute I break free. Count on it."

He helped her tidy the clothing he had rumpled in his grope, and walked her out, cheerfully greeting the cleaning crew as if it were nine-thirty in the morning instead of nearly ten on a Friday night. "Have at it. I'll be back in a few."

The town's gossip hotline would be on fire by midnight.

****

Saturday morning, brunching together, Memory told Mac she continued to be puzzled by Laurel's death.

"The police did a thorough job at Laurel's apartment," he said. "They determined no struggle took place there. Detectives took her address book from a kitchen drawer and a calendar from her bedside table, neither of which provided any revelations. The rest of her belongings they left intact, dishes rinsed and left in the drainer beside the sink; clothes tossed across Laurel's unmade bed, and other evidence of the life she lived."

Memory picked up the conversation. "Until she didn't any more. I want to go there anyway. Please. I have a feeling. Call it woman's intuition. I want to pursue it."

Mac didn't press for more, so she didn't explain further.

Like Memory, Laurel had been an only child and a shining star to her mother and father. Unlike Memory, she had portraits and pictures of herself everywhere. They transformed every wall in the apartment to a vanity display.

Through high school, Laurel had often mentioned keeping a diary, and encouraged others to do the same, to write down their most private thoughts and emotions and, of course, to record events. Memory thought of that as she wandered through the five-room apartment. As different as they had been, she saw indications that she and Laurel had much in common. Both were raised by doting parents. Both had nice wardrobes—Laurel's more expensive, of course. Both were members of the state and national honor societies, and were popular with their classmates.

Memory wandered about the bedroom and as she moved, her browsing developed a purpose. Where was Laurel's journal? Women far less self-centered than Laurel kept diaries in high school and continued the practice later, referring to diaries as journals. Memory felt certain Laurel had considered her every activity, her every thought, worthy of note, as she often posted details of her life online.

As if her fingertips would sense the presence of the volume she sought, Memory brushed her hands over the surfaces of desk, dresser, headboard, and night stand. After several minutes, her lack of success did not dissuade her, nor did Mac's occasional stops in the doorway to check on her. She simply ignored any would-be distractions, from within or without. She curled a leg under as she settled onto the armless, child-size rocking chair and used the other foot to push, creating an easy motion. The seat slipped. Memory stopped rocking and allowed a little smile. She stood and lifted the fitted seat from the chair. There, between the cushion and the support webbing, lay a book.

Having guessed correctly, when no one else had, gave Memory a boost. Maybe she could help untangle this mystery. Her mood lightened. A thorough search by the police had not turned up the journal. She had.

Again she curled a leg under her and eased back into the small chair as she opened the book.

Laurel's entries were sporadic. She made frequent references to "Q," which Memory assumed was Quinton Ressler.

"What is that?" Mac asked, wandering into the bedroom. She held up the book, as if defending herself, using a thumb to mark the page she was reading.

"Laurel's journal."

He smiled and shook his head, clearly missing the significance.

"We used to call them diaries," she said. "Every girl had one, from second or third grade up, a place to record your most private thoughts."

He gave her a questioning smile. "Did you keep a diary?"

She shrugged. "Several, but mine are full of drivel. Rereading them, I found I made profound discoveries, stumbled upon life's truths, apparently forgot them, then had the same eureka moments when I turned up the same important finds second, third, and even fourth times. I discovered some truths half a dozen times before they finally sank in."

"Oh, yeah, like what?"

"Silly things like thinking I must be in love with John Berry because my heart fluttered and my stomach churned when I saw him one afternoon. The next day's entry reported I had to stay home from school with the flu. So much for physical responses defining true love."

Mack gave her an appreciative chuckle and a jaundiced look. "You couldn't tell the difference between being in love and a stomach virus?"

She felt the sudden obligation to defend her naive earlier self. “Well, as it turned out, the symptoms are nearly identical.”

“You can tell the difference now, I suppose.”

Their eyes met and held in a mute communication. Memory was first to lower her gaze, turning her attention back to the journal without bothering to answer, relieved that Mac didn’t pursue the question. Vaguely, she hoped the subject might come up again when they were in more intimate circumstances. He wandered out of the room, leaving her alone with the diary. Obviously, Mac didn’t realize the entries were current. He probably thought Memory was reading words written when Laurel was young. Memory would tell him the truth…later.

She thumbed through, skimming the pages, all written in Laurel’s small, precise hand.

*C’s foreplay is boring. I need stimulation. I like a man to force me. Q choked me tonight. I came just before I passed out. It was the most exciting sex I’ve ever had.*

Memory flipped a couple of pages.

*I tied Q spread eagle last night and used the feather to get him going, then I blindfolded him and used the leather thong. He liked it at first, then he said I was playing too rough. I didn’t feel like stopping. I liked hearing him beg. He hurts me all the time, often on purpose. I wanted him to see how it felt to be helpless and have someone work you over. I was careful, but I couldn’t help laughing when he whined and finally started bawling. I got tired and let him go. He might not let me tie him up again for a while, but next time, I’m going to play rough. I loved making him cry and beg. I wonder if C will let me tie him up. C is more of a man than Q. I don't think he'll let me, but it would be fun. Maybe sometime.*

The last entry was on August 1, the night she died.

*I hate M. She's got Q acting totally stupid. He thinks he can sleep with her—annoying enough—but tonight she went into her helpless Annie routine with D. Made me want to heave. We picked her up in a rainstorm walking on the side of the highway. She was a mess, but D got all hot and bothered. We got rid of her and came to my place but he wouldn't come in. I wanted to teach him a game, one a really bad boy like him would appreciate, but he wouldn't. Damn M's 'perfect' self.*

Memory stared at the page as a theory took shape. Laurel and Quinton had a peculiar relationship. They sometimes had rough sex. If he had driven her back to the country club that night, he might have put her out on the side of the road to humiliate her, payback for making him cry. Tit for tat. A game: one-upping each other. Memory was beginning to understand their friendship. Still she was glad she was not reading these pages out loud to Mac. She gave the chair another push, rocking and reading again.

*M's not right for D. She has no sense of style. I could make something passable out of her, I suppose. A playmate for all of us. I might. It would look like a kindness. If I could get her trusting me, maybe she'd let me do…things.*

What had Laurel meant? "I don't even want to go there," Memory muttered, keeping her voice low. Memory squirmed in the little rocker chair and gave it another push with her foot.

*She looked like a drowned rat on the highway in the rain. I couldn't believe D stopped. I hate that Sir Galahad hang-up he's got. M got on my absolutely last nerve. I wanted to hurt D. What is it with men? They're looking to score with every female. He was hot to trot but it was M he wanted, not me.*

*I do not want C around her, not that she would appeal to him, but I couldn't bear to see him go goopy over her. That might cause me to tell everybody the truth about her.*

Memory shifted her gaze from the pages in front of her to the floor. Someone reading that journal might think Memory had a reason to keep Laurel from exposing some big secret. Of course, Memory's lone secret was no secret at all. It was obvious to everyone that she was, and had always been, out of step. Everyone in Astrick had long-ago accepted her as a super nerd. A geek. The last member of an eccentric family. No one would suspect Memory of trying to keep Laurel from revealing what everyone in town already knew. Except maybe "C." Now who in the world was he? Someone new to Astrick, it sounded like. Someone Memory didn't know.

Also, she didn't like Laurel's comments about "D," David…Mac. She made him sound like a sex fiend. Laurel thought he was hot for Memory. At Flanagan's, wearing bed sheets, Memory had given him every opportunity, but he hadn't been interested.

However, now she seemed to be wearing him down.

She shivered and smiled at the thought of what could transpire between them, eventually.

Laurel's written ramblings about Mac's

background might look like a motive, except everyone knew his reputation. Teachers and parents alike considered him a thug.

She flipped through the rest of the journal's empty pages before she laid it aside.

"What were you smiling about a minute ago, and why are you frowning again now?" Mac asked. "What'd you read in there?" He indicated the journal.

"Nothing."

"Did you find something in the diary I should know about? Anything from her youth that might reflect on things going on today?"

Her eyes narrowed as she looked at the journal lying closed on the bedside table. "It's not old stuff. This is Laurel's current diary and she mentioned you—at least on a page or two."

He reached for it, but she put a hand on top. He eyed her suspiciously and she removed her hand, yielding the journal. He studied her, less interested in the diary than in the quiet challenge in Memory's eyes.

"Every small town has its dirty little secrets," Memory said, and indicated that he sit on the end of the bed in the quiet of Laurel's bedroom.

He complied, saying, "I'm sure that's true. To which of ours are you referring?" He'd get to the journal containing Laurel's opinions and complaints later.

"Well, there's the disappearance of Quint's first wife and his marrying Doris for what Mrs. Flanagan believes is an extortion scheme on Doris's part. Suspicions grow if you factor in the mysterious safe deposit box that Mrs. Flanagan told us about, and what it may or may not contain.

"Then, there's Quint wanting to buy my dad's farm. Quint has no interest in farming or ranching. Besides, he already has all the land he'll ever need if he should develop that interest.

"Then there is Laurel's death and, of course, the lame attacks on me."

"Oh, those dirty little secrets. Come on. Lie down here a minute and let's talk secrets."

Memory laughed. Then, eyeing him, she began unbuttoning her blouse, prompting Mac's full attention.

"What are you doing?"

"You invited me to lie down on Laurel's bed, didn't you? I assume you expect me to take off my clothes. Isn't that how you and Laurel did it?"

Mac grimaced. "I don't want us to have sex here."

"Because it's a place for Laurel's dirty little secrets, not ours?"

He leaned back on his elbows and narrowed his eyes. "All right, you win." She smiled, and went back to reading the journal.

"Memory, would you marry me?"

She didn't even look up. "Yes."

He rolled up to sit on the side of the bed. "When?"

She flipped another page. "Whenever you say."

"Today?"

Finally, she glanced at him, her expression fond, but focused. "Sure, Mac, but why don't we clear up the questions around Laurel's death first?"

"What questions are you talking about?"

"The circumstances that brought about her death. The death of Quint's first wife. Quint wanting to buy my dad's farm. Someone's hiring of Dicky Steam. Do you think it's all related?"

Her focus brought him back to the subject. "I do. And Quint seems to be the most basic common denominator," Mac said. "If Quint killed Laurel, that would clarify things. Laurel's dad told Horsely she and I were about to get hitched," he said, apropos of nothing. "But since we're throwing wild ass questions and theories out there…He thought I might have gotten cold feet and knocked her off so I wouldn't have to marry her."

Tired of the small chair, Memory stood and bent from side to side, getting the kinks out, but not taking her eyes from Mac's face. "I heard that rumor, too…that you and Laurel were getting married."

A teasing grin spread over his face. "Did it make you jealous?"

"It might have given me a twinge."

"Really?"

She shrugged, walked to the window without answering, but posed another question. "Tell me more about the D.A.'s hypothetical list of suspects. So Quint is the primary. Who else?"

"Doris Ressler, Quint's wife, who might have a serious motive if she thought Laurel was a threat to her marriage."

"Was she? Laurel, I mean. Was she a threat?"

"No more than she's always been. Quint and Laurel had been sleeping together off and on since high school, but he married Doris. I figure that made his wife feel secure enough."

"Unless she just found out about them."

"Their ongoing affair has been broadly discussed for years."

"Isn't the wife always the last to know?"

"Not this wife." He studied the pattern in the carpet somberly. "I guess Doris is a possibility, but I don't think so."

"Anybody else?"

"There is you, of course." He arched his eyebrows.

"Me? You're kidding."

"Insanely jealous cuts both ways. You might have thought Laurel was coming between you and Quint."

"That's just as good as suspecting you."

"Horsely did suspect me at one time. No more, though."

Memory knew David couldn't be guilty. She was still hung up on the idea of someone suspecting her.

"Do you think I'm capable of…?"

"No, I never have thought that. It's a theory some law enforcement guys who don't know you very well were bouncing around early on."

She stared at him for a moment in disbelief. "Okay, who else could it have been?"

"It gets pretty far-fetched." He looked apologetic, at having told her.

"More far-fetched than thinking it was me? Give me a break. Let's have it."

"Dicky Steam looks like an obvious suspect."

"I forgot about him." Memory turned back from the window and straightened to scowl at Mac.

"You'd forgotten him?" Mac looked skeptical.

"I mean as a murder suspect. It now looks as if there's no connection between my experiences and Laurel's death."

"You could be right," Mac said.

"Give me your off-the-wall guess. Who might have hired him and why. Not to kill Laurel…or me."

“How about…Laurel hired him to scare you off?”

“Laurel?”

“Let’s say he was watching you and saw you go stomping off, walking down the highway. Maybe he thought about it and decided you were vulnerable out there and he could get rid of you permanently and it would look like an accident.”

“You’re right, that theory is pretty far out.” Memory glanced at the bed, then walked over to settle again in the small rocking chair.

“Maybe it took him a while to come up with that plan and by the time he got around to it and spotted a bedraggled female wearing a white sweater trudging beside the highway, he wasn’t as discerning as he might have been. Wouldn’t it be ironic if he wound up running over the very person who hired him?”

“That fits with the theory that someone dumped her out on the highway after she was already dead.”

“Yeah,” Mac stared as he began to pace. “It’s possible that Dicky came along and ran over her after the actual killer drove off.”

“Do you mean maybe she was standing on the shoulder of the road wet but alive?” Memory shook her head, staring at Mac’s face, wondering if he were serious while entertaining the idea that the theory was plausible. “Ironic?” she breathed. “Like Alfred Hitchcock. She hired the assassin who killed…her.”

“Yeah.”

“Dicky Steam won’t say who hired him?”

“No. Before the trial, I suggested to Horsely that we offer to reduce the charge in exchange for a name, but Cliff said there would be no way to verify it, if he named Laurel. Of course, Cliff’s right about that. Steam could lie, get a deal from us, and still not expose the person who really set this up."

"You're saying we'll never know who hired Dicky Steam?"

"Maybe not. Crimes are like that sometimes. They don't get solved so much as they just sort of dissolve."

Memory was quiet for several ticks of the clock, frowning with the beginning of a headache, before she looked at Mac again. She pointed at Laurel's journal, which he had picked up. His index finger marked a spot where he apparently had stopped reading.

"Okay, then," Memory challenged, "who is C? Did he play any part in this?"

He glanced at the journal and back at Memory with a frown of his own. "I was just wondering about that. Laurel didn't show much imagination in concealing the identities of the people populating her diary. Q was Quint. M was you. D was Doris."

"Or David."

"Right."

"She didn't refer to you as M."

"Laurel didn't call me Mac. She didn't like nicknames. She thought they made a person sound common. I didn't want her to call me that anyway."

"Why not?"

"We weren't that close."

"You were sleeping with her, rumored to be about to marry her."

"She mentioned that marriage thing to several people, but never to me. She knew how I felt. If I had wanted to get married, Laurel would not have been in the top ten candidates."

"You never intend to get married?" Memory

studied his expression.

"I didn't say I never intend to get married." He returned her serious look. "I've been waiting for the right woman to ask me."

"I thought men did the proposing."

"Not since the pill. That's about the time women started wearing the pants in public, figuratively and literally. Haven't you heard? Women are equal now. Gals call guys for dates, pay for things, even carry condoms."

She flushed and lowered her gaze, embarrassed. "I see."

"Obviously you haven't been doing it right." He tilted his head to see her face.

"I guess not."

"You don't ask guys out?"

"No."

"I guess that means you haven't asked anyone to marry you yet either?"

"Have you?"

His expression softened as he studied her a long minute. "Not until recently."

He was talking about her. Memory blushed again and focused on a ragged fingernail. "We probably should uncover some of Astrick's other dirty little secrets before we get bogged down in mush and personal stuff."

"Memory."

She looked up. His eyes captured hers and held for a heartbeat before he smiled and winked.

"Okay, back to business."

"Laurel wrote a lot about C," she ventured. "According to her journal, they were sexually involved."

"I've asked around. Even the best sources for gossip in town could not tell me anyone else she might have been dating."

"Meaning you checked with the ladies' church circles?"

He arched his eyebrows at the slur. "And barber and beauty shops. Some people guessed, but none of their ideas panned out so I'm sort of back to my initial thought."

"The person you suspect, is it someone here in town?"

"Yes."

"Male?"

"Yep."

"A Charles or Chester or Carl somebody."

"Or Clark or Chambers or Collins."

Memory scowled. "I didn't think about the C referring to a last name. But the references in her journal are never arm's length enough for it to be his last name. She waxes poetically and often about the way C touches her. One entry said he made her feel like a well-loved cat."

"I'm skipping the mushy parts," Mac said.

"Then you may miss important clues."

"Like what?"

"Like he's something of a celebrity."

"We don't have any celebrities in Astrick."

"Apparently we do."

"Like that washed up musician who used to play jazz with some big-named entertainer?"

"No, this is someone who has enough starch left to be romantic and to satisfy a woman as sophisticated as

Laurel."

"Yeah? Well, that's gotta be one great lover then, because Laurel was one tough mama to satisfy." He suddenly looked contrite. "At least that's what I heard."

"Like you wouldn't know from personal experience."

"I thought women admired men who kissed and didn't tell."

She twisted her face to disapproval and stared at him. Not to be deterred, Mac continued to concentrate on the question. "What do we know about him?"

Dropping the subject of Mac and Laurel's involvement for the moment, Memory shrugged. "Well, I think we can be pretty sure he's married."

"Why would you say that?" He sat on the bed again.

"Don't look at me like I'm being catty. If Laurel had a man she could call her own, she would have advertised it. Therefore, since she sneaked around and didn't even write his name in her journal, I think it's safe to assume he is married."

"Hmmm. Solid deductive reasoning, Watson. What else?"

"A married celebrity that pleased Laurel in bed and didn't have to worry about repercussions from Quint Ressler. That should narrow the field."

They sat quietly for a few moments, each caught up in the revelations of the last few minutes, before Memory said, "It's too bad we don't have Laurel's old journals, going back several years. We might be able to find when she first started writing about C, if he's not from here or if he was gone for a while becoming a star before he came back here."

"We do have her old journals. I found a box of books that look like this one in a cabinet in the back of her carport."

Memory's quick movement brought Mac to his feet. Without another word, he pivoted and led the way to the complex's covered parking.

"Where do you want to look at these?" he asked as he hoisted the box of books to his shoulder.

"Would it be all right if we continued using her apartment?"

"Probably. I'll see if I can clear it with the police."

"It seems more appropriate to keep her personal belongings in her place rather than strewing them all over town." Memory led the way across the parking lot and up the stairs to Laurel's apartment.

Mac studied her. "Also, being in town is more convenient than being out at your house. And you feel safer in a dead woman's apartment than you do at my place."

"I didn't say that." She opened the apartment door and stepped aside to let him carry the box into the living room, then hurried ahead to move a stack of magazines.

"You're not arguing." He placed the box on the game table Memory had just cleared.

"No." It was her turn to look contrite. "I'm not sure you're right, but I'm not saying you're wrong."

## Chapter Twenty

"Do you want my help?" Mac asked, as he eyed the box of journals.

"No." Memory smiled. "The evidence might be mixed in with some mushy stuff and I know how sensitive you are."

"Depends on who's getting mushy." He sidled closer. Memory retreated a step, putting a hand in front of her mouth to staunch the giggling.

"No way, sweet pea, are you going to dodge this." Mac was pleasantly surprised that Memory opened her arms and, when he stepped into them, she wrapped him tightly in her embrace. It was the first physical contact they'd had all day. He never knew with Memory whether to try to pick up where they'd left off or start all over again. Each avenue had its delights. But today he was content to hold her at first, until nerves began jangling awareness in other parts of his anatomy. "You've got some tall explaining to do, little girl," he said, trying to suppress his carnal awakenings. He attempted to step out of her arms, but she held onto him.

"What are you talking about now?"

"Trust issues."

"Mine or yours?" She caught and held his gaze with her innocent one.

"Mine, of course. You trust everyone."

He kissed the tip of her nose, which set her giggling. The bubbling laughter became groans as he nibbled to her ear and down, settling in the nape of her neck. His groans mingled with hers as he pushed her a little away and set his lips to following the curve of her neckline. Tipping his face, he kissed up to take her pert little chin fully into his mouth. His breathing became panting until he pushed her to arms' length.

"What now?" Memory rasped and dabbed her fingers lightly to Mac's kiss-swollen lips as he continued to hold her in the circle of his arms, their pelvic areas pressed together firmly.

"My place. Your place. Some place." Mac knew he sounded rabid—and felt that way, too—but the sound of his voice was calm compared with the clamor going on inside him. This was definitely the wrong place. He didn't want his first complete sexual experience with Memory to be in Laurel's apartment—a shrine to a dead woman—but he was quickly reaching the point where he didn't much care about the where as long as the what happened.

"So you do want to have sex," she said.

He gave her his best, most incredulous look. "Of course I do!"

"When?"

"Now would be fine."

"What I mean is, where?"

"At the moment, I'm not all that particular."

"You want to do it here?"

He closed his eyes, considering the many posed pictures of Laurel strategically placed by the deceased woman in her apartment for her own pleasure and enjoyment. He heaved a resigned sigh. "No, not here."

"You look…defeated."

"How would you like me to look?"

"Sexy." She pursed her mouth, obviously annoyed.

He grinned. "Okay. How do I do that?"

"I don't know. Like you usually do. You know. Slant me that lean, hungry look."

"Memory, I rehearse facial expressions in front of the mirror. I've practiced shock and angry glares, set my mouth just so to give jurors skepticism and guilt-trips, but I have never, ever once tried to look sexy. That one must just come naturally."

"You don't dial it up like you do the others?"

"Apparently not. If I could, you'd be seeing it on this kisser right now."

She frowned at her fingers as she ran them together. When she spoke, her voice was low. "Of course, you look sexiest when you're using props."

"What props?"

"A sheet wrapped around your middle. I dream about your bare chest. It's impressive. Also, you've got great pecs and amazing abdominal muscles." Without looking at him, her hands still interlocked, she pointed both index fingers at his waist. "You know, props, that make a girl's mouth water."

"Then yeah, this definitely is the wrong place."

She looked stricken. "And the wrong time?"

"Possibly."

"Are we the wrong people?"

His salacious grin returned. "No, we are definitely the right people. I'll work on putting the rest together."

"When?"

"There's no rush."

"Earlier you were in a big hurry."

"That is correct, but that was before I realized…"

"I'm a virgin?"

Mac's brain came to a complete standstill. "You are?"

"Well of course, silly."

His mouth opened, then shut again. Several times, in fact. No doubt his expression was one of a man who had no idea what to do, or say, which was unheard of for David McCann. His color might have even changed a bit, as well. The air suddenly felt a whole lot warmer.

"Mac? Are you all right?"

He shook his head, as if to clear it of cobwebs. "Fine. I'm…fine."

She eyed him suspiciously. "Does it bother you that I'm…you know…a beginner?"

"Oh, hell, no!…I mean, no…not at all," he tried to reassure her, almost frantically. Good God, he felt like he'd just won the lottery. "But…listen, Memory…I'll find us the right place and reserve us some time. I mean, you want to do this thing right, don't you, first time out and all?"

"I didn't know there was quality control involved."

"Oh, yeah. Doing it right the first time is crucial."

"No one's ever mentioned that."

"Leave it to me, Memory. I'm into quality and good taste when it comes to…to us. Trust me on this. I'll make sure we get it right the first time. Will you do that? Will you trust me to plan this for us?"

She looked as if she might have more questions, ones she refrained from asking. Mac was glad about that. He wanted carte blanche to make these arrangements.

She nodded. "Let's go read the diaries."

## Chapter Twenty-One

When he appeared for his criminal trial, Dicky Steam's arm was still in a sling. He had fresh bandages on his neck and a new tape over the bridge of his nose. Memory wondered if he had used stage makeup on his eyes, which still looked badly discolored even two months after he had forced her to inflict his last injury. He should be healed, after all that time. He was probably trying to play on the jury's sympathy. Mac suggested he might also be trying to lay some groundwork for his civil case against her.

Oddly, District Attorney Cliff Horsely took on the case himself, rather than turning it to one of his assistants.

On the stand, Memory, in a pinstriped business suit and sensible dark heels, looked and sounded professional as she described her initial meeting with the defendant, the incident during which she protected herself with a can of spray paint.

Horsely was studiously grim as he focused on a juror who appeared to smile at Memory's account and shoot sly glances at the defendant. It was only natural for the jurors to compare the size of the combatants and the D.A. paced his questioning to allow for the comparison without directly calling attention to the fact that, while Memory might be taller than the defendant, he had at least a one-hundred-pound advantage on her.

Demoted to second chair at the prosecution table, First Assistant District Attorney David McCann kept his face stoic and his eyes riveted on the witness. Memory's expression did not reflect any recognition during her occasional glances at him.

"Tell us about the second time you met this man." Horsely encouraged in a kindly tone.

Memory sat very straight and looked as if she were trying to keep her wits about her. "The second time, I was again alone in the house…"

"Just to clarify this point, Ms. Smith, in whose house?"

"My house, Mr. Horsely. My family home. The farm house where I grew up."

"All right, you were there in your home where any reasonable person might expect safety, privacy and security?"

"Yes, sir, at least I always thought so. Anyway, I was in my nightgown, brushing my teeth in the upstairs bathroom, when I heard what sounded like glass breaking downstairs. The noise sounded like it came from the front of the house.

"Was your car there?"

"Yes. It was clear someone was home."

"And so you heard glass breaking."

"It sounded like someone was breaking in, again. I panicked.

"The upstairs bathroom is the only room in the house with a lock on the door, so I slammed and locked the door. Unfortunately, one of the reasons that bathroom feels so secure is that there is no window."

"So there is only one way in or out."

"Correct. It didn't take long to realize I had trapped

myself in a room with no alternate escape route, without a weapon, or even a cell phone. I looked around for something to fight off an intruder. It was instinct, I guess, to want to have something in my hands. That's when I noticed the hair spray."

The woman juror whose mouth had twitched at the story of the spray paint, smiled openly as if anticipating what was to follow.

The prosecutor gave the woman juror an approving glance, arched his brows, and nodded as he addressed Memory. "And?"

"He figured out where I was, came up the stairs, and began trying to break down the door. It took him several tries. That bathroom door was solid oak. It held for a while as he battered away."

"Then what happened?"

"It gave. The door itself didn't. The doorjamb splintered. Just before he blasted through, I turned off the light, hoping darkness might give me an advantage.

"He exploded through that door, stumbling and off balance. I guess he didn't expect it to be dark inside and he was wearing another stocking on his face. He staggered for a second, like he was trying to get his balance. By the time he got his feet under control enough to backpedal, it was too late. I aimed for his eyes and let him have it with the hairspray."

The woman juror made a spewing noise and ducked her head, clapping a hand over her mouth. Her reaction was contagious as other jurors and spectators in the courtroom—mostly the women—sputtered. When one man in the audience let loose a bawdy shout of laughter, the judge sobered, but he appeared to be struggling to control an inappropriate reaction of his own.

"We'll have order in the courtroom," the judge said finally, then hiccupped and quickly took a sip of the water kept on a shelf under his bench.

With dramatic timing, Horsely allowed a pregnant pause to let the room again become quiet before he continued. "What happened then, Ms. Smith?"

"I ran."

"Of course you did. Down the stairs and straight out of the house, didn't you?"

"Yes, but I didn't stop there. I hit the back road and ran all the way to Charlie's Station on Highway Thirty-two."

"Barefooted?"

"Yes, sir."

"In your nightie?"

"Yes."

"And you summoned help?"

"Yes. Luckily there was a quarter in the change coffer on the pay phone because, of course, I wasn't carrying any money or a cell phone or anything."

"Did the sheriff come and arrest the intruder?"

"No, sir. The guy was gone by the time the law enforcement people arrived."

"So you had seen the man twice—had been within arm's length of him, or should we say spray-can range?" Horsley paused to allow for the expected muted laughter before he continued. "Do you see that man in this courtroom today?"

"Yes." She looked directly at the defendant. "It's the defendant, Mr. Steam."

"Now, did you have occasion to see Mr. Steam under threatening circumstances again?"

"I'm afraid so. Twice."

The defense attorney leaped to his feet. "Objection, Your Honor."

"Okay, Merritt, hold your water," the judge said. "Everybody here's eventually going to know there were four attacks."

"I object to your terminology, Your Honor, specifically your use of the word 'attacks'."

"Overruled."

Merritt Overstreet sat back in his chair. From the city, Overstreet was a fairly high-dollar criminal lawyer with a reputation for successfully defending people charged with crimes. During the arraignment and preliminary hearing in this case, he had grumbled to anyone who would listen about getting hometowned in Astrick, saying the judge kept siding with the locals at the early hearings on his motions to suppress various pieces of evidence. He hinted that an appeal of the ruling here was a done deal.

"Let's get on with this," the judge said.

The prosecutor followed with his next question as if there had been no interruption. "Ms. Smith, when did you have occasion to meet this man again?"

"At Quint Ressler's office about eight-thirty the next morning. Tuesday."

"What took you to Mr. Ressler's office that time of day?"

"Karen, Mr. Ressler's receptionist, gets there early, and I went to pick up some belongings I had left during the time I was updating their computer programs. Karen needed to run an errand and asked me to answer the phones while she was gone. A few minutes later, I heard the bell indicating someone had entered the reception room from outside. When Karen didn't call out, I started toward the front. Here he came again."

"Objection," Overstreet bellowed. "Who is this 'he' to whom the witness is referring?"

Without waiting for the judge's ruling on the objection, Memory stretched out her arm and pointed her index finger. "Mr. Steam, the defendant. The man sitting right there beside you."

"Was he masked?" the defense attorney snapped.

It was the judge's turn to bellow. "Mister Overstreet, I don't know where you've been practicing law, but here in Astrick, the court allows the prosecutor to finish questioning his witness before the defense begins its cross examination. You will have your turn, sir. I'll see to it. Now sit down."

Overstreet took a breath as if he planned to respond, but the judge slanted him a warning look. "I'm a hair's breath away from finding you in contempt, sir. You'd be wise to consider if what you are about to say is worth the fine I might impose."

Squinting his defiance, bold because such a look could not be taken down by the court reporter, Overstreet sat. Then he jutted his jaw and settled a threatening glower on the witness, a look which he continued until the exaggerated rustling of papers at the prosecution table diverted his attention. The distraction was the D.A.'s first assistant noisily tearing sheets from a legal pad and wadding them up. He wasn't looking at the tablet. He was glaring directly at Overstreet.

Meanwhile, Memory's testimony continued at Cliff Horsely's prodding. "Was the man in Mr. Ressler's office wearing a stocking over his face?"

"Yes."

“Still you had no doubt about his identity?”

Memory gave the defendant a sympathetic look and was surprised when he shot her what appeared to be a bashful grin. She stiffened and turned to regard the D.A. “No. By then, we were pretty well acquainted. I would have recognized him just about anywhere, with or without the mask.” She ventured another look at the defendant. “As you can see, his build is…distinctive.”

The jurors’ eyes shifted to the defendant and their thoughts played across their faces, transparent even to the casual observer. They validated Memory’s suggestion that the man’s squatty physique and dwarf-like proportions would make him easy to pick out, even in disguise.

“Did he pursue you there, in Mr. Ressler’s offices?”

“Yes. He came to the hallway door, the door right beside the door to my temporary office. I was trapped in Mr. Ressler’s office. All he had to do was keep an eye on both doors. So I checked the top drawers in Mr. Ressler’s desk thinking he might have a gun or some kind of weapon, but there wasn’t anything.”

“Go on.”

“Again, I was frantic to find a way to defend myself.”

“Did you come up with something?”

“Yes. Mr. Ressler has a dartboard. I grabbed a handful. I’m not very good at darts, but I figured a man was a bigger target than the usual bulls eye and maybe I could hit him. Besides, I had four sets of darts to work with.”

Several jurors snickered.

“Did you?” Horsely asked, “hit the larger target?”

"Yes. But first I gave him fair warning. I held them up and hoped he could see them, even through the stocking. I didn't think it would be fair to throw metal pointed darts at a person without letting him know I planned to do it."

"Did your warning slow him down?"

"Not a bit." She gave the defendant a puzzled look. "In fact, he smiled."

The defense attorney leaped to his feet, but before he could object, Memory added, "I could see his teeth through the mesh of the stocking. His smile looked more like the Cheshire Cat than the Grinch."

The defense attorney sat down as Memory continued speaking.

"Mr. Steam had an oversized pistol in his hand and he pointed it at me. I figured he could blow me into a million pieces with a gun that big. While he was taking aim, I threw a dart. I aimed at his chest, but the dart lost momentum at the end and nose-dived. it stuck in his thigh. I think it went pretty deep, because it shivered and didn't fall out."

"How did Mr. Steam react?"

"He screamed and yanked the dart out of his leg. That distracted him and he didn't fire his gun at me, at least not right then. When he recovered a little and it looked like he was going to try shooting me again, I threw another dart. He dodged. It hit the wall behind him and fell on the floor."

"What thought ran through your mind at that time, Ms. Smith? Were you in fear for your life?"

"Objection," Overstreet said, again leaping to his feet. The jurors looked startled and maybe annoyed by the interruption. "He's leading his own witness, your

Honor."

"Sustained."

"What were you thinking?" Horsely prompted again.

"My mind went off on a tangent. Mr. Ressler is very proud of his offices. He had told me the walls were genuine mahogany, imported from South America. For a split second, I thought if this guy didn't kill me, Mr. Ressler probably would for putting dart holes in his beautiful wall."

Spectators and jurors alike seemed to exhale a collective sigh.

"Your Honor," Overstreet pleaded.

"Are you objecting, Mr. Overstreet?"

"Yes."

"State your grounds."

"What's the use?"

"If you have no grounds, don't bother objecting, sir. It only delays the proceedings."

"Right."

Horsely bowed his head and rubbed a hand back and forth over his mouth, but when he straightened, there was no sign of emotion. "Ms. Smith, did you think of calling for help? Summoning the police?"

"Not until I ran out of darts."

"Did any of your other darts hit Mr. Steam?"

"Yes. Altogether, four of those darts did, but they didn't stop him. During that time, he fired his gun but, to my amazement, it didn't make a loud noise. Another surprising thing was it didn't shoot bullets. It shot darts, too. It only fired one shot at a time, then he had to reload. That slowed him down, which is why I had a chance to throw all my darts at him."

"What happened when you were out of darts?"

"I threw a stapler and the electric pencil sharpener and the paper clips in a holder. He turned his back to me to load another dart in his gun. Darts he had fired out of his gun lay on the floor next to the wall. I picked one up. By then, I pretty well had him bracketed and I wasn't shaking quite so badly. His back was to me and his shirt had pulled up out of his trousers so there was bare skin showing. I took aim and hit him right in that meaty part."

"You hit him with a dart from his own gun?"

"Yes."

"Then what happened?"

"I threw a second of his darts."

"And?"

"He jerked upright, then he twisted around. He looked startled for a couple of seconds, then he just sort of wilted. What I mean is, he folded onto the floor, like an inflatable figure that had sprung a leak."

There was muffled laughter in the audience, but a sharp glance from the judge quieted the offenders.

"Did you call the police then?" Horsely asked.

"No, I didn't. I ran for the parking lot just as Karen drove in. She did it before I began thinking clearly. She called them on her cell phone."

"Did they arrive before the man regained consciousness?"

"No. By the time the police arrived, he was gone."

"Did you see him leave?"

"No."

"Thank you. Now, I believe Mr. Overstreet has some questions."

Horsely returned to the prosecutor's table.

Overstreet stood at the podium rather than approaching the witness. "Ms. Smith, what is your relationship with Quint Ressler?"

David's low growl seemed to issue a challenge to everyone in the courtroom as he stood. "Objection. Irrelevant."

"I'm laying groundwork which will make the question relevant," Overstreet said.

The judge looked solemn. "Maybe you'd better establish your relevance first."

Overstreet regarded Memory again. "Are you a Miss, a Ms., or a Mrs.?"

"Objection."

"I don't know how to address the witness, Your Honor."

"Overruled."

"I prefer Ms.," Memory said.

"Ah, then you are one of those enlightened champions of women's rights. Are you a lesbian?"

"Your Honor," David said, standing again, "does Mr. Overstreet have any questions for this witness that have any bearing on the charges against his client?"

The judge shifted uncomfortably. "Mr. Overstreet, perhaps you should move on to a subject that's germane to these proceedings."

"When they put Mr. Steam in jail, Ms. Memory," Overstreet smirked as he addressed her, as if he were oozing southern charm, "did that meet with your approval?"

"Yes. It meant he wouldn't be coming after me anymore."

"Do you know what charges were filed against him?"

"I believe they finally decided to charge him with stalking and assaulting me."

"Did you sustain any injuries at my client's hand, Ms. Smith?"

She looked surprised. "No, I didn't, but it wasn't…"

"A simple yes or no is sufficient."

"Okay. No."

"The first time you met Mr. Steam, was he wearing bandages?"

"Not that I could see, but it would have been hard to see bandages behind the stocking covering his face and head."

"Was that a 'No?'"

"I didn't look him over all that carefully then, Mr. Overstreet, so I cannot give you a yes or no. He had just broken into my house. I was frightened."

"Your Honor," Overstreet wailed, appealing to the judge.

His Honor gave him a sheepish shrug. "She merely answered your question to the best of her ability, counselor." The judge addressed Memory. "Were you aware of any bandages on the defendant during his first assault on you, Ms. Smith?"

"No, sir, I was not aware of any."

Overstreet gave the theatrical sigh of a man tried to the end of his patience before he turned his attention from the judge back to Memory. "How about the second time you met? Were you any more observant on that occasion?"

"I don't remember seeing any bandages that time either. He looked fit and I suppose he probably was because that's when he broke down the bathroom door that was made of solid oak."

Overstreet turned to the judge. "Your Honor, will you please instruct the witness to answer the questions."

Horsely started to object, but David touched his arm and looked oddly satisfied, indicating he should allow Memory to fend for herself.

"I believe she's trying to," the judge answered. "Perhaps you should be more specific so she'll know which of the four times he attacked her that you want her to describe."

Overstreet gave the judge a look of exaggerated disbelief, took a breath as if he planned to object, then appeared to change his mind and set his attention back on the witness who was making his life so difficult. "Each time you and Mr. Steam met, he was the one who came away battered and bruised, wasn't he?"

Memory looked thoughtful. "Yes, it did keep turning out that way, but that was never my intention. I would have thought he'd have been put off, but bad results didn't seem to discourage him one little bit."

Overstreet studied her for a long moment, then lowered his voice to a confidential tone. "Wasn't there a fourth incident, one Mr. Horsely conveniently omitted?"

"Yes, there was."

"Why don't you tell us about that meeting, Ms. Smith?" Overstreet gave the jury a triumphant look.

"He broke into my house again."

"Again?"

"Yes. Again. It was the fourth time he had come after me, the third time he had broken into my house."

"Why, in heaven's name would a man who had

been turned back so viciously ever want to lay eyes on you again?"

Memory shook her head from side to side and lowered her voice, matching his confidential tone. "I have thought and thought about that, Mr. Overstreet, and I cannot, for the life of me, think why a sane man would do such a thing."

Overstreet's eyes rounded dramatically. "Are you suggesting my client is insane?"

"I'm not qualified to say, but even you seem confused about what in the world he was thinking. Isn't that why you asked me?"

Jurors ducked and covered their mouths, eyeballing the defendant, and smiling at the odd exchange. David McCann ran his tongue along his teeth in an effort not to smile. He had never seen a more entertaining cross-examination. Memory's dumb act was very effective.

Overstreet's jaws clenched and unclenched. "I ask the questions here, Ms. Smith. That's not your job." She folded her hands in her lap and lowered her eyes looking contrite. McCann bit back another smile. Who would have imagined Memory was such an accomplished actress?

Not wanting to quit at a disadvantage, the defense attorney plowed on. "My client sustained serious injuries that night, didn't he?"

"I don't know. Again, I'm not really qualified to say."

"What deadly device did you use against him that time?"

"The lid from the back of the toilet." She shrugged. "You know, the cover over the tank part."

Muffled laughter from the jury box drew a frown

from the judge, but ducking his own head, he did not call them to order.

Overstreet kept on, as if trying to redeem his position. “Your assaults on him escalated with each encounter, didn’t they, Ms. Smith?”

“Someone had taken everything else I could have used out of the room, Mr. Overstreet—toothpaste, soap, sprays, everything. He had even unscrewed and removed the shower rod and the towel racks. He’d gone so far as to remove the spool from the toilet paper dispenser. There wasn’t anything left in there to use to defend myself.”

“So you savagely, and with no pangs of conscience, slammed a fellow human being upside the head with the twenty-pound top off the toilet tank?”

“Is that how much it weighs?” She clamped a hand over her mouth. “Sorry. I have no idea how much it weighed. It was terribly heavy, but I think twenty pounds is an exaggeration.” She rolled her eyes as if trying to recall. “I did have to stand on the toilet seat to get enough leverage to swing it, and I could only swing it very slowly at that.”

“As soon as my client was in the room, you slammed that apparatus into him without any hesitation or thought for his well-being?”

Her face twisted into puzzlement. “He broke down the door again, just like before. It was the third time he had broken into my house, actually the fourth, probably, because someone had stripped everything out of the bathroom between the time I left home that morning and the time I returned that evening.”

“After you hit him, did you take even a moment to see how badly your victim was injured?”

"No, I didn't." Her answer was matter-of-fact, without a hint of remorse. McCann glanced at the jurors, most of whom were nodding with half smiles on their faces.

"Did you summon immediate medical assistance for him?" Overstreet pressed.

She frowned and bit her lips, looking repentant. "No, sir, I did not."

"What did you do?"

"I jumped over him and ran as fast as I could down the stairs and outside. I got in my car, locked the doors and took off for Charlie's Station. I called David McCann, the assistant district attorney there, and told him the guy in the stocking mask had broken into my house again."

"What did you expect Mr. McCann to do?"

Memory's gaze drifted to Mac. He smiled and gave her a slight nod of encouragement. Obviously Overstreet was annoyed by the exchange.

"You did not call for medical assistance for my client, did you?"

"Well, yes, indirectly I did. I just told you, I called Mr. McCann. I told him exactly what happened. He said he would call the police and an ambulance, and I was to stay right where I was at Charlie's."

"What did the emergency crew find when they arrived at your house?"

"I suppose they found glass from the broken pane in the front hallway and the door standing wide open, the way I left it, and another broken bathroom door."

"Was there any sign of my client?"

"Yes, he was there, too."

Looking as if he finally had the upper hand,

Overstreet pursued what he perceived to be his advantage. “Mr. Horsely failed to ask you about that incident, your final meeting with Mr. Steam.”

“Yes.” Memory’s eyes followed Overstreet’s and she, too, gave the prosecutor an inquiring look.

“Well?”

“Do you want me to tell you why Mr. Horsely didn’t ask me about it?”

“And our juror friends here.” With a sweep of his hand, he indicated the members of the jury panel. His expression and his tone indicated he was being sarcastic. “They’d like to know as well.”

“Honestly, Mr. Overstreet, I don’t know.”

“Is it because you intentionally lured my client there, Ms. Smith?”

Her eyes popped wide. “Lured him? No. I never had a conversation with the man, never even saw him when he wasn’t wearing a stocking mask. Why in the world would I have wanted to lure him? How do you think I could have lured him?”

“Didn’t you use your feminine charms to entice him?”

Memory darted a quick glance at the defendant. Her mouth twitched as her face assumed various expressions: uncertainty, humor, then blatant disbelief. “You’re kidding. Right?”

“Why do you think I am being facetious, Ms. Smith?”

She frowned as if uncertain about what the lawyer was hoping she might say. She had injured the man repeatedly and was not inclined to ridicule him in front of everyone. She framed her answer carefully. “Well, I’d have to say because Mr. Steam is not really my type. I mean, my tastes run to guys who are…well…taller and younger and, well…"

"Yes?"

"Less intense."

Jurors giggled again, eying the judge, who suddenly leaned behind the bench as if to tie his shoe. Observers in the audience chuckled openly. Overstreet paced the room and again appeared to be vexed. Approaching the matter from a different angle, he said, "Once you had injured this man, you gave no thought to helping him, thinking only of yourself, of saving your own skin rather than taking time to assist a fellow human being. That is typical hit-and-run mentality, Ms. Smith. Did you spare any thought for him?"

Memory looked apologetic. "No. I wasn't concerned about his welfare. I didn't think how badly he might be hurt until I got to Charlie's and calmed down. I guess I didn't consider Mr. Steam's injury might be life threatening. The other times, he vanished before the law enforcement people arrived. I had already seen him bounce back three times before. I had begun to think of him like…"

"Think of him like what?"

"Well, like a cockroach, if you must know. You know, you swat and swat the little boogers, but no matter how hard you try, they just keep coming back. It's like they refuse to be gotten rid of."

Snickers erupted in the jury box, although people covered their mouths or ducked their heads and avoided looking at the attorneys, or the defendant, or at Memory.

Everyone in the courtroom sobered as one juror, an older woman, began trembling as if she were having a seizure. When the judge motioned the bailiff to find out if she were ill, she fairly exploded, convulsing with laughter.

"Your Honor, I ask that this juror be disqualified," Overstreet shouted.

"On what grounds?" the judge asked.

"Apparently, she has taken ill."

"No…oh no, Your Honor," the woman said, flapping a hand and dabbing her mouth with a tissue. "It's the pictures…you know…of these two."

Overstreet bristled again. "No pictures have been introduced into evidence, Your Honor. I object, if this juror has gained access to…"

"No, no," the woman interrupted, flapping harder. "It's the mental pictures of this sweet-looking young woman beating off her assailant, time after time. That's the picture that keeps getting me so tickled. It's really and truly Mr. Overstreet's fault, Judge. He's putting the pictures here in my head, and making them lifelike with the questions he's asking."

Overstreet flashed the juror what he no doubt considered a threatening look, but his evil glower only increased her giggling. She pointed at him with the index finger of one hand, and clamped the tissue over her mouth with the other. Her muffled laughter triggered other jurors and spectators. The judge disregarded them all as he tapped his gavel for order.

The jury took only ninety minutes to return a verdict, finding Dicky Steam guilty and recommending he be sentenced to five years in prison for his repeated assaults on Memory Smith.

## Chapter Twenty-Two

The courtroom battles, however, did not end with the Dicky Steam verdict. Overstreet pursued the civil suit against Memory on Steam's behalf, claiming she owed him five hundred thousand dollars for medical bills and his pain and suffering.

"I don't have five hundred thousand dollars," Memory reminded Mac over the telephone when he called that evening. "I don't even have fifty."

"I told you, Memory, it's a nuisance suit," Mac reminded. "He's just trying to get under your skin. Don't worry. I'm on it. Who knows, he might take five hundred bucks to settle today."

"I've already admitted under oath that I injured him."

"Memory, honey, there is in the law something called contributory negligence. The point is, dear old Dicky would never have gotten injured if he had not insinuated himself into places he was not invited and had no business being."

Memory sniffled and sounded as if she were recovering. "Like my house?"

"Exactly. And Quint's office. This frivolous lawsuit may be a face-saving measure."

"What do you mean?"

"I imagine other inmates in the county jail are riding him about his criminal moves being foiled by an unarmed female. He may be trying to regain some respect before he gets shipped to the big house where he will reside among serious criminals. His lawsuit is clever, if you think about it."

"You mean you admire him for suing me?" Her spirits took a nosedive. "It seems like we'll be in court forever. We still have the hearing coming up on Laurel."

The reminder dealt Mac a blow, too, but he opted to bluff it through. "Why would you worry about that?"

"Because if either of us is implicated in causing her to be walking on the highway that night, we are going to have to alibi each other, which means the whole world will know we spent the night together at Flanagan's."

He forced a laugh. "Devastating for you, sweet pea, but that revelation's only going to make people around here admire me." He was quiet for a moment. "Memory, I'll try to steer things away from our whereabouts. It may not even come up."

****

As the investigation evolved, however, Memory and Mac were questioned separately. While Mac tried to sidestep, Memory simply told the truth. The two detectives in charge mentioned her disclosure to their captain and their cohorts.

Following that trail, they talked to Mrs. Flanagan, who verified Mac's whereabouts at specific times, though she was not able to say for certain that he remained in the motel room continuously until five a.m.

"All right, McCann, can anyone say where you were at five a.m.?"

"Yes." He waited for someone to ask straight out.

"Okay, who?"

"Memory Smith."

The detectives gave each other a knowing look, before they realized he wasn't finished. "And Quint Ressler."

"What?" they chorused.

"He called the motel room a few minutes after five."

"From where?"

"I don't know? Ask him, or maybe check phone records and find out. You can do that, can't you?"

****

Ressler didn't own up to making the call at first, pretending he didn't know what the detectives were talking about when they invited him to their offices for questioning. It was early in the day, but he complained of having "a major headache."

As they escorted him down the hall, he stopped. "Is that Memory Smith's voice? Is she here?"

Both detectives responded by shaking their heads, no.

The interrogation room was hot and smelled of human waste, and the offered chair was an ancient metal folding chair. Quint was complaining again as Assistant District Attorney David McCann sauntered into the room.

"Does he have to be here?" Ressler asked.

"He may be prosecuting your case. Yes, he needs to be here," Detective Bryant said.

Without speaking or acknowledging Ressler, Mac pulled another folding chair to the table. It screeched as he turned it and sat down.

The detectives took turns grilling Quint Ressler

while Mac sat quietly. In his discomfort, Ressler apparently believed it easier to answer their questions honestly than to think up other versions.

"What's the big deal," he said finally, when they honed in on the early morning phone call to Memory. "Big whoop. I admit I called Flanagan's on my cell phone from home. My wife was right there. She can tell you all about it."

"Your wife was up at five a.m. and listening while you spoke obscenities to Memory Smith on the telephone?"

"No, she wasn't up. And she doesn't eavesdrop. What I mean is, she can verify I spent the night at home and woke up in my own bed the next morning."

"Do you and Mrs. Ressler share a bed?" Detective Bryant asked.

"I don't think a married couple's bedroom preferences are any of your damn business," Ressler said.

"They are if you don't sleep in the same bed, or in the same room, or even in the same house."

"What do you mean?"

"It's common knowledge, sir, that you and your wife are in the process of getting a divorce. Generally, that means you sleep in different physical locations."

Ressler jutted his chin. "It just so happens that we were not estranged on the night in question."

"Meaning you were still sleeping together?"

His heavy chins quivered and melted. "Well, no. We are not in the habit of sleeping in the same bed."

"How about in the same room?" the second detective, Wayne Green, chimed.

"My snoring disturbs her rest."

“So your wife cannot swear that you were at your house the morning in question.” The comment, more a statement than a question, preceded Detective Green’s renewed scribbling in his small, spiral notebook.

Ressler’s chin folded into its second layer. “No, I suppose not.” He spoke as though he didn’t know if she would verify he was home that night, even if she could. Then his expression brightened. “I also spoke with David McCann that morning. As it turned out, he was at the motel with Memory. I suggest you ask him what he and she were doing in that motel room together all night long. I think you’d better follow up on that.”

Neither detective even glanced at McCann. “No, sir, we lost interest in them after we established they were there together. What consenting adults do in a motel room isn’t our concern. What we are interested in is finding out is who caused Ms. Dubois’ death.

“For instance, if a person—someone like you—put her out of his car on the highway, that person’s got no problem because, although it isn’t nice, that is not a criminal act. If, however, he saw or was involved in a vehicle/pedestrian accident and didn’t report it, he is culpable and we definitely are interested in that.

“What I’m saying is, it would be better for that person if he stepped up voluntarily, before we put in the man hours and resources required to run him to ground.” Green gave Ressler a significant look. “That person would be much better off if he came clean and told us about it now.”

Ressler frowned into the detective’s face. The lawman lowered his voice and his gaze at the same time. “Was it you, Mr. Ressler? Did you cause Ms. Dubois to be out on the side of the highway that night?

Did you hit her with your car, then leave the scene without notifying anyone or summoning aid?"

"I did not." Quint looked at his sweaty hands clenching and unclenching in his lap. "I can tell you positively, my car was not involved, as far as I know."

That statement piqued Mac's interest. "Quint, what do you mean, 'as far as you know?'"

"I mean, I had been drinking."

"Did you see Laurel at the country club?"

"Yes, earlier. You saw her, too. All of us were there."

Mac leaned over the table, closer to but not touching Ressler. "Did you pick her up in your car later at her condo and take her back to the country club?"

"That's the part I'm not sure about."

"What's the problem? Did you or did you not drive Laurel Dubois back to the country club?"

"I put my car in the garage. I didn't take it out again…but…" His gaze shifted to Detective Bryant's face. "My car was almost out of gas." He frowned and squinted hard at the blank wall. "I might have driven her back up there…later, or I might be remembering a different night. They all run together."

"So you cannot say if you did or didn't pick her up at her apartment, take her to the country club, then drive her home?"

"I could have taken her up there, but I left without her, because I went straight home, if it's the time I'm thinking about."

"Maybe you left without her and went back to get her? Could it have happened that way?"

Detective Green stood, drawing the attention of the other three men in the room. "Let's back up a little.

You took Ms. Smith to the country club for dinner."

"That's right."

"Where was her car?"

"At my office. In employee parking."

"Did you return her to her car?"

"No. I do remember that. We argued. She took off on foot, out into the rain."

"Very good, Ressler," Mac said, then he looked at the detectives. "He's right. It was raining. He does remember. Okay, Quint, now go on. Did you stay at the country club?"

"For a while. Had to keep up my image. Couldn't let everyone think I had offended Memory. I had a couple of drinks, then drove home. My car was almost out of gas and our usual station was closed.

"You needed gas?" Mac's voice was quiet in the still room. Quint looked startled.

"That's right! I remember, now. I parked my car and drove my wife's. I have keys to her car on my key ring."

Detective Bryant wrote furiously in his notebook. McCann schooled his expression to indifferent as Ressler blurted what he remembered.

"Laurel had been at the country club, but when I was ready to go, she'd left. I went to her apartment. I was on my way back there when I saw emergency lights and a big hullabaloo beside the highway."

"What time was that?" Detective Bryant asked, still writing.

"I don't know."

"What was going on?"

"They'd found a woman's body. Some guy recognized Memory's sweater. It was hers, all right. I recognized it. I verified it belonged to her. There was a lot of blood and gore. I didn't want to get too close. I saw enough to know that was Memory's sweater. An ambulance was there. One of the medics pronounced her dead. I was devastated."

"You identified the body as Memory Smith?"

"Actually, I identified the sweater. That must be what started the rumors. That's what threw me."

The two detectives consulted quietly—not including either McCann nor Ressler—then Green folded his notebook and left the room.

"Mr. Ressler, my partner is going now to impound your wife's car."

"Why would he do that?"

"It may provide evidence regarding the hit and run accident."

"Doris wasn't even out that night."

"No, but you just said you were driving her car later in the evening, when yours got low on fuel."

"Hers has more bells and whistles than mine. I wanted to make up with Memory. I wanted to drive the better car."

"Did you pick up Laurel instead?" Again Mac's baritone voice shattered a stillness in the room, but he couldn't keep the volume out of it.

"I could have." Ressler looked puzzled for a moment, before his expression became a frown. "Laurel made me mad, you know. She sat there wearing Memory's sweater and had the gall to accuse me of being unfaithful to her. I have a mental picture of that. She offended me by insulting our friend Memory. I made her get out of the car."

He glanced up as if expecting Mac's approval. "I

pulled over and stopped, but she wouldn't budge. No cars were coming." He rolled his eyes and frowned. "I put the car in park. I leaned over and opened her door and shoved her out. The bitch. She scratched and fought me, trying to get back in, shrieking and screaming. Hell, it wasn't even raining any more. I was really angry. I got the door closed and hit the lock. It served her right."

Ressler took a deep breath and shivered. "She called me names. I drove slowly at first, to irritate her, you know."

Quinton ran the fingers of both hands through his hair then propped his elbows on the table. When he looked again at his interrogators, tears dribbled down his face. "She screamed. It was just like her to make a big scene out of the least little thing. Then she did something that wasn't like her at all. She…" His voice caught. "She ran alongside. She pounded on the door, trying to get me to stop. Her being so hateful that way made me madder. I floor-boarded it. She couldn't keep up. She shrieked and the next thing I knew I heard this loud bumping and thumping, like I had a flat. I kept driving. I knew I was probably ruining the tire, maybe even the rim. It was all Laurel's fault for being so stupid."

"You know now what happened to Laurel, don't you?" Mac asked quietly. There was a long silence.

Ressler's shoulders slumped and he dropped his chins to his chest. "In my heart of hearts, I knew something…was…well, was wrong. I mean, it wasn't like Laurel to run like that. I looked at the passenger door." His voice rose to a queer falsetto and tears washed his cheeks, which quivered. "A piece of

Memory's sweater…was there. It was just like Laurel to do something spiteful like that, to try to stop me by slamming Memory's sweater in the door. Didn't she know how…how stupid that was? It wasn't my fault. She never should have tried to stop me from closing the car door after I shoved her out. How short-sighted was that?"

Silence enveloped each of the men in the interrogation room.

"We need to check the passenger side of Doris Ressler's car for body damage." Bryant addressed no one in particular. Mac heard someone in the observation room open a door. Bryant raised his voice, obviously making sure the people on the other side of the mirror heard him. "Dust the inside thoroughly. If there's so much as a hair from Laurel Dubois' head, I want it found."

A door closed and Mac heard footsteps move hurriedly down the hall.

In the interrogation room, Ressler began to sob openly. He didn't bother to mop the slobber sliding down his chins.

"What did you do after that, Mr. Ressler?" Detective Bryant asked.

He raised his head and gave the officer an accusing glare. "What do you think I did? I stopped the car and opened the damned door. She pulled the sweater free."

"Did you see her?" McCann asked, clearing his throat.

"I didn't look."

"Did the sweater pull straight out of the door?"

"It sort of slid down and out."

"What did you do then?"

"I pulled the door shut and drove. I didn't want to face her, listen to all the yammering and name calling. I figured someone would give her a ride. But I guess someone might have run over her after that, in the dark. They might have killed her."

The detective looked at McCann, who didn't meet his eyes.

"Why didn't you call to get her some help after you left her?" McCann asked, clearing his throat again. "Anonymously."

"It probably wouldn't have done any good. She probably got hit before anybody could have gotten there. What good would it have done to call and incriminate myself?"

"You knew she was dead, didn't you?" McCann stood. Ressler kept his eyes averted.

"No. She pulled that sweater out of the door the minute I opened it. She couldn't have done that if she'd been dead."

"What if she didn't pull it out? What if when you opened the door, gravity pulled it free?"

Detective Bryant didn't wait for an answer. Instead he followed McCann's question with a statement. "It doesn't make any difference. The law is clear. Anyone who causes an automobile accident involving an injury, or even witnesses one, is required to stop and render aid. You're a lawyer, for God's sake, Ressler. You know that. The penalties for turning your back on a person who's been injured are harsh and they're that way for a reason. Your cell phone was right there. Why didn't you call someone?"

"I don't know." Ressler rasped under the deluge that overcame him. "I didn't know…" He covered his face with both hands, muffling his voice.

Detective Bryant closed his notebook. “Mr. Ressler, you need to own up to what you did. Ms. Dubois was a prominent citizen in town. At the very least, you contributed to her death.”

“I did not. Hell, I didn’t even remember seeing her that night until he got me talking about it.” Ressler glowered at McCann.

“One more question, Mr. Ressler,” Detective Bryant said as he turned to leave.

“What?”

“How did you happen to call Ms. Smith in that motel room at five-fourteen that morning? How did you know she was there?”

“She was a registered guest, I suppose.”

Bryant gave him a cautioning look. “The room wasn’t in her name. It was in Mr. McCann’s.”

“I guess I was calling him.”

“No. Mrs. Flanagan said the caller asked if she had a woman staying there who had checked in after midnight. Also, the language you used was not intended for a man, Mr. Ressler. We have a detailed account of what you said to Ms. Smith.”

Ressler sniffed and sat straighter. “What do you suppose Memory Smith and David McCann were doing in that room?” His voice was a murmur, as if he had little hope of resurrecting that subject.

“As I told you earlier, Mr. Ressler, we neither know nor care what they were doing. What we want to know is how you happened to call that room at that motel at that time of day, particularly after you had identified the dead Jane Doe as Memory Smith? You should know that making an intentionally erroneous statement to the police at the scene of an accident is a felony?"

"I didn't make any false statements. I identified Memory's sweater. I only told them what I knew at the time was true. The body was wearing Memory Smith's sweater."

"If you thought the victim on the highway wearing the sweater was Memory Smith and said so to bystanders, how did you happen to call the motel looking for Memory Smith not three hours later?"

"Someone I saw later must have mentioned that Memory was staying at the motel. I can't really say who. As I've already told you, voluntarily, I'd been drinking. The events of the night were fuzzy. Confused. Like a bad dream. I saw and spoke with dozens of people at the country club during the evening, and many more later, at the scene of the accident."

Bryant hadn't made detective by being easily sidetracked. "Mr. McCann told us that, as far as he knew, only he, Ms. Smith, and Ms. Dubois knew Ms. Smith was at Flanagan's. Ms. Smith was there hiding out, specifically from you. We spoke with her. She thought she had good reason not to reveal her whereabouts."

"How about McCann?" Ressler asked.

"He went to the drug store, verified by the clerk. Back at the motel, Mr. McCann had a conversation with Mrs. Flanagan in the motel office. He did not mention to either of them that he had taken that room for Ms. Smith. Which takes us right back to my earlier question: Why did you call the motel and why did you say all those sexually explicit things to Ms. Smith when she answered the phone? She said you addressed her by her name. You didn't know Mr. McCann was there, did you? You didn't expect him to take that phone, did you?"

Ressler's mouth dropped open. "I resent the hell out of the implication there. I am one-hundred-percent heterosexual. Get that straight right here and now. I don't want to hear rumors to the contrary."

"Yes, sir, but you still haven't answered my question."

Ressler looked mystified. Bryant had a reputation for being a bulldog with obstinate suspects. "Who told you either Ms. Smith or Mr. McCann might be in that room? Which one of them did you call?"

"I told you, someone must have told me she was there."

"Could that someone have been Ms. Dubois?"

"I don't know. I don't remember. How could it have been her?"

"Mr. McCann said he and Ms. Dubois picked Ms. Smith up on the highway, drove her directly to the motel, and that he took Ms. Dubois straight home from there. Did Ms. Dubois contact you after Mr. McCann dropped her at her apartment?"

"She might have. Laurel and I frequently spoke on the telephone in the evenings."

"Why was that, Mr. Ressler?"

"She and I were old, old friends. I believe we even dated some back in high school."

"I see." Bryant reproduced his notebook and again began scribbling in it. "We have it from several sources that you and she often were seen in each others' company."

"Yes, well, my wife and I have what some people

term an open marriage. That is, we allow one another some flexibility."

Bryant nailed him with a stare. "Are you saying participants in an open marriage date other people?"

"Well," Ressler fidgeted, "I wouldn't call it dating exactly."

"You allow one another to see other men and women socially?"

"Doris has never really gotten interested in anyone else."

"But you have?"

"That's what I meant when I said Laurel and I went back a long way. We dated before I was married the first time, and after my first wife disappeared." Seeing the puzzled look on the detective's face, he paused.

Detective Green stepped back into the interrogation room as Bryant's cell phone rang. Bryant stepped out of the room.

"Because you dated Ms. Dubois before you were married, you considered it all right to continue dating her after you were married to someone else?" Green said, picking up the questioning as if he had been listening before entering the room.

"That may be an over simplification."

"But that's the gist of it, right?"

"I guess you could put it that way, generally speaking."

"Is that why you think your wife will or will not corroborate your story about being home?"

Detective Bryant stepped back into the interrogation room. "There are dents and damage to the side of Mrs. Ressler's vehicle. They also found evidence that Ms. Dubois was in the car. Also, Mrs.

Ressler has given us a statement. She says neither Mr. Ressler nor his car were at home early that evening and that he apparently returned his to their garage and took her vehicle out sometime after midnight." He looked at the suspect. "What do you have to say to that?"

"I have to say she is even more vindictive than I thought. If you found evidence in her car, she may be your prime suspect in the death of Laurel Dubois."

Both Green and Bryant snorted their opinions of that theory. Staring at the floor, McCann did not respond. Listening to Ressler's story, he realized, Memory had had a close call that night. Too close.

## Chapter Twenty-Three

When Memory answered the door at her home at eight-thirty that morning, Mac lost himself for a minute in her smile, fascinated by her unrepentant pleasure at seeing him. After a long moment of fueling his ego, he said, "Hi."

She studied his face several ticks, before she said, "Come in. What's going on?"

He had fixed his expression with a pleasant look. "I've got a story to tell you."

"Okay." She led him into the living room and indicated he should sit on the sofa. "Do you want coffee? I just made it."

"Maybe later."

Memory ran the fingers of both hands together, then asked an opening question. "Okay, tell me. What did Quint tell the police?"

"He was confused about the sequence of events. He recalled he was on his way back to pick Laurel up when he saw the commotion at the scene on the highway where they had found a woman's body."

"I don't understand."

"He told them 'Some guy recognized Memory's sweater,' that he didn't identify you as the victim. He said he only identified your sweater."

"But they said…"

Mac waved off her words, providing his own. "I

know, he had it out of sequence, but he was drunk. Booze can play tricks with your head. Witnesses said Ressler was the guy who identified your sweater, and told them the victim was you."

"He called me at Flanagan's a long time after that. What was that about?"

"Apparently, as he sobered up, Quint remembered Laurel was wearing your sweater the last time he saw it, before he saw it on the mangled body on the highway."

"Did he also remember…?"

"I don't know. What I do know is he called you at the motel later thinking you were alone. I wondered if he planned to lure you out and take you some place where he could have you to himself. After all, no one would be looking for you if everyone thought you were dead. He would have all the time in the world with you at his mercy."

"Oh, Mac, that is scary."

He gave her a somber look. "Yes, it is."

He went on to tell her Quint's entire tale. She listened quietly, but tears welled in her eyes more than once.

****

Mac hadn't forgotten Dicky Steam. Facing a five-year sentence might make Dicky more cooperative; maybe willing to shed additional light on events.

Mac didn't mention his plan to his boss or to Memory. No use getting people upset.

"Big deal. So I admitted it was a she," Steam conceded when Mac confronted him in the visitor's room at the medium security prison. "I let that slip on purpose."

"Sure you did. Did she give you her name?"

"She didn't say and I didn't ask."

"So, what'd she look like?"

"Never saw her."

"How did she pay you?"

"Cash. Left an envelope with a key inside. Left it in a drop spot at different places in town, then she'd call and tell me where to look for it."

"Key to what?"

"A locker. First time it was a locker out at the airport. The next time it was in the locker room at that futuristic looking rock and glass truck stop out on the bypass."

"Are there lockers in service stations?" Mac asked.

"Yeah, for truckers passing through who want to stow their stuff while they shower."

"She left you money twice?"

"She was supposed to pay me in three installments, first one was to get me started. The second payment got postponed when I screwed up—and the third. I threw in the fourth time to make up for not getting the job done before. She still owes me for the third one, though."

"How much?"

"Three hundred thirty-four dollars to get me started. Three hundred thirty-three the other two times."

"A thousand dollars to kill someone?"

"Well, now, I wasn't hired to kill anyone. I was only supposed to scare her. Get her to leave town. The way I looked at it, if the mark left town after I scared her once, a thousand would have been plenty."

"But she didn't." Mac stared at the man.

"Right, which is what made it complicated."

"How did you happen to do the hit and run out on the highway?"

"I already told you, I didn't do that. I didn't even know that woman. I wouldn't have anything to lose now by telling you if I had done that, but I didn't, so I'm not gonna say I did. Of course, if it had been the gal I was supposed to scare, I might have considered it. That Memory person made me 'bout mad enough to kill her. I mean, she knocked me around pretty good. Made me look incompetent. I wanted to hurt her before we was finished, but I didn't have no grudges against the other woman, the one that got run over out on the highway. No, sir, I didn't have nothing to do with that."

McCann thought about it. Obviously Dicky did not realize that the woman killed on the highway was most likely his secret employer. "There's been a problem about collecting your last payment, right?"

"Well, yeah. She hasn't paid me the last she owed me yet, but I expect she's having to wait again. I had to wait on the first payment for her to have some cash come available."

"When was that?"

Dicky scratched his chin. "Oh, yeah, I know when it was. My birthday's July twentieth. That's the day she was supposed to make the first payment. My birthdays have always been a big disappointment. It's a family tradition, you might say. She came through a couple of days later."

"July twenty-second?"

"Yeah, about then."

"Did you start stalking Ms. Smith after you got the first payment?"

"Following her around, yeah. But I didn't do nothing."

"Until when?"

"Until my employer made her second payment. I got her instructions in the mail the day after it finally rained. I was still hanging around waiting for her to tell me where to pick up the rest of my money when I got assaulted and arrested."

"Through no fault of your own?"

"Right."

"I see." Mac stood up without looking at Steam, pushed his chair under the table, and rapped on the door, signaling the guard.

The timing was right. The harassment began the Saturday night after Laurel was killed—the night it finally rained. Laurel lived on an allowance. It paid late in the month. The twentieth.

The guard opened the door and Mac sauntered out without either speaking to or looking at Steam again. He saw no reason to tell Dicky that he probably wouldn't be getting the third installment on his pay because it was likely his employer died August first.

## Chapter Twenty-Four

Memory did not like Cliff Horsely. Word was that, although Horsely had assumed first chair in Dicky Steam's trial, he rarely troubled himself with the preparation and trying of cases; left most of the grunge work to his assistants. While he didn't help with the day-to-day grind, the D.A. did sit at the prosecutor's table on the high-profile cases, most of which he assigned to Mac.

Relieved that she no longer needed to be concerned about Dicky Steam or unwelcome attentions from Quint Ressler, and comforted by Mac's assurance that he would work out the time and place for her sexual initiation, Memory was feeling charitable when she accompanied Mac to a party that night honoring law enforcement. Honorees included everyone from state supreme court justices down to the newest foot patrolman in the police department.

Mellow beside Mac, Memory was particularly annoyed when, circulating by herself, she overheard Horsely speak boisterously about his second in command.

"David McCann is a scrapper," Horsely said. "Belligerence is ingrained in him, animal instinct that makes him go straight for the jugular. While that attitude makes him effective as a prosecutor, he's like a Doberman. Someone's got to keep a firm hand on his leash, and muzzle him in polite society. McCann will never be domesticated enough to hold the top job. He's gone about as far as he needs to go."

Sidling over to stand beside Horsely, Memory put on what she considered her innocent look. "Why, Mr. District Attorney, whatever are you saying? There is no sweeter, more mannerly gentleman in this room than David McCann."

Obviously startled to realize one of Mac's champions had overheard his comments, Horsely covered his perfidy with a phony chuckle. His artificial laughter galled as he pretended to think she was kidding. He slid an arm around her shoulders, but Memory deftly slid out from under his arm, not bothering to hide her annoyance.

"Now, Miss Memory," he said, "you are not famous for your sense of humor. Is this a new dimension you're trying to develop?"

People were staring. Maybe she needed to tone it down a little.

"What I mean to say is, I emphatically disagree with your dark appraisal of David McCann. As you observed about me only a moment ago, you are not known for your sense of humor. When you speak disparagingly about David McCann, it's probably a poor attempt at levity, right?"

Horsely summoned some righteous indignation of his own. "I merely put into words, my dear, what everyone in town knows: that McCann is unschooled in the ways of polite society and has no chivalry."

Memory gave him a phony smile and tilted her head to one side, playing the coquette. "You described a dangerous animal rather than a caring man like Mr.

McCann. In my opinion, you do not deserve that man's loyalty. I wonder if he would be so steadfast if he overheard the snide remarks you make behind his back."

Horsely rolled his eyes, as if he did not want this conversation to get any louder or draw any more attention than it had already. Lowering his voice, he flashed her a conspiratorial smile. "You are as refreshing as everybody says you are, Miss Memory, and obviously just as naive."

His patronizing tone spiked her temper another notch, until she noticed his wayward glances at bystanders within earshot. Memory suddenly adopted a patronizing tone of her own.

"Maybe I am naive, Mister Cliff," she crooned, imitating the southern affectation of his title. "I shall demonstrate my point."

He inhaled as if to launch an objection, but Memory was having none of it.

"I'll do it right here and now so your friends can see your error without moving a step."

His smile appeared forced as Horsely's eyes roved from one individual face in their immediate company to the next, scanning them as if trying to bolster his confidence with their admiration. He obviously took heart from their nodding reassurance.

Memory flashed what she hoped was a confident smile. She never went out on a limb like this, especially not endorsing the behavior of someone who could be as unpredictable as David McCann. She knew Mac fairly well, however, and was gaining confidence in the kind of man he had become.

"As you can see," she said, "Mister McCann is

interested in the conversation in that cluster of people. I'm going to walk over there, and I want you to observe his body language. You can evaluate his sensitivity, his beautiful manners, and his chivalry without my saying a word. I doubt that he will speak to me as I approach—certainly not if someone else is talking. He is too much a gentleman to interrupt. If he ignores me, observe how he ignores me. You are about to witness the ideal behavior of the ultra sensitive alpha male in polite society today."

The district attorney faked a bawdy laugh, igniting polite, if not convincing, asides from his minions.

Working her way around other conversational clusters, Memory traversed the room. Mac glanced at her once, when she was about halfway, but looked as if he were not consciously aware of her. As she got closer, however, and his animated conversation with Bill Dodge continued, Mac pivoted slightly, just enough to indicate he was aware of her approach, even while his attention remained focused on Dodge.

As she worked her way closer, Mac shifted his drink from the hand nearest her—his right—to his left. When she was only a few steps away, he extended his free arm, effectively welcoming her into the group of half-a-dozen people, all engaged in such lively conversations that Memory wondered if any of them heard what any of the others was saying.

She positioned herself within the circle of Mac's arm before he gave her an inquisitive frown, then glanced behind her. She supposed he was looking for whatever threat might have sent her there. What he saw instead was only a gaggle of faces, including his boss's, all of which appeared to be focused on Memory at that moment.

Mac gave her a tentative smile and tightened the arm draped around her shoulder. He spoke in a quiet undertone. “Do you know everyone here?”

Five other people in the cluster stopped talking long enough to nod, almost en masse. Some said hello before they resumed individual conversations, airing opinions on the burdens of air traffic controllers. Memory took advantage of their preoccupation to raise her chin and smile smugly back over her shoulder, giving Horsely and his followers an I-told-you-so glance.

Horsely raised his glass, miming a toast, conceding the point. Memory snuggled closer under Mac’s arm, movement that earned her another curious look and prompted one more sweeping glance behind to see if she had come to him for protection.

## Chapter Twenty-Five

"Do you and Cliff Horsely get along?" Memory asked Mac as he drove toward her dad's house later than evening.

"Most of the time."

"Do you consider him a friend?"

He smiled at the question, but didn't look at her. "Again, most of the time, as close as an employee and an employer usually get, I suppose. We disagree occasionally and sometimes loudly on run-of-the-mill stuff like what charges to file, what kind of deal we'll offer, just generally how to approach a case."

"I have yet to hear you complain about him."

"He's the boss."

"Does he defer to you?"

Mac gazed out at the darkened highway for a moment. "Sometimes."

"Often?"

"Often enough. Why? What are you driving at?"

"He made some derogatory comments about you during our trial preparations. He isn't nearly as loyal to you as you are to him. That makes me not like him."

Mac grinned. "He's made some veiled references to my being from the west side of town, right?"

"Yes."

"Horsely's a snob, Memory, and it's silly, with his history. His dad was a miner and Cliff was one of twelve kids. He grew up a lot more deprived than I was. The house they lived in didn't have running water until Cliff was in his last year of high school. He puts me down sometimes to draw attention from his background. It doesn't bother me. It's not important."

"It is important. To me it is."

"Why? Everybody around here knows who came from where. I'm not fooling anyone wearing eight-hundred-dollar suits. Neither is Cliff. If tearing me down makes him forget or forgive himself for his beginnings, it's okay with me."

"Well, it's not okay with me."

"What does it have to do with you?"

"I don't know." She focused on her hands clasped in her lap. "I just can't stand for people who lack character to pretend they're superior to people who obviously have it. Character, I mean."

Mac's laugh was genuine. "Memory Smith, I think you're crazy about me."

"Yeah, well, you're probably the only one who hasn't noticed."

Memory was quiet as Mac pulled up in front of the farm house. Muted lights burned in several rooms, both downstairs and upstairs.

"Good idea, keeping some lights on."

"Come on in."

Mac eyed her suspiciously. "What are you up to?"

She smiled. "Nothing. I want to show you something."

He got out of the car, then walked around and opened her door. She wrapped an arm around his waist and snuggled as they climbed the porch steps. The porch light was not one of those Memory had left burning.

"Do you want me to fix us a drink?" he asked when they were inside. She locked the door and used the new deadbolt.

"Not right now, thank you." She took his hand and led him toward the stairs. "I have something to show you."

"Something upstairs?"

"Umm," she hummed affirmatively. He smiled, but she wouldn't meet his eyes.

"In your parents' bedroom," he asked as she bypassed her own room. "What is it?"

"It's self-explanatory."

The glow of muted light made the room ethereal. Everything looked properly made up, except… Mac did a double take when he noticed the two large, white squares folded in the middle of the queen-sized bed.

"What's all this?" he asked, but couldn't contain a grin.

"I'm tired of waiting, McCann. Two weeks ago, I bought condoms in a drugstore in Metcalf."

"Had you ever been in that store before?" he said, grabbing her hand to keep her from slipping beyond his reach. She laughed.

"No, and I don't plan to ever darken the doors there again."

Still holding her hand, he walked to the side of the bed and smiled down at the two folded bedsheets.

"Klan clothing?"

"Togas," she corrected.

"When?"

"Now. You can dress in here. I'll use my room."

Memory was still tugging and tucking the sheet as

she returned to the master bedroom. Mac stood at attention in a darkened corner, his sheet secured at his waist. "Now what?"

She twisted her face comically. "I hadn't planned much beyond this."

"This, being?"

"Looking at you. You have got to have the best looking upper body anywhere."

"Is looking enough?"

She exhaled. "Not exactly."

"Come on over here and check out the merchandise."

"Okay." She took small steps allowed by the toga around the bed, stopped in front of him, and patted his stomach. "Oh, yeah. This is good," she whispered.

"There's more."

"Right."

"Go ahead. Braille me."

Mac closed his own eyes and fisted his hands as Memory ran her fingertips over his chest and followed the contours of his ribs to his waist, her movements accompanied by a humming sound. "You are beautiful," she sighed. Without permission, she pressed her lips to his chest.

Mac's hands closed at her waist to lift. He sat her in the middle of the bed and tugged the end of the sheet she had tucked over her shoulder. He unwound the sheet covering her breasts, then stepped back to feast his eyes. "*You* are beautiful," he said, repeating, reemphasizing her words and joining her on the bed.

They took turns unwrapping one another, touching, fondling, kissing every inch of flesh as it was bared. Neither of them spoke as their breathing quickened and their bodies heated.

Mac tossed his sheet first, then removed and tossed the last wrap covering her.

Passion burned as he laid a hot, hard hand in her midriff, then pressed, moving it lower, titillating, tantalizing, opening her. He stepped over to fit himself between her long, quivering legs, and lowered his torso. She whimpered and the sound incited him. He situated himself above her carefully. This was his moment, the crowning achievement of his life, one he would remember forever.

He caught the little squeal from her mouth in his, an exchange, nearly as intimate as the movement below as he entered her. He held a moment, waiting. As she relaxed, he pumped once, slowly, gently, in and out, allowing her time to accept him. She rocked, a tiny, encouraging movement, signaling. He lowered himself into her again, his biceps bulging. Memory wrapped her hands around his arms and moaned with pleasure.

He liked pleasing her. He pumped again, deeper. She writhed and pulled herself up, scrubbing her breasts to his chest, arching her body, raising it to encourage more of him.

His arms locked as he held himself above her, waiting, but she was already ahead of him. She called his name as she powered her body, her legs lifting her hips. She groaned as he broke through the last resistant membrane and rocked into her. The rhythm set, they moved in sync, as lovers do. Rocking, soaring, they traveled together, high into the heavens, where neither of them had been before. Mac tried to hold her there, at the pinnacle, only to allow a groan of his own as the spire broke and they plunged together, back into the here and now.

As their heavy breathing slowed, he saw her tears. Memory clawed to pull him down on top of her. Instead of yielding, he lifted himself up and over to the side where he stretched, facing her. She covered her nose and mouth with both hands and her shoulders shook. He responded to her devastation with a light laugh.

"Don't be sad, sweetheart. We are perfect together."

"Was that a…home run?"

"Yes." He laughed at her concern.

"Will we ever be able to do that again?"

He smiled. "That and better, again, and again, and again."

She turned a horrified stare on him. "We forgot the condom."

"Are you afraid you'll get pregnant?"

"Aren't you?"

"No. You did say you'd marry me." He didn't want her to see how important her response was. She uncovered her face and stared at him wild-eyed.

"You still want to marry me?"

He laughed. "I do. Absolutely, the minute you set the date."

"But where will we live? Where will I work?"

"We'll live right here. You can work for me in the district attorney's office. If you don't want to work for me, you'll probably have your choice of judges or law offices. Or I can go into private practice.

"What about the rest? How will we manage?

He grinned. "I predict we'll live happily ever after. How are you thinking we'll manage?"

Her anxiety turned to giggling. "Happily ever

after? Mac, those words sound silly coming from you."

"I know. Who'd have thought I'd ever use those words? Happily ever after. Not only that, I believe it's going to happen."

## Chapter Twenty-Six

Their first effort was not their best. Mac and Memory polished their love-making through the night, with one home run after another, then slept until daylight streamed across her parents' bed to rouse them at seven-thirty.

While Memory bathed, Mac went to the kitchen to make coffee. Snooping, he found a coffee cake in the freezer and preheated the stove to warm it. Wrapped in the bedsheet, he kicked the trailing corner as he turned to see Memory come through the door barefooted, but wearing slacks and a pullover shirt.

"Going formal, are you?" he said, smiling.

"I've been thinking. "

"Oh, dear."

"About Helen Mouser."

"Who?"

"Quint Ressler's first wife. The one who disappeared."

"Ah."

"We seem to have done well figuring out Laurel's murder. I thought maybe we could try a cold case."

"Cold case?" David smiled and decided to indulge her. "Hold that thought."

Half an hour later, after he had showered and dressed, he lifted the warmed coffee cake from the oven, and poured two more cups of coffee. Memory grabbed the milk and poured a little into her cup, then added and stirred a generous portion of sugar.

"You take your coffee like a sissy," Mac said, smiling.

"No hair on my chest. I thought you'd noticed."

"Is drinking coffee black what puts hair on your chest?"

"Obviously. You have it. I don't."

"Deductions like that prove you are a natural-born detective."

He put his arms around her and began fondling her breasts again.

"Mmmm… If you keep taking us back to bed, we're never going to accomplish anything worthwhile," she said, but she was smiling.

He nuzzled her ear. "Raincheck?"

"Yes."

"Okay, then, I guess we can get back to crime-solving…temporarily. Where do we start?"

"Do you think it's odd how much Cliff knows about Laurel's personal business?"

"You've been thinking about this since last night."

"Well, yes, but not, you know…when we were…involved."

Mac nearly snorted coffee through his nose. "I should hope not, but to answer your question, I'm sure they were acquainted. They both grew up here."

"She was our age, and Horsely's much older, isn't he?"

"Probably ten years."

"Mac, Laurel referred to the unidentified lover in her journal as 'C.'"

"So?"

"Could her secret lover have been Cliff Horsely? Be objective, now. Cliff begins with a C. Laurel refers to everyone in her journal by the initials of their first names. We agree that he knows a lot about her. I mean, he told you someone gave her a Persian with a pedigree. You had been dating her and you didn't mention her having a cat."

"I didn't know she did…have a cat."

She slanted him a telling look. "Cliff Horsely did."

"Yes, he did." Mac scowled. An hour ago he'd come downstairs, hoping to find some food and coffee and take it all back to bed. But Memory was on a tear. He loved that about her, her intensity when she felt passionate about something. He just wished more of that passion was focused on him this morning. He waited a couple more heartbeats, but she wasn't through.

"How many people knew Laurel had had her wisdom teeth extracted that week? That's an odd subject for a dad to mention to his golf cronies."

"It's funny you should mention that, because I asked Ressler. He neither knew nor cared that she had had those teeth out, certainly had no idea when."

"Cliff also knew she'd haggled over the price of her Camry, that she'd gotten an especially good price on it because it was a year-end model. He's also the one who speculated that she wouldn't have been driving her new car in the rain the night she died because she wouldn't have wanted to get it dirty."

"Exactly what are you trying to say?" Mac said.

"I don't know." She took a bite of coffee cake. The move raised her shirt exposing her midriff. The flash of skin prompted Mac to put a hand on her thigh. Then he picked up her bare foot and propped it on his knee. She wiggled her toes and giggled, then frowned. "So who hired Dicky Steam?"

"I'm almost certain it was Laurel."

Memory paused, fork in mid air. "You're thinking Laurel hired a killer to murder her?"

Mac looked deeply into her eyes, his expression serious. "Not her."

Memory set her fork aside. "Oh."

"Then again, I could be wrong," Mac temporized. "Trying to link the killing and the stalking may have been my first mistake. So…since we're just brainstorming, I do have a couple of theories I'd like to try out loud, if it's okay with you." He needed to get her mind off of the possibility that Laurel had wanted Memory dead.

"Okay. Shoot." She slid into the chair facing his.

"First, let's go back ten years. Laurel and Quint were an item after high school, but the Dubois' were not nearly as prominent as the Mousers."

"You're saying Quint fell in love with the unsophisticated Helen Mouser?"

Mac waved that idea off. "Quint's always been most in love with himself, but his relationship with Laurel worked. Regardless of that, he gave in to his parents and married Helen. After all, marrying someone else didn't necessarily mean he had to give up Laurel. Get the picture?"

Memory didn't say anything, her silence giving him permission to continue.

"They'd been married six months when Helen vanished. Did you know about that at the time?"

"Yes. Mom sent the newspaper clippings when

Helen disappeared and updated me as the hunt progressed. Do you think Quint had something to do with her disappearance?"

"I do."

Mac's cell phone vibrated and sounded. He answered it on the fourth ring, listened a moment, said, "Yes," and hung up, before he spoke. "Get your shoes on, woman, while I clear the dishes. Our public calls."

****

Twenty minutes later, Mac pulled under the overhang at Flanagan's. He and Memory walked into the office where Mrs. Flanagan had cups of hot cider and gingerbread cookies on a plate. The three of them greeted each other warmly. Memory declined a cup of cider or anything to eat. Mac hoped she wasn't still thinking about Laurel's possible intentions. Mrs. Flanagan motioned them to sit on the too-soft sofa, which they did.

"I want to tell you something," Mrs. Flanagan said as she passed the cookies to Mac. "Laurel had a tiny guard on her national honor society pin. She always had it on the zipper pull of her everyday purses. When they delivered her purse to her mother, the first thing she noticed was that no guard was attached."

"Investigators found the guard inside Doris Ressler's car," Mac said. "That pretty well confirmed Quint's story earlier." And Ressler's chances of going to prison.

Mrs. Flanagan wasn't to be distracted. "Talking about it got me thinking about Quint and the disappearance of his first wife, Helen, and all that."

Memory and Mac glanced at each other before Memory nodded toward Mrs. Flanagan. "We were just talking about that. Do you see a connection between the missing wife and the missing emblem?"

"Never mind," Mrs. Flanagan said, deflated. "I thought maybe it was important."

"There may be a connection, Mrs. Flanagan," Memory said. "Don't give up so easily. When Quint had his first wife—Helen—declared legally dead, were people suspicious?"

"It caused a stir," Mrs. Flanagan said, easing into the overstuffed chair. "Mr. Mouser got a court order to search the area where the Resslers have their cabin, looking for her body, but they didn't turn up anything. I heard Quint's in-laws, who never liked him, wanted to lynch him, but they couldn't come up with evidence that he was involved in their daughter's disappearance."

"Were Quinton and Laurel still an item?"

Mac responded. "Hotter than ever."

"But he didn't marry Laurel the second time either," Memory mused.

Mrs. Flanagan spoke up. "People didn't know much about Doris Weddle. She was several years older than Quinton. She began her career as a butcher at the meat market. After that she was a waitress and a bartender. She had no family or money behind her. She was a moderately attractive, broad-faced country girl. No one could figure out what Quinton saw in her, but they got married at the courthouse one Tuesday afternoon, middle of the week, mind you."

Mac cleared his throat, and Mrs. Flanagan paused to sip her cider. "There was a rumor that Doris knew something about Helen's disappearance and used that to make Quint marry her," Mac said.

Memory's eyes rounded. "Why didn't you say

something?"

"I didn't know we were going to have this conversation."

"But don't you see?" Memory insisted. "If he killed his first wife, being a blackmailing second wife might be dangerous."

Mrs. Flanagan answered. "A teller at the bank says Doris has a safe deposit box in her name only. She never uses it."

"So, you suspect she's got something in there that would point to Quint if anything happened to her?" Memory asked.

"I don't know anything, except she has a box at the bank in her name only. She pays for it before the rent on it comes due, once a year, regular as clockwork, and she never uses it."

Memory gave Mac a hard look. "You knew about the box, too, didn't you?"

"What's that got to do with the price of eggs?"

"Does any of this have anything to do with Quint Ressler trying to buy my dad's farm?"

It was time to stop deflecting. "Yes."

"Do you think that's significant?" Mrs. Flanagan asked.

Memory nodded. "I don't know anything, of course, except our farm shares a property line with the land where the Resslers have their cabin. Could Quint's first wife be buried on my dad's place? Quint tried to buy it from Dad several years ago. Dad wouldn't sell it. Quint was friendly with Dad after Mom passed away, and was attentive to me after Dad's death—until that Friday night. Several times, he offered to take the farm off my hands. He went so far as to have it appraised. He offered more than the appraised value. Said he wanted to help me out. I wondered about that at the time."

"You really don't want to sell it?"

"I could sell the surface, probably, someday, but I want to keep the mineral rights. Quint insists on buying both."

"Are there any gas wells out that direction?" Mac asked.

"No, but companies occasionally offer to lease an acreage."

Mrs. Flanagan peered into her cup. "Do you suppose he's afraid someone drilling out there might dig up something Quinton doesn't want found?"

Memory studied Mac's face which showed no reaction, Mrs. Flanagan nodded, but didn't offer to continue, so Memory picked up the speculation.

"Six or eight weeks ago I was offered a drilling lease on ten acres over by the Resslers' property line. What if Quint got nervous about someone drilling there and told his wife? Doris might have hired Dicky Steam after all. Maybe they wanted to scare me into selling, and Quint's generous offer was on the table. His buying Dad's place might solve several problems at once. It would get rid of me, guarantee they would control the drilling and/or enable them to remove any evidence before it was unearthed, so to speak."

The three of them were silent for a moment. Mrs. Flanagan looked stunned. Memory sank back onto the sofa, her expression indicating she was entertaining morbid thoughts. When she finally glanced up, Mac's scowl captured her attention.

"What are you thinking?" she asked.

"That what happened to Laurel came dangerously

close to happening to you. You made Quint angry by spurning his advances and by not selling him the farm. You refused to leave town and you were thinking of leasing that acreage to the drilling company. You probably made him feel impotent. He made a play for you, and you turned him down. That was a real slap in the face for a guy who brags about his success with the ladies."

So much for keeping her mind off the idea that someone wanted her dead. *Way to go, McCann.*

"So what's going to happen to Quint?" she asked instead.

"Prison." He'd personally see to it.

"For accidentally killing a friend?" Mrs. Flanagan asked.

"Happens all the time, Mrs. Flanagan. It's called manslaughter." He looked at both women. "There's a lesson in that. Choose your friends wisely. Hang with people who don't drink or do drugs, who won't accidentally knock you off."

"I'll try to remember that," Memory responded dryly, and it was good to see a smile on her face again. "Now, what's the connection between Laurel's death and Dicky Steam stalking me?"

"None."

"You mean one has nothing to do with the other?"

"Right."

"When did you figure that out?"

"Quite recently."

## Chapter Twenty-Seven

Back at Memory's house much later that evening, Memory handed Mac a glass of wine. She wrapped both hands around her cup of hot spiced tea, then curled one leg under her as she eased onto the sofa beside him. She drew a deep, contented breath.

She thought Mac looked smug, probably pleased that she so obviously trusted him. Okay, she could give him that. Owed him that.

Mac reached to right Memory's teacup that tipped precariously. He took a sip of his wine, then arched his brows regarding the glass. "Where did you get this?"

She gave him a knowing smile. "At the liquor store. I asked what wine you preferred and Mrs. Migdat told me. Then I asked if they had a smoother version."

"More expensive, you mean?"

"Yes." She beamed. He was pleased.

He righted her cup again. She ignored his correction, lost the grin, and frowned into his face, ready to get back to discussing the events of the day. As if by mutual agreement, they had concentrated on other things during their lunch at the diner after leaving Mrs. Flanagan's, and then they had split up for several hours, Mac claiming he had some work to do at the office.

Mac said, "Your tea's getting cold."

She raised the cup and took an obligatory sip. "I don't suppose anyone believes that after Quint and

Doris Ressler married they lived happily ever after."

He sighed. He'd hoped she'd let sleeping dogs lie for the evening. "No, but they have gotten along surprisingly well. Doris cleaned up nice and kept to her end of the bargain. Also, she was shrewd in looking out for Quint's interests, which, of course, became her interests too. So yes, I got curious about the safe deposit box at the First National."

"That again?"

"That again. Since there was so much smoke—speculation—about what she had tucked away in there, maybe evidence of murder, I got a warrant this afternoon. Without a warrant, of course, no one else could get into that box unless Doris died, at which time a bank officer would inventory the box with Doris's next of kin."

"Quint couldn't have inventoried the box without a witness?"

"Correct." Mac drained the last of his wine.

"Do you want some more?"

"No. We may go to the club later for a drink and a turn around the dance floor." He gave her time to respond, but Memory held silent, staring at the wall.

"What was in the box?"

"Nothing."

"No papers or valuables? Deeds? Anything?"

"No."

"So the new Resslers did live happily ever after?" she said.

"Until you showed up."

"Me? What did I do?"

"Aside from making both of the ladies in Quint's life jealous? A year or two ago when oil companies began leasing minerals, Quint had no problem with them leasing his land, but when they approached your dad, Quint got nervous. He was just as worried when the land belonged to you. A lot of people wondered why Quint cared about a company drilling on the Smith's property."

"Wondered what?"

"Why it mattered to him. Why should Quint care about people digging holes on his neighbor's property? When they asked, he said he wanted to preserve the serenity of the lake and the area around his family's cabin."

Memory felt the blood drain from her face and she whispered, "But he was really afraid they might dig up human remains? Is that what you think? Here? On Dad's farm?"

"Yes, which is the real reason I told Quint I had a warrant to search Doris' bank box. I told him I inventoried the box and the jig was up; that I was going to get a new warrant, one to dig for Helen's remains on the Smith property. If he made me spend district funds going to all that trouble, I was going to be really mad by the time I found what I was looking for. He was going to pay the price for making me mad, maybe pay by drawing a lethal injection. He caved. Said he'd take us to her grave."

Memory put her cup on the side table, stood to straighten her slacks, then sat back down and pulled her knees up to her chest. Mac patted her knee. She looked teary, and he wished the subject had not come up.

"Did you find her?" she asked.

"We did."

She looked away for a long moment before turning

back to him.

"Why did Laurel have to die?"

"That was unplanned. Spur-of-the-moment. Manslaughter, not murder. Ressler said she was jealous of you and threw a fit. She threatened him saying she knew he had murdered Helen."

"Laurel didn't really know that, did she?"

"I don't imagine she believed it, either, but it got a rise out of him and that's what she was after, a way to get his attention. He wasn't in the right frame of mind for it that night. When she wouldn't shut up, he made her get out of the car. You know what happened after that."

"He didn't plan to kill her?"

"No, although he was responsible for her death, either directly or indirectly. We don't know for certain if any other vehicle or vehicles ran over her after he left her on the side of the road. They might have. As you know, her body was unrecognizable."

"Quint misidentified her on purpose. That was a big part of his crime. Then Steam began stalking you, as agreed, but instead of abandoning ship—leaving town—you took him on."

"I probably wouldn't have if I hadn't gotten you." She looked startled by her own words. "I mean, hadn't gotten you involved."

He gave her a telling smile. "Oh, yeah, baby, you got me involved, all right, all the way up to my eyeballs."

Her expression clouded and again she looked like she might cry. Mac shifted, pulling her shoulders, positioning her to face him. He studied her several seconds, then lowered his mouth to devour hers.

Memory's lips held stiff for a moment before she yielded, relaxing into the kiss. Mac ran one hand inside her sweater and followed the warmth of bare skin to fondle her.

His behavior prompted Memory to launch a welcome survey of her own. She pushed both her hands under the waistband of his knit shirt and up as she inhaled. She counted his ribs with her fingertips, up and down, a massage that nearly drove him wild with the need to be inside her.

He eased her down, flat on her back, and positioned himself above her.

"I won't ask for anything else," she wheezed, breathless. "Just one more home run."

"Baby, you're never going to have to ask me for anything else again. Starting now, I'm going to provide everything you need or want for the rest of your life."

"You don't have to make promises," she rasped. "I'm convinced…you are the sexiest man in town."

"Is that all? Then by morning, Ms. Smith, I intend to have expanded that opinion. I'm going to make you believe I am the sexiest man in the world."

A wicked laugh burbled in his throat. Releasing her hand, he slipped his fingers up under her sweater again, sliding them over her bare skin, released her bra, and skimmed bra and sweater up and off. He pushed her back onto the couch. Trying to conceal her exquisite breasts with her bare arms, she maintained a secret smile. He knelt on the floor to tug her shoes off baring her feet. Before she could react, he slipped his hands between her knees, following with his body, then lifted his own shirt up and over his head.

Memory studied his marvelous chest a moment

before her secret smile opened to a broad grin. She threw open her arms and arched her back, welcoming him. He caught her waist with both hands, and pulled her close to plant his mouth against her warm, scented flesh. She moaned as his lips roved from her waist up. She cried out when his mouth took a nipple, then sucked, as if to consume the entire breast. Her hands, braced at the back of his head, tugged encouragement as he inhaled her. He might suffocate—a delicious way to die—but he didn't plan to end it all just yet.

Her flesh felt feverish, pressing closer and closer, inviting him, not just inside her clothing, but inside her. That was his plan. Memory was still a beginner and beginners needed foreplay. Oh, yes, she did, and he was going to provide all the foreplay she wanted for as long as she wanted it.

He spread his hands to the glorious globes of her delectable bottom, which were still clothed, while he continued mouthing her bared breasts and midriff. Gripping her tightly, he mouthed lower, down the front of her slacks. Her moaning became a plea as his lips reached her vortex. Tantalizing, teasing, he nipped at her. She clawed at the fastener on her slacks. She was frantic. Her fingers were clumsy.

"Help me," she whined. "Please…help me get these off."

"Yes, sweetheart, I'll help you. When it's time, but it's not time yet."

"Mac, please, it is time." Her words softened to a whisper. "It's years and years past time. We have a lot of catching up to do."

"Not yet." He tugged her hips and blew his hot breath into the front of her slacks. "We have more exploring first."

Her pleas became a wail and she stammered. He laughed at her torment. "Come on, let's go upstairs where we'll have plenty of time and privacy for the main event…or events."

With less coaxing than he expected, he stood and pulled her to her feet. "Can you walk, or do you want me to carry you?"

"We can do it here."

"We want to do it right."

"We already did it right."

"There's more." He looked down at her bare breasts and bit his lips. For all his bragging, he didn't know how long he could maintain the foreplay. She deserved long, slow, exquisite loving. They would make love so well and so often that she would never want anyone else, ever. That was his plan.

He caught her around the waist and lifted to slip his other arm under her knees. She kicked, but he pulled her high and kissed her. She kissed him back, wrapping long, bare arms around his shoulders.

In the master bedroom, he sat her on the side of the tall bed, then unbuttoned and unfastened button and fastener, stripping her. There was no conversation, only nonsensical whispers, and touching, and moans of anticipation.

He stretched her on her back, then watched her reactions as he stripped himself, losing shoes and socks, then sliding trousers and shorts down and out of the way.

Mac stretched beside her where he examined her slowly, using only his fingertips to explore the lines and hollows, the crevices and hidden places where no other hands had surveyed before. When she frowned or wiggled as if to escape his touch, he paused to allow her time to adjust.

Once she became accustomed to his fondling one area, he set his mouth to trace the same paths established by his prying, probing fingers. Her responses guided him. As her breathing accelerated from long, deep draughts, to quick, desperate gasps, he intensified his efforts, always evaluating, heightening the stimuli as indicated. His own pleasure swelled with hers until he was scarcely able to breathe.

Like a hand working its way into a glove, Mac's body fitted itself into hers…and then they began to rock.

****

One year later, Astrick's bad boy, David McCann, married Memory Smith, the miracle child. He became district attorney of Bacone and two adjoining counties the following July, winning the election without an opponent. Eventually, he would become district judge.

His appeared to be an idyllic life of successes. In spite of reaching lofty career goals, Mac sometimes teased his wife that his finest achievement was waking up next to her in her parents' queen-size bed the morning after they first made love, holding her as she babbled happily about "going all the way home."

Without manipulation or artifice, Astrick's miracle child restored the town's greatest skeptic, filling her husband with confidence and making him trust a woman—a Memory—he would never again live without.

## A word about the author...

A former newspaper reporter, Sharon (Thetford) Ervin has a B.A. in Journalism from the University of Oklahoma. She lives in McAlester, Oklahoma, is married to attorney Bill Ervin, and has four grown children. She works half-days in her husband and older son's law office as probate clerk, bookkeeper, and gofer.

*MEMORY* is her twelfth published novel.

Sharon belongs to PEO, the General Federation of Women's Clubs, Alpha Phi, Romance Writers of America, Sisters in Crime, the Oklahoma Federation of Writers, Inc., The Texas Writers Guild, and McAlester's McSherry Writers.

She can be contacted on her Website: http://sharonervin.com, on Facebook, Twitter, or directly at ervins@sbcglobal.net.